Rhys Wilcox was born in Luton on 'decimilisation day' and feels deprived of missing out on shillings by 24 hours.

He started writing sometime between his first and second birthdays and has never looked back. Literature took a serious turn at Portsmouth University whilst reading Media & Design; he found he had a lot of spare time on his hands so wrote a few plays for the drama society, started his first novel and tried his hand at stand-up comedy.

He thinks he's funny and has only had his primary school maths teacher tell him otherwise.

He lives in West Sussex with his wife, Melanie, and daughter, Natasja, whom he is raising.

BLOOD LUST

To Juliette

Rhys Wilcox

Blood Lust

What light?

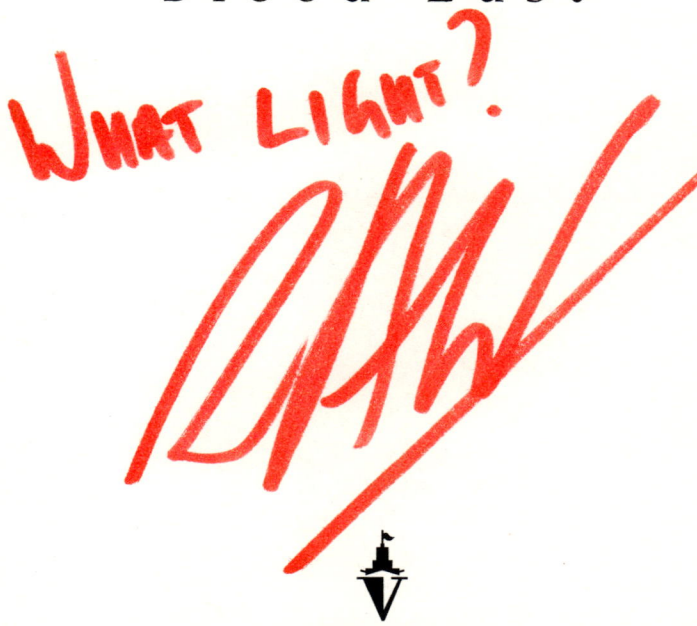

Vanguard Press

VANGUARD PAPERBACK

© Copyright 2002
Rhys Wilcox

The right of Rhys Wilcox to be identified as author of this work has been asserted by him in accordance with the Copyright, Designs and Patents Act 1988

All Rights Reserved

No reproduction, copy or transmission of this publication may be made without written permission.
No paragraph of this publication may be reproduced, copied or transmitted save with the written permission or in accordance with the provisions of the Copyright Act 1956 (as amended).

Any person who does any unauthorised act in relation to this publication may be liable to criminal prosecution and civil claims for damage.

A CIP catalogue record for this title is available from the British Library
ISBN 1 903489 85 7

Vanguard Press is an imprint of
Pegasus Elliot MacKenzie Publishers Ltd.
www.pegasuspublishers.com

First Published in 2002

Vanguard Press
Sheraton House Castle Park
Cambridge England

Printed & Bound in Great Britain

Dedication

For Melanie and Natasja.

The characters in this book are all based on people I have met and hate.

You all know who you are.

Only your names have been changed to make everyone paranoid.

Before the Beginning...

It had been a good party. At first he had not wanted to come, what with everybody being at least three years younger than himself. Because despite what any older generations may think about 'young people', there is even going to be a generation gap when a large group of only-just-twenty-year-olds and one person who is rapidly approaching mid-twenties and, in their eyes, impending middle age, get together.

Yet, as with most awkward meetings and such, inhibitions and unease were broken down by the diplomatic powers of alcohol. He talked to someone he had never met before and would probably never meet again, about a subject he had no interest in, no knowledge of and no memory of ever after he had sobered up.

The worst part about the evening was the fact that people actually wanted proper conversations with him, what with his recent graduation and all. All he wanted to do was get over the fact that when he had reached the legal age of consenting sex, the girl he was talking to was only just entering secondary school, and get off with her. All she wanted to do was find out about housing rates, hours of study, and what 'A' levels were needed.

Sod it, he thought. "'A' levels are wank," he had told her. "You lot get piss easy GCSEs to arse around with and then they have to make 'A' levels piss easy as well to keep their figures up. When you go to uni', it's not so easy. Major fucking culture shock. You don't get told every little thing you have to do to get by, you have to do it all on your own." He paused for thought. "Unless you do some Mickey Mouse, some fucking media degree, in which case you've just got to be an oppressed minority of a fucking Marxist to suck up to and impress the lecturers. If you're female you just say 'But how does that relate to women?' to every issue under the sun and you come out with an easy 2-1 and a head full of bullshit."

He stared at the girl blearily and noticed she was frowning.

"What?" he asked.

"I'm going to do a media degree actually, and it isn't easy. You have to be able to interpret underlying messages that are prolific in today's society. It's not 'Mickey Mouse'."

"I *did* the degree. No you don't and yes it is." He suddenly realised, 'Crash and Burn!' as she turned tail and stormed off.

There came a loud laugh from behind and he turned to see his mate, the guy who had invited him, in fits of hysterics at his performance.

"Piss off," he said and his mate screamed even louder.

He walked over to him and patted him on the shoulder. "Cheer up man. There's plenty of better girls than her, trust me," he said and tried to wink. He blinked.

He scanned the room and his eyes focused on someone he would normally describe as, "Phwoar! Fit!"

"Who's she?" he asked and pointed with his pint glass.

His mate stared at the area he was indicating with his wavering hand; it was encompassing about a dozen women. "Who? The tall one?" he guessed.

"Yeah."

"A friend of a friend and out of your league."

"How much?" he asked, a wager was completed and destiny had put the boot in.

Later, still before the Beginning but perhaps a leading contributor to the development of the Beginning, he fell in love.

***

Much later. A beginning...

It was going to be a surprising day for John Settle; it was going to be the day that he discovered he was dead.

Will be dead.

Is dead.

Whatever.

He was forty-three, slightly balding, slightly paunched but nothing to be overly concerned with. He had a wife, two children aged nineteen and seven, a boring job and a Damocles of a mortgage of which he was trying to discuss with his bank manager.

"Mr Settle," the banker said, "you are currently five months in arrears of payment. If the money is not forth coming within the next two weeks then we will have no choice but to foreclose on your mortgage."

"Two weeks!" John squealed. "I couldn't raise fifty pence from the back of the sofa in two weeks, let alone this much."

"Then I suggest you concentrate your efforts on finding a new home Mr Settle." The banker smiled that kind of a smile that just begged to be punched.

John was not the sort of man who would give in to that sort of pleading. He was a believer in justice; he believed that every man, woman and child would get what was coming to them. He believed this quite vehemently – he had to – because of all the men, women and children who had abused him in one way or another in the past and he had not had the spontaneity to do anything about it. He did not have the bottle to do anything about it. John was one of those poor saps in the world who could not handle direct and immediate confrontations; that is why, as he walked down the street away from the bank, he was thinking of all the things he could have done and should have done.

It is called *l'esprit d'escalier*. It is French and therefore sounds very romantic. There is no word for it in English apart from the direct translation 'the spirit of the stairs'. Whose side of the 'better language' argument that would be for is uncertain. It is a disorder that affects all of us. Even those amongst us who are quick enough to come up with some sort of witty retort. Sometimes they walk away from a situation with their teeth in their pocket and their nose smeared up their forehead thinking, *I should not have said that*. From the simple decisions in life; *I wish I'd said yes to seconds*; to earth shattering life changers; *'Still be friends'? Should've said, 'Fuck off and die, whore queen from hell!'* From political meetings, *I should have said no to that war. Oh well*; to John Settle; *Should have dived across the table, rammed my fist down his throat and pulled out his heart*.

Being of the literary kind, this description does not pay full credit to the images he was creating in his fevered brain.

Ripped off his head and shat down his neck.

In his mind's eye the banker was still smiling *that* smile but his head was rolling around his 'IN' tray and John was squatting over his blood-spurting neck, straining off a load. In reality, however, John had simply wandered aimlessly in to the park.

"I should have at least sworn at him," he said out loud.

He became aware of his surroundings and of the girl who was watching him from the bench. She stared blankly and John stared back. He sat next to her, still staring. He put his hand on her thigh; neither of them looked away from the other. His hand moved up her leg, over her hip, up her waist to her breast. She leaned forward and pressed her lips roughly against his. Their mouths opened, her tongue was cold and bitter against his. They moved their bodies closer together and embraced tightly, her hands slid over his back and down to the front of his trousers, he was obviously aroused. She unclipped his belt and trousers and moved her hand inside to free his erection. He pulled away from her demanding lips and drew in a long breath of air, she transferred her mouth's attention to his neck and took large sucking bites out of it, her hand pumped hard on his cock. Her bites were becoming more fierce, causing so much pain that heightened the sensation and freed his mind from all of his immediate concerns. Her teeth felt so sharp as they scratched against his skin. Her hand moved faster and his breathing quickened, her teeth split the skin of his neck – the pain was unbearable but excruciatingly ecstatic – she sunk them further in and he felt his blood gush out the wound and down his front.

He felt the most overpowering orgasm ever as he was released from his mortal constraints and earthly worries. Then blackness followed.

He should have at least sworn at him.

***

It was dark, John was cold and he knew he was dead. He was in a tight metal box.

They've buried me, he thought and started to panic. He screamed and punched at the sides of the container until, suddenly, light streamed in and John was pulled, feet first, out. He was lying on a bench in a mortuary. Two shocked nurses stared at him with their jaws agape.

John was panting heavily, slowly calming down and getting to grips with the situation. He hurt, his body ached and his neck stung like a bastard. He felt incredibly hungry.

The two nurses turned to each other, each wanting the other to do something. They were shocked, and to put it frankly, shit scared. This man/corpse had been brought in only fifteen minutes ago, his body completely devoid of blood. Not a drop could be found in him. Outside, there was quite a bit, but in? Nary a corpuscle or platelet could be detected.

John could tell that the nurses were scared, they were as white as a white shirt washed in 'Wonda Whites NEW Whites Wash washes whites so much better than the old Wonda Whites, we wonder what sort of wankers you were to buy the old stuff'. He wanted to say something to reassure them that everything was all right but his throat was too dry to speak. He needed a drink but had no way to ask for it.

He pulled himself off the bench and reached out to the nurses, he felt so weak. The nurses jumped back, their hearts were pounding so heavily in their chests that it was almost deafening.

And that caused him a moment's pause of thought – their heartbeats deafening them would be perfectly rational under normal circumstances given this abnormal circumstance, but deafening to him? The deep bass pounding of muscle pumping, the snapping of atrium valves preventing the backward flow of life's liquid. It was turning John's brain into a burning mush of hunger and insanity. He needed to stop that noise.

Eventually it did stop and when the mists of anguish had cleared from his muddled brain, John knew that although he was not properly dead, he was at least damned.

***

It had been a surprising day for Cameron Mortice. This morning he had been sleeping peacefully in his Edinburgh flat when his door came, suddenly, crashing to the floor. The reason for this extreme and sudden transference of what is commonly regarded as a vertical object, to being horizontal, was because of the appearance of the two big brothers of the two biggest rugby forwards you have ever seen. They inflicted a minimal amount of violence upon his person and ejected him from the building. He was left standing in the street in his T-shirt and boxer shorts. He thanked someone somewhere that it had not been a hot enough night to warrant sleeping *á la buff*.

The morning commuters paid little attention to him. Cameron staggered around in circles trying to wake up and work out what to do. He rubbed his knocked about head, he looked at his reflection in a window; a couple of bruises on his face; his fair hair still suffering from night time pillow damage; a nasty twinge in the nape of his neck that gave the signal of an impending headache. Still, mustn't grumble.

The two steroid abusers loaded up their van with what Cameron considered to be 'all his worldly possessions' and they climbed into the cab. Cameron deemed it safe to return to his flat and did so. On the door he found a card; 'BRUISE BROTHERS BAILIFFS'.

"Piss," Cameron said.

The bailiffs had removed everything he owned and everything he had acquired over the last six years that he had spent here. Some councils take non-payment of utility bills very seriously in certain places around the country.

This left him with no choice any more. He had been putting off the inevitable for far too long now; he was going to have to go home to his family. But how? It was whilst staring at the floor in a mire of self-pity that he realised his feet had taken the initiative and had started walking.

As the morning continued and his journey progressed, he was surprised that he did not get arrested or even more severely beaten up; as he stuck his thumb out and began hitch-hiking he was even more surprised when a car actually pulled over to pick him up.

"Just because the driver's female doesn't mean she isn't a psycho," Cameron said to himself before getting in.

"Where are you going?" the driver asked. He noticed her look at his bare legs and shorts and suddenly felt very vulnerable.

"Sussex, eventually," he replied, "but Leeds for now."

She started the car. "I'm going as far as Newcastle. You'll have to get another lift from there."

"That'd be great, thanks." Cameron said aloud but was thinking, *Please let me live to get another lift.*

He was therefore surprised to be dropped off on the A1 junction at Washington without a scratch.

"Maybe life isn't such a bastard after all," he said as the police car pulled up beside him.

An hour of interviews and half an hour of story corroboration later, Cameron was allowed to go on his way. The police, being fine public servants, supplied him with more appropriate travelling attire: trousers two sizes too small and shoes two sizes too big. He thanked them all the same and only swore at them under his breath for fifteen minutes.

His second lift was a male driver. "Just because he's a bloke doesn't mean he is a psycho."

The hour-long journey passed uneventfully, except for a riveting debate on the Euro elections that Cameron contributed to with such enthusiasm. The driver's destination was York so he dropped Cameron off and gave him some change to call Leeds, which he went to do as soon as he found a phone.

He stood in the telephone booth reciting numbers silently to himself. It had been a while since he had called this one and he was slightly wary as to what sort of reception he would receive.

"What's the sodding number," he muttered under his breath. "Oh-double-one-three-two, erm. Now was it... no." In the end he just dialled the numbers that came into his head and hoped for the best. Five-five-five, five-five-five.

The line was connected. "Hello?" a girl's voice enquired.

"Can I speak to Gillian Kildress please?" Cameron asked. "It's Cameron Mortice."

He looked out of the window of the phone box at the town he had been dropped off at. His attention was drawn back to the phone.

"Hello yes? She isn't? Well what time does she finish? Well can you tell her I phoned and that my life has fallen apart and I'm currently stuck in the arse end of nowhere in some toss hole called Wetherby and -"

The girl on the other end interrupted him.

"What?" he asked incredulously.

He listened intently to the repeated statement.

"Why should I give a rat's arse about the British Legal Deposits Library?" he asked her and listened to the reply.

"I know I've got time on my hands," he squealed then exasperation calmed him down. "Please, just tell Gillian I'll call again later." He hung up quite forcefully. "Piss!"

The thumb emerged once more at the A58 Junction towards Leeds and he started walking.

Ten miles later he entered the city of Leeds with new and improved blisters on his feet. He made his way to the first cafe and their phone. He dialled and eventually the phone was answered.

"Gillian? Thank god. No, I'm in Leeds now. In a place called Bernie's Caff on Roundhay Road. I don't know. The top half I imagine. Can you come and get me and I'll explain everything later. Okay. Bye."

He hung up and sat down at a table. A waitress walked up.

"What can I get you?" she asked him.

"Coffee please," he said and she walked off again.

He looked up at the clock on the wall, he had been on the move constantly for the last eight hours and he was absolutely knackered. He did not even have the energy to tell the nutter who sat down opposite him to piss off.

"I don't have any change," Cameron automatically muttered when his uninvited guest opened his mouth.

"Well, that makes two of us then," the nutter replied with an over accentuated English accent and he placed his walking stick across the centre of the table.

Cameron shook his head with bewilderment.

"You seem to be a bit down, had some trouble?" He seemed to have some sort of continental intonation in his voice.

"That would be an understatement." Cameron replied.

The waitress brought Cameron's coffee over and dropped it in front of him. She did not seem to notice the nutter. Cameron studied him, silver unkempt hair, dirty face, white stubble, and the bluest crystalline eyes. He could have passed for a sixty-year-old at an idle glance, but close inspection would have narrowed it to somewhere between thirty and forty. The ageing processes had had practically the opposite effect on Cameron; at a quick glimpse you might have said twenty at a push, but what with him graduating from Edinburgh two years ago said he had to be about twenty-three. He would then have told you that before his three-year course he had taken two years off after his 'A' levels.

"What do you believe?" the nutter asked.

Cameron came back to attention with a start. "What?"

"I just wanted to know what you believed in."

Cameron laughed to himself and tried to catch the waitress's eye to come and save him. He had to settle for pretending the nutter was not there and drinking his coffee.

"Do you believe in UFOs, fairies, ghosts, what?"

Cameron's patience finally snapped. "I believe that I must have some sort of sign over my head that says that if there's any shit in the world then it should come and pay me a great deal of time and attention."

"Do you really believe that?" Nutter asked.

"At this present moment in time, yes."

Nutter looked to the empty space above Cameron's head. "A sign? Do you know, I think I can see it."

Cameron calmed down again. "Somehow, I thought you might be able to," he said.

"Belief is a very powerful thing."

"Really." Cameron could not even be bothered to hide his disinterest.

"If you really truly believe in something, it will exist somewhere in the world and it will try to find you."

"Really."

"What do you really, truly believe in?" Nutter stared at Cameron without a trace of madness. He was serious.

Cameron could not help but answer. "I believe in one true love and love at first sight. I believe that your true love's laugh will sound like an angel's song. I believe in the sanctity of marriage and the honesty of relationships. I believe that you never forget who your real friends are and that you should make your enemies think they're friends so you can keep an eye on them. I believe that any government will fuck it up somewhere for someone and that those in power shouldn't be. I believe in living for the moment but not to be stupid about ignoring the future. I believe in ghosts, UFOs, heaven, hell, life after death but not fairies."

Cameron watched his inquisitor for a reaction, Nutter simply widened his eyes as if to say, 'Is that it?' An image suddenly flashed across his mind and he blurted, "I believe in vampires."

Nutter raised his eyebrows. "What made you say that?"

"You asked, I answered," Cameron replied unconvincingly and decided it to be a good move to bury his reddening face in his coffee cup and start drinking again.

"They are out there and they will try to find you," Nutter warned and raised himself out of his seat. "Watch your back Cameron Mortice. I hope we will not have to meet again."

"Not even half as much as me, pal," Cameron said and continued drinking. He stopped and looked up. "How did you...?" but Nutter had gone.

The door to the cafe opened and a young woman entered. She was in her mid twenties, slim and about six foot tall. She had shoulder length red hair and a pale clean complexion. She turned her emerald green eyes in his direction and stormed towards him. Cameron got up to meet her. They embraced affectionately and parted only to lock lips. Cameron pulled away sharply, yelping with pain, rubbing one of the bruises by his mouth.

"You've been beaten up," she said and slapped him across the face.

Cameron leapt away further, yelping louder. "What was that for?"

"I don't know. You just deserved it. Let's go, I'm double parked outside."

"You're going to have to pay for my coffee, Gillian," he said and edged out of arm's reach.

"You're crap aren't you."

Gillian paid the bill, they left, got in her orange mini and drove towards the city centre.

"What happened?" Gillian demanded.

"I got kicked out. I lost everything." He hung his head in shame.

"And you came all the way down here to me. What am I supposed to do with you?"

Cameron edged his way to the door. "Just put me up for the night and I'll be on my way tomorrow." He did not move far enough away. He yelped and rubbed his dead arm.

"You bastard," she spat, "what about all your mates in Edinburgh?"

"They've all left. I don't know anybody up there any more."

They drove in silence for a while, Cameron still looking at his feet, Gillian gritting her teeth.

"How long have we been going out with one another?" she asked.

"Are you talking literal time wise, or physical time that we've spent together?" he asked.

"Both," she replied.

"Well, we first got off with each other at Danny's party last Easter, so time wise it's been about a year and a quarter."

"And physically?"

He wrinkled his brow in concentration. "That weekend, the weekend you came up to see me,"

"You were stoned the whole time so it doesn't count," she interrupted.

"All right. About a fortnight in total over the summer, a weekend at Christmas, another party at Danny's the next Easter, and now."

"A grand total of twenty three days Cameron. Hardly the basis for a stable relationship with a promising future."

Cameron's bottom lip popped out and he puffed his cheeks. "Have you been seeing someone else? Owwww!"

"You know damn well that I'm not like that." Gillian flexed her aching knuckles.

Cameron rubbed his arm and winced in pain. "Are you trying to say you want to end it then?"

"No you stupid idiot. I'm saying I want to make a more positive try of things." She pulled the car to a halt at a red light and turned to look at him. "Don't go home straight away, stay here for a while."

"I want to," he said, "but I didn't want it to look like I was running to you now the shit's hit the fan."

The light turned green and Gillian pulled off again. "So what would you call this then?"

Cameron smiled sheepishly. "I'm sorry I'm so crap," he mumbled and Gillian laughed aloud. Cameron thought he heard a choir of angels sing.

Gillian was living in typical student accommodation; not too messy, but then again hardly what would be described as a clean house, which she shared with three others of a similar age group. Cameron was slightly amused to recognise many of the characteristics of the abode as similar to his own experiences in student accommodation. The obligatory road works flashing lamp (not working), tattered umbrella (unusable), discarded cricket bat (unused), and a collection of various videos and video cases under the television set that had probably looked quite neat at the beginning of term when they had been displayed on the owner's shelves. A large wooden clock chimed loudly on the hour as he stepped through the front door.

The only male in the house (considered himself extremely lucky) was Daniel Night, the party host responsible for Cameron and Gillian's meeting. He was slightly taller than Gillian and built of brick shit house proportions. He had brown hair neatly parted above a handsome, permanently tanned face. Needless to say, the girls loved him (so did some of the boys), and the boys hated him (except those who loved him).

Cassandra Twee was Danny's girlfriend. She was about half his size but everything was in good proportion. Meaning that both of her legs were of the same length, and stuff. Anyway, what she lost in height she made up for in black belt martial arts. She was Danny's bodyguard. She had shoulder length green hair, which tended to turn red in the winter, and a rather striking array of earrings, approximately ten in each ear. People feared for her safety during thunderstorms.

The fourth occupant was Penny Helsine; the female to whom Cameron had spoken to earlier. She was what could be described as having the appearance of a stereotypical feminist; she had a severe crew cut, and dressed in Doc Martens and dungarees all the time. Although having an almost harsh and intimidating appearance, Penny was probably the nicest person out of everyone you have been introduced to so far (especially John). She was nice. There was no real other way of describing her. She would listen to what you had to say, no matter how stupid, irritating, or boring, and appear genuinely interested. She could make intelligent conversation after six pints of Scrumpy *and* be able to see you home all right.

It is because of her niceness that would explain why everyone got so emotional when she had gone. But that is not until later.

Cameron was ushered into the house and reintroduced to everyone. Pleasantries were exchanged and embarrassing silences endured until Cassandra did the unsociable thing of turning the television on to catch the end of a mindless Australian soap. The conversations began to flow.

"Who was that?" Cameron asked.

"God, when was the last time you saw this?" Cassandra snorted.

"About three months ago," he replied.

"Oh no," the household groaned in unison.

"You're not going to sit there and ask who everyone is as they walk on are you?" Gillian asked.

"Don't worry about it Cameron," Danny said, "I've been watching this shit for the past three years and I still don't know who everyone is."

"I only wanted to know who that one was," Cameron reiterated.

Penny came to his rescue. "That was Anny. She's John's daughter but not really. She's living in the street with her daughter Sally, and stepdaughter Tina. She's applying for a divorce from her husband Frank who is now running the guesthouse."

"Where are the twins?" he enquired.

"Oh puhlease," Cassandra chirped. "What planet have you been living on? Carol's gone to Hawaii and Pauline went to America after her fling with Raoul."

"Has Seeda had her baby yet?" Cameron asked nonchalantly, trying to make out he did know some of the up to date plot lines.

Everyone laughed. "Even I know that's 'Family And Friends'," guffawed Danny.

"Oh yeah," Cameron said quietly and sank back in his seat, not a word passed his lips until the final credits. "They've changed the theme music," he announced.

"Loser!" the household chanted.

"Bollocks to the lot of you," he declared in the face of defeat. Everyone laughed.

***

Neil Abbot was a bastard and he loved it. In the entire history of the company, he was the only employee to ever attain the position of bank manager before he was thirty. He achieved this by keeping an eye on everything that went on around him. Every little indiscretion that took place, he noted down. Then, when a company inspector came to visit, he pounced. The then manager was fifty-eight and was due to retire soon anyway. Neil had not held himself personally responsible, apparently it was a well-known fact that he had a dodgy heart. The way was paved.

His phone rang and with the reactions of a cobra he picked it up. He enjoyed hearing the shock on the caller's voice when he answered so quickly.

"Yes," he said. "Again? Yes, very well, show him in."

Neil got up from his desk and opened his filing cabinet. He took out a file and put it on his desk.

There was a knock on the door and he opened it.

"Back so soon Mr Settle, I did give you a fortnight," Neil smarmed.

He was still smiling as John showed him his still beating heart.

***

"So what am I supposed to do while you're revising?" Cameron moaned.

"Go out somewhere. Danny and Penny have finished. Go out with them."

"Gillian," he whined.

"No. I've got this exam tomorrow first thing and I've hardly done anything for it. Take this and buy yourself some drinks." She handed him a five-pound note from her pocket.

There was a knock at the door and Penny stuck her head round. "Danny and I are going now. Are you coming Cameron?"

"Suppose so," he replied and trudged out of the room.

"See you later Gilly," Penny smiled and left.

"Don't you wait to be asked to enter a room?" Cameron asked Penny.

"What do you mean?" she enquired.

"Just now, you walked straight in. We could have been doing anything."

Penny snorted. "I don't think so."

"What's that supposed to mean?" Cameron demanded.

"Later," she replied.

Cameron frowned and followed in silence.

The three of them left the house and walked fifty yards before entering The Black Dragon Inn. They got a table in the corner of the pub and sat down with their drinks.

Danny stood up suddenly. "Fancy a game of pinball?"

Cameron and Penny declined his offer and he walked off alone.

"How's it going between you and Gillian?" Penny asked.

"Okay I think," Cameron replied.

"She likes you a lot, you know that don't you?"

"Ish."

"What's that mean?"

"I sort of know. Had a suspicion," he said uneasily.

"How do you feel about her?"

"What is this?" Cameron asked in semi-mock irritation, "Oprah Winfrey or something?"

"I was only asking, I didn't think you'd get this upset about it," Penny explained.

Cameron calmed down. "I'm not upset, I just want to know what's with all the questions. Has Gillian been saying something?"

"Well, sort of." It was Penny's turn to feel uneasy.

There was a knock at Gillian's door.

"Yeah," she called out and Cassandra walked in.

"Well?" Cassandra asked.

"Well what?"

"Did you say anything?"

"No, not yet," Gillian said and turned her attention back to the books on her desk.

"For crying out loud Gillian. You said next time you see him."

"It's been nearly two months and he suddenly turns up on my doorstep from over a hundred miles away, the first thing I ask is not going to be, 'How come we've never shagged?'"

The uneasy stick was passed back to Cameron. "Er. Bloody hell."

"I don't know why, but it seems to bother her." Penny was still holding one end of it.

"I don't know, it's never actually come up before." Cameron was staring intensely back through the mists of time.

"You're impotent?" Penny asked.

Cameron was abruptly brought back to reality. "No! I mean the topic of sex has never come up before. I haven't rushed into things because of, well, you know."

"No."

Cameron's face flushed red. His eyes darted around the room searching for a possible escape route while his brain searched for the appropriate words without using the only words it had available.

"I'm still a virgin," he finally blurted.

Cassandra's eyes were as wide as plates. "You're not."

"Yes I am." Gillian's face was turning the same colour as her hair.

"What, never?"

"Never all right?" Embarrassment was giving way to annoyance.

"Blimey," Cassandra declared.

"Yeah well, it's not as if I've not done anything sort of associated with sex," Gillian protested. "I've messed around, you know."

"No."

Cameron was getting a bit upset. "We've done stuff. Slept together, played around. I never wanted to put any pressure on. I've always been too scared to say anything."

"Do you love her?" Penny asked.

Cameron started fidgeting, getting more uncomfortable. "Well, yeah, I suppose. Perhaps."

"What do you mean 'perhaps'?"

"It's hard to say, I mean, it's not as if we've been seeing each other for very long."

"Twenty three days to be precise," said Gillian. "He just seems so casual that I don't want to make an idiot out of myself."

"Not really a lot I can suggest," Cassandra shrugged.

"How did you and Danny get together?"

"Fresher's Ball. We both got extremely pissed, got off with each other and shagged out in the car park behind the bowling alley. A couple of weeks later I bumped into him again to tell him I thought I was pregnant and he said he'd come to the clinic with me. I just fell for him straight away."

"Because he went to the clinic with you?"

"And the fact that he's got a really big willy. I mean huge." She indicated "huge" with her hands.

Gillian looked bewildered. "Does that really matter then? The size?"

"God yeah."

"But I thought..." Gillian was getting more confused.

Cassandra took a deep breath. "Look it's quite simple, any bloke that tells you 'size isn't important', is suffering from a severe case of fish bait if you get my drift."

"But I've heard girls say it as well," Gillian told her.

"Well, either they wouldn't know a big willy when they saw one, or they have trouble parking cars."

"What?"

"They can't judge distances," Cassandra explained. "They think six inches is a foot."

Gillian looked even more concerned that ever.

"How big is Cameron's?" Cassandra asked.

"Cass!" Gillian shouted.

"I only asked."

Gillian shrugged her shoulders. "I don't have anything to compare it with. Except for what you say 'huge' is."

"Huge. Enormous. Gigantic," Danny announced.

"Good game was it Danny?" Penny asked.

"The highest score I've ever got. Who wants another drink?"

Penny and Cameron raised their empty glasses to him.

"Shit," he said and slouched off to the bar.

Penny turned back to Cameron who was looking everywhere else but at her.

"How did you two get together?" she enquired innocently.

"We sort of knew of each other at school, I was two years ahead," Cameron said.

"I thought Gillian came from somewhere around Oxford – Didcot – and you're from Sussex."

"She does and I am," Cameron nodded. "Oh! Me and Gillian. I thought you meant me and Danny."

Penny's eyes rotated skyward and she tutted.

"It was one of Danny's parties last Easter. Her and Cassandra came down. A couple of my mates bet me I couldn't get off with Gillian so I turned on the charm, introduced myself, spiked her drinks and won the bet."

Penny's jaw dropped. "That's disgusting," she screeched.

"What's disgusting?" Danny asked and put three pints on the table.

"How him and Gillian first met," Penny explained.

"Oh that," Danny chuckled.

"You know?" She was becoming more amazed by the second. Cameron thought she was going to dislocate her jaw if it dropped any further.

"I still owe him a fiver for it," Danny said.

Cameron was waiting for the 'pop'.

"Does Gillian know?" Penny asked.

Both men nodded and drank their pints.

Any second now, he thought.

"What does she think about it?"

"She had a bet with me that she wouldn't be able to score," Danny said. "As soon as she pays me the five quid she owes, Cameron gets his."

Penny shut her mouth, drank her pint and dropped the subject for, as far as she was concerned, forever.

Gillian had abandoned her books for more disreputable reading material; magazines for the discerning woman.

"I didn't know you had stuff like this," she said, unable to drag her eyes away from the glossy pages. "Does Danny know?"

"Yeah. It was his fault that I started getting them."

"Why?"

"Because of all the jazz mags he collects. It's a big kinky thing for us."

Gillian turned to the centre page. "Dear god," she exclaimed.

Cassandra peered over her shoulder. "Danny's is bigger than that."

"How big is this?" Gillian asked sheepishly.

"I'd say that was pretty big," Cassandra replied. "How does it compare to Cameron's?" Gillian turned the magazine ninety degrees. "It's hard to say. The photo's at a strange angle. I didn't think magazines were allowed to show, you know."

"What, willies?"

"No. Upright willies." Gillian was blushing again and Cassandra giggled. "Don't laugh at me," Gillian whined.

"Sorry," Cassandra sniffed, looked at Gillian and burst out laughing again, curling up on the floor. "'Upright willies'," she howled.

Gillian smiled upon hearing how ridiculous she must have sounded. "All right then, stiff cocks," she said.

Cassandra laughed even louder.

Eventually she calmed down a bit and looked at Gillian with absolute sincerity. "Look, it doesn't matter how big he is. All that matters is how you feel and how he makes you feel."

Gillian smiled but still looked uncertain.

"There's nothing to worry about," Cassandra tried to

reassure her. "The first time you do it will be so scary because it's nothing like you could possibly imagine, and it hurts like a bastard to start off with. If you get as pissed as a fart before hand, try to relax and let him get on with it, it will be over before you know it and you'll wonder what all the fuss was about."

"I don't want him to go off me because I'm no good," Gillian said.

"Then the next time you'll have a better idea of what to do. It's all so natural and easy, it just develops by itself."

Cassandra leant over the magazines and hugged her friend, Gillian whispered, "Thanks," into her ear and they sat back again looking down at the array of erect members on show.

"Penis envy my arse," Cassandra said. "I can't imagine why any woman would want one of those things stuck to her."

"It's not meant literally," Gillian corrected.

"Fancy a smoke?" Cassandra asked.

"Yeah all right," said Danny stuffing his fifth packet of crisps into his mouth. "One more and then we can go back and skin up."

"Danny," Penny chastised, "not so loud."

"Sorry," he said and spat crisps.

Cameron stood to go to the bar. "You might as well count me out, Gillian doesn't like me doing that sort of stuff around her."

He walked up to the bar. "Two pints of Flowers and a pint of Strongbow please," he requested. In his head he was planning the rest of the evening.

They go back to the house and while Penny, Danny and Cassandra stay downstairs to have a smoke, he goes upstairs to find Gillian still working. She turns to look at him as he enters the room. He locks the door behind him and she smiles knowingly. She gets up and meets him in the middle of the room, clothes fall from their bodies like the autumn leaves. They wrap each other in a tangle of exploring limbs. They fall to the bed and he enters her, thrusting with an unrequited passion. He comes before she realises that they are doing anything.

"Shit," he hissed and handed the barman his five-pound note. He collected the meagre change and returned to the table with the drinks.

"No crisps?" Danny complained.

"Sorry. No money," Cameron replied.

"Are you okay?" Penny asked.

"I'm scared," Cameron whispered.

"What's going on?" Danny interrupted.

Penny turned to him. "Well you know how Gilly's been complaining."

Cameron suddenly sat up. "You said she only mentioned something."

"What about not getting any?" Danny asked.

"She told you as well?"

Penny nodded to Danny. "Well it's because Cameron's still a virgin."

"Oh Jesus."

"No!" Danny gasped and Penny nodded. "I figured it had something to do with his preferences."

"You thought I was gay?"

Penny dismissed Danny's beliefs with a wave. "He's just scared you know."

"Hello, people. I am here," Cameron called. "You can talk to me."

"My first time was hilarious," Danny laughed. "I was so scared that I'd get caught afterwards."

"Where were you?" Penny asked.

"In my parents' room."

Cameron had ceased his complaining and had become enthralled with the story.

"Where were your parents?" Penny questioned.

"My dad was downstairs watching the football." He bobbed his head in silent laughter.

"Weren't you scared?" Cameron asked.

Danny shook his head, still smiling. "Too excited. I guess I can understand apprehension if you were planning it, but this just sort of happened."

"What?" Penny and Cameron demanded in unison.

"I was seventeen when it happened and I was just going into my parents' room to get a pair of socks out of my dad's cupboard."

"Cut out the details," Penny urged, "get on with the important stuff."

"Okay. I went in the room and she was just standing there, naked."

"What? An au pair or something?" Cameron asked.

Danny shook his head.

"Not your mum?" Penny asked.

"Gross," Danny yelled. Penny and Cameron sighed with relief. "My parents are divorced. It was my step mum."

Penny and Cameron said nothing. They simply stared.

"They'd only been married for about six months and she was obviously already bored with him. Anyway, she saw me come in and she just stared at me." Danny looked at the two staring at him now. "Not quite like that, more sexy. I said sorry for just barging in and was about to go when she told me not to. She wiggled towards me (I had a real horn by now) and we started snogging. Then we did it."

"On your dad's bed," said Cameron in disbelief.

"With your dad's wife," Penny said in utter amazement.

"Yeah," said Danny and laughed. "Is that totally mental or what?"

"And then some," Cameron agreed whilst Penny simply looked horrified.

"When was your first time Penny?" Danny asked.

Penny came back to her senses. "A long time ago," she said.

"Yeah? How old?"

She looked at Cameron; he was obviously embarrassed about a female discussing sex, he was pretending to not really pay attention by drinking quickly.

"About thirteen," she said.

"You weren't raped or anything were you?" Danny asked bluntly and Cameron nearly drowned on his cider.

"'Thirteen'? I hadn't even got my first pubes at thirteen," he squealed and returned his attention to his drink.

"No," she replied flatly. "I was playing 'Doctors and Nurses' with the boy next door. It just went a bit too far."

"As far as 'gynaecologists and lonely house wives'?" Danny asked but Penny simply eyed him with disdain.

"Our parents weren't impressed," she continued.

"No shit?" commented Cameron.

"I was raised in an atmosphere of devout Catholicism and my father thought I'd been possessed or something. I was sent to a boarding school run by strict nuns who were told exactly what had happened and I was caned every night for five years."

Once again Cameron was struck silent and, for once, Danny joined him.

"I never saw my parents again," she said matter-of-factly. "I haven't had sex again since then either."

Silence ruled the table.

"Sorry," Penny finally said. "You did ask though."

"I know I did," Gillian protested, "but I didn't think you were going to be so graphic." She took another drag from the joint and inhaled deeply. She coughed.

Cassandra returned her skirt to its proper place and sat down on the magazines. A penis caught her attention and she pulled it towards her. "He is fucking gorgeous. I wouldn't mind working up an appetite with him."

Gillian started giggling uncontrollably. "Do you," she panted, "do you 'spit or swallow'?" She screamed with laughter.

"I swallow," Cassandra answered and looked at her bewildered.

Gillian fell over she was laughing so hard. She was writhing in a sea of swollen two dimensional cocks. "I'm a sperm," she announced between shrieks.

Cassandra leaned over her incapacitated friend and removed the joint from her convulsing hand; she giggled to herself. "Sometimes, after I've been down on him, I pretend to swallow and go to kiss him and spoon it all into his mouth."

Gillian was not breathing properly. "Please stop," she gasped. "I can't, I can't take any more."

"Okay, calm down," Cassandra soothed.

Gillian sat upright, flushed and panting heavily. She wiped the tears from her cheeks. "How was your first time?" she asked.

"I got pissed out of my face and passed out half way through. I couldn't even tell you who did it to me. I woke up with a splitting headache, a split fanny, and a split condom by the bed."

"What happened to the bloke?"

"He had split."

The two girls roared with laughter.

Silence had resumed its command in association with embarrassment. It was finally decided by all to return home and try to change the conversation.

From the top of the street they heard the screaming from the house.

"What the hell is that?" Cameron asked.

"Cassandra's stoned," answered Danny. "She always screeches like that when she's been spliffing." He suddenly took off up the street and into the house.

Cameron turned to Penny. "Doesn't he like her smoking?" he asked.

"It's not that," she replied, "he wants to get there quickly before she smokes it all."

They entered the house and heard Danny call from upstairs. "Hey guys, up here. You're not going to believe this."

They jogged upstairs into Danny's room The sight before them was a Dalian nightmare; two women rolling around a carpet of turgid todgers and bizarre sexual toys, laughing uncontrollably and gabbling unrecognisably.

"They're both wasted," Danny announced.

"You fucking hypocrite Gillian," Penny shouted. "All those years of self righteous preaching, and now this." She pointed at all the cigarette butts amongst the peachy bare butts.

Cameron did not think he could handle any more shocks this evening. "You've been smoking, Gillian?"

She looked up at him. "Show us your willy," she yelled and began convulsing again.

Danny and Penny looked to Cameron. Cameron just stared at the ceiling and shook his head in disbelief.

Neil had woken up with a pain in his chest, something was not right. It was dark and humid and he was wrapped up tightly in plastic. He started to panic; he could not catch his breath. He stopped panicking when he realised that he did not need to breathe. It was then that he knew that he was dead.

A silver line slowly came into focus in the darkness about an inch above his face; it ran down the length of his body. It looked like a zip. He pushed at it and the body bag he was in split open; much to the surprise of the police, ambulance men and bank staff.

Their was a scream, two people passed out, jaws dropped, heart beats increased, the noise was deafening to Neil. He forced his hands over his ears, attempting to block out the bass beat of life. The pain was unbearable. He screamed and windows shattered.

The onlookers were watching a man with a gaping hole in his chest writhing in pain, and screaming. His eyes had turned crimson red and his teeth were growing. Each time he screamed at the sky, the awe struck audience witnessed his canines pushing further and further out through his gums.

The pain had subsided, what was left was an aching emptiness. Hunger. The beat was still hammering at his eardrums, but instead of hurting, it made him crave sustenance, he needed to feed.

Leaping to his feet caused some of the more sensible onlookers to run. A few could not move.

A police officer came to his senses, although not his senses of survival. He stepped forward. "All right sir," he said, "if you'll just calm down we'll get the doctors to take another look at that injury." With hindsight he would have considered this to be a very stupid thing to say. Alas, he was not going to get the chance for hindsight.

Neil flew across the room at the officer, ripping his helmet and forehead off.

The officer stared blankly, his throat emitted choked, gagging noises. The last things to go through his mind were Neil's teeth.

Neil sank his mouth into the pink fruit of thought. He sucked back and swallowed the juices of remembrance. "Ah, sweeter than pomegranate," he declared to his horrified audience, "and none of those annoying seeds that stick between your teeth."

After finishing his appetiser, Neil turned to the rest of the crowd who were now, no longer there. Instead stood a lone man, silver unkempt hair, dirty face and the bluest crystalline eyes. Something about the man nagged at Neil's memory; something about the way he leaned on his walking stick produced an instinctive feeling of fear.

Neil smiled, blood dripped from his mouth. "I've tasted a red head, let's see if blondes are more fun."

Once again he seemed to fly across the room, Nutter just stood his ground but pulled ever so slightly at the handle of his stick which released a thin epee.

There was the briefest flash of silver and Neil felt severe pain. He span wildly across the floor clutching at the stump of his wrist. His hand twitched at Nutter's feet; it seemed to age rapidly before their eyes and eventually crumbled to dust.

Neil pulled himself off the floor. "I'm going to make you wish you hadn't done that."

The stump of his arm began to swell. It gently pulsated as it grew; when it was the size of a fist, five fingers grew out of it. His new hand established its proper form on his arm with a popping noise as the new bones snapped into their appropriate places.

"You've learnt quickly," Nutter said. "A pity you will have no time to teach anyone else." He lunged forward, his sword sliced through the air and into Neil's chest. He rocked on the spot.

"A sword... through the space... where my heart should be?" Neil enquired in disbelief.

"Whatever you believe will work," replied Nutter and he extracted his sword from Neil's chest.

"A... wooden stake... through the heart normally," Neil coughed.

"You are dying though, aren't you," Nutter said.

"I... believe so."

The wound in Neil's chest opened wider, a shaft of light poured out of his thoracic cavity. His entire body folded in on itself, into the light. He was gone.

Nutter was gone.

John was bored. In the period of one day he had considered

his life over, got his rocks off, had his throat ripped out, come back to life, fed, then fulfilled the ultimate dream of killing his bank manager. What on earth was there left to do?

A memory of a person suddenly flashed through his mind, and with it came a worry. He had better phone his wife; she would probably be getting concerned as to his whereabouts.

Locating a phone box, he entered it and searched his pockets for change. None.

He lifted the handset and dialled the operator. "Reversed charges for five-five-five five-five-five-five please," he said and waited. Eventually the call was put through. "Honey, it's John. I just thought I'd... What? Your husband John. Yes I know they probably did but if you'll let me explain... Patty? Don't hang up. Patty."

The line went dead.

"Fuck!" John swore. He had not taken into consideration the fact that the police, upon discovering his body and identity, would have located his next of kin and declared his demise.

He would just have to go round there and explain in person. He stepped out of the telephone box and began rising into the air. He did not know how he was doing it; it just came as a natural action.

He was slowly rising above the trees. He discovered that he had lost all sense of direction so lowered himself back to the ground to get his bearings.

Fairly confident of his location, he ascended once more and flew in the general direction of home, keeping a careful eye on the streets below and on any low flying aircraft.

The cool evening air rushed past his ears, the low clouds condensing on his clothes and face, stinging his eyes. For a brief moment – whilst he was completely deprived of all external sensory information – he thought.

I'm dead. I'm really dead. I've died and become an undead; a vampire. I've killed, drunk blood and created more. Why? How? Where have we come from?

Then, as if on command, answers began to filter into his mind. Memories from someone else's mind transferred into his and suddenly he was remembering thoughts, experiences and actions that did not belong to him. Experiences that came from thousands of others, from times thousands of years before his own and from places that he never knew existed. This sudden cerebral information download was overwhelming, dizzying. He forced his mind to close itself off to everything other than his own thoughts and then he gently lowered himself to the ground to compose his state of mind.

He took a couple of deep breaths. "Altitude sickness," he put the symptoms down to. "Thin air and a lack of oxygen to the brain."

He looked around him and noticed the landmark of his local corner shop a bit further down the road.

"I can walk from here thanks very much," he muttered to anyone who might be listening in and picked up a brisk pace down the road and took the second turning on the left after the post box.

He reached his front garden and deftly vaulted the fence landing softly on the grass; he admired his newly discovered athletic prowess as he walked up to the front door and searched his pockets for his keys but found none. He rang the doorbell and waited.

He heard muffled voices from inside, the sound of heavy footsteps approaching the door and then the chain lock being removed.

The door opened and a man's face peered round.

"Hello, George," said John.

"Holy shit," said George and slammed the door.

"That's not very nice, George," John shouted at the door, "this is my house after all."

John pressed his hand against the door and pushed it open again. He walked into the hallway where the man called George was fearfully backing down.

"You're supposed to be dead," George said. "The police came round, told Patricia you'd had your throat slashed. I came and identified the body, for Christ's sake."

John was getting closer. "What can I say," he shrugged his shoulders, "I got better."

George was obviously scared, John could hear it in his voice. "What happened, John?"

A woman stepped into the hall. She was middle aged and

had been crying; her cheeks were heavily stained with tears and run mascara.

"Hello Patty," John said and she fainted.

George's heart beat quickened dramatically, so much that John began salivating and his eyes turned to that distinct shade of red.

"John, what the hell are you?" George spluttered.

John smiled; his canines had extended to razor fangs. "It's such a long story," he said, "so much easier if I just showed you."

George wanted to scream but was too startled to find John biting through his oesophagus.

John's children were startled to see their mother on the floor, their father still alive, and seemingly necking their uncle.

"Just keeping it in the family, kids," he told them. "Blood being tastier than water and all that."

The scene had changed slightly; all five of them were sitting on the floor now. Candles were lit along the desk, cupboard, chest of drawers and across the floor. The magazined manhoods had now been joined in unholy matrimony with an array of photographic fannies. Danny had decided to bridge the sexual equality gap by displaying his own collection of specialist reading.

A production line of joints were being rolled, Danny and Cassandra sat opposite each other, rolled one each then passed it to the person on their left.

Cameron and Gillian sat next to each other; Gillian looked extremely tired. Penny sat opposite them; she took a drag of a cigarette and inhaled deeply.

"The trouble with parents," she blew the smoke from her lungs, "is that they forget what it's like to be young."

"That's the same with lecturers," Danny added. "They've been to University, they know what it's like being a student but they still expect you to do work."

Penny continued unperturbed. "Take my father."

"Where?" quipped Cassandra and giggled to herself.

Penny eyed her disdainfully. "He's so high and fucking mighty. I make one mistake when I'm too young to know otherwise and he disowns me."

"Same with me," added Cameron. "My family think I'm a loser,"

"You are," mumbled Gillian and rolled to the floor.

"But I know different," he ignored her. "I'm going to be something special, I'm going to be immortalised somehow."

"Be careful what you wish for," Penny warned, "immortality may not be anything special. You'll see all your friends and loved ones die around you."

"You've seen 'Highlander' too many times, Penny," Danny said.

Cameron shook his head whilst inhaling the intoxicating fumes. "It's not a wish. It's a fact. Some bloke told me that if I believed in something hard enough, it'll happen." He passed the cigarette to Gillian who had passed out so it went straight on to Cassandra.

"Who was this bloke?" she asked. "Obi Wan Kenobi?"

"Screw you, dope head," he retorted.

"Seriously," said Penny, "who did say this?"

"Some nutter I met in the cafe whilst waiting for Gillian to pick me up."

Danny chuckled to himself. "Red Five, I'm going in," he announced and fell backwards into the sea of genitalia.

Gillian sat bolt upright. "I'm going to be sick," she declared and everyone moved.

They backed against walls and doors; Cassandra had jumped onto her bed. They froze and stared at Gillian as she sat in the lotus position, pupils dilated and vacant.

"False alarm," she said and fell to the floor again.

Everybody sighed with relief and resumed their seats. Cameron raised Gillian to the upright position once more. "I'd better get her to bed," he said.

"Yeah, right," sniggered Danny.

"She's in the right mood for it," added Cassandra.

"What are you on about?" Cameron asked and lifted the protesting Gillian to her feet.

"Ignore them," said Penny. "See you in the morning."

"Okay. Good night," he said and dragged Gillian out of the room.

Half way down the hall her eyes shot open. "I'm really going to be sick this time," she declared.

Cameron managed to get her to the bathroom and throw her head down the toilet just as she began retching. He sat beside her, rubbing her back and saying soothing things. "That's it," he said in a soft voice, "get it all out."

"Cameron," she gasped between mouthfuls, "stop rubbing my back. It's really annoying."

"Sorry," he said, stopped, and let her get on with it.

Cameron's earlier fantasy of how the evening was going to pass had given way to the reality of Gillian vomiting for two hours then passing out hugging the toilet bowl.

What with him not being a particularly muscular bloke, and Gillian not being a particularly small woman, he found it practically impossible to prise her from her lavatorial embrace. He left her to it and went to bed.

***

Outside, a storm was brewing. Dark clouds gathered over the city, occasionally flickering in the darkness. They rumbled a deep stomach hunger that needed satisfying.

The populace of Leeds were in for a rough night.

***

The doorbell rang and John Settle Junior, nineteen years old, answered it. He opened the door an inch and looked at the policeman standing on the porch.

"Er, hello," said the policeman, "we've had reports of a disturbance here. Is everything all right?"

"Yes," John junior replied.

"Can I speak with your mother?" he asked.

"Just a minute," the boy said and closed the door.

It returned to the same open position and Patricia Settle peered through the gap. "Yes?"

"Sorry to disturb you Mrs Settle, but we heard..."

"There's no trouble, officer," she interrupted, "we're all just a bit upset that's all."

"If you're sure?" he inquired.

"Yes," she answered and closed the door. The policeman shrugged his shoulders and strolled back to his car. Had he noticed the faint palm indentation in the door and the slightly splintered doorframe around the lock, he might not have walked anywhere ever again.

The hallway to the house was covered with blood; it was smeared down the walls, pools stained the carpet, and Tracy Settle, seven years old, was still lying in a small puddle of her own.

John Settle was sitting in a large armchair that was positioned in the centre of the room and you could tell it was 'his' seat. His body moulded perfectly in the leather embrace; it had been placed directly in front of the television with the ideal angle to benefit from the surround sound of the digital stereo 3D dog's bollocks audio system; and it had the remote control resting on the right arm for minimal elbow and wrist exertion against maximum channel changing efficiency. His son had sat down on the adjacent sofa which was positioned with its back to a large set of French windows; these opened out to a well cared for garden with a neatly mown lawn, trimmed borders and busy eco-friendly vegetable patch.

John watched his son for any sign of emotion and/or reaction to this sudden turn of events, but his face showed nothing except, perhaps, the preoccupation of self-indulgent, deep thought. The boy's blood-stained pyjamas were already filling admirably; he had always been concerned for the physical state of his post pubescent boy – his gawky, lanky body and unfortunate facial skin disorder had been, if we were going to be honest, a disappointment to John. What father did not, would not, want his son to be a handsome, popular, athletic *uberman* rather than a geeky, possibly homo, ugly twat. Apologies for the harshness of a father's description, but he recognised the characteristics from the twats he knew when he was a boy. It was unfortunate, but a fact of life. Now his boy was beginning to live up to his expectations.

John drifted his gaze over to his brother-in-law, George, who had adapted to the change far more casually than John junior. Now there was a disappointment, both in life and death, the sad, fat, balding, perverted son-of-a-bitch was still sad, fat and balding. He hoped to god (not necessarily The God, any god would do) that the perversion may have cleared up with the change. John studied the relaxed man and frowned, George had actually accepted his fate far more casually than *he* had actually done. George had not shown an iota of a second thought, doubt or misgiving to his sudden change of species; he had been human, he had died and now he was a vampire. As simple as that. 'Nuff said.

John could not decide whether this was a good thing or not – straight acceptance against moral and ethical turmoil, it was probably a good thing for George. These thoughts brought John's attention back to his child; no longer just a son – an individual who had been created by half a cell created automatically by him – but an immediate offspring of his, a being for whom he was directly, solely and deliberately responsible.

Patricia walked back into the room and the three males looked up at her; she had become even more beautiful to John now than she had ever been before. Physically, she had slimmed and perted making her a socially contrived vision of female perfection; but also emotionally, John now felt closer to her than ever before. She was still his wife whom he loved; she had become more than the girl he had fancied as a youth; and was also – like his son – a creation of his. A child to protect and nurture.

Pride washed over his entire being as he rejoiced in his new family. He had managed to bring them together in a way that no blood ties could ever claim – they all shared a death bringer in him. They were the perfect family unit.

"Who wants some?" Patricia asked, and gently lifted the front of her skirt revealing her knickerless state of undress.

John choked.

"Was this how the subject was broached to Oedipus?" John junior asked rhetorically.

George leapt to his feet, pulling his trousers and pants down in the same movement, and releasing his very erect cock.

John double choked and his son buried his head in his hands.

"Christ almighty," John junior groaned.

"You," John shouted, and pointed at George, "sit the fuck down and put that," he pointed at George's point, "out of my sight."

George did what he had been ordered to do, but at no time did he take his eyes off his sister's none-of-his-business.

John stood and hurried to cover up his beloved. She wrapped her arms around his neck, stared deeply into his eyes and smiled sexily.

"Do you want me?" she asked him, then noticed that he was not returning her gaze with the same affection attached. "Master?" she added.

John did a mental double-take. *I know I called them my creations*, he thought, *but 'Master'?*

He was brought back to life with his wife rubbing at his crotch.

"Christ, Patty! What's the matter with you?" he demanded.

She recoiled suddenly from his verbal reprimand.

"Sorry, Master," she pleaded, and cowered away from him. "Sorry."

He turned to catch the attention of George and John junior. He needed a rational reaction from someone else and it was not going to come from Patricia. He quickly ruled out George as well so directed his intent at his son.

"Look, all I want to do is sit down and talk about this for a minute," he told them all. "Try to make some sort of sense out this whole situation."

John junior nodded his approval; George and Patricia looked at each other somewhat bemused.

"Talk about what?" George asked.

"This," John replied and waved his arms around the room indicating those all within it. "What has happened to us."

George and Patricia exchanged bewildered glances again.

"We're vampires," Patricia told him.

"Yes," John affirmed with the intonation that he expected a bit more than that. Patricia just smiled proudly because she had got an answer right.

"But why?" John howled and sent his wife cowering in the corner again.

"Because you killed us," George told him, "and you are a vampire."

John was just about to completely lose his rag when his son stood up and distracted his flow to anger.

"What dad wants to know is not totally dissimilar to the ultimate question about life; Why? How? and Who? Why have we become vampires – not the simple logistics involved," John junior pointed at George before he had the chance to butt in again with the vampire version of "because mummy and daddy loved each other very much", "- but for what purpose have we become vampires. Is such a monumental alteration in our physical selves just another 'fact of life', or is there a higher meaning?

"How did we become vampires?" Again he pointed at George as a pre-emptive interruption. "What has physically and spiritually happened to us to become undead? What are the religious connotations involved? Are we inherently evil? Or do we still possess the ability of free will?

"Finally, where does the buck stop? Who was the first? Who is the creator of all of us?"

George and Patricia pointed at John as if they had been asked a really stupid question.

"But who made him?"

John bowed his head to hide the potential embarrassment that was rising.

"Who made her?"

Lucky guess? John suspected and thought for a second that his son shook his head in reply.

"Who is at the end of it all?" John junior continued. "The ultimate creator."

He sat down again.

John eyed the boy with unashamed suspicion. That was exactly what he had wanted to know but part of the overriding frustration had been the inability to present his thoughts and questions with the clarity just demonstrated. He was unable to ask the specifics because he could not analyse them to such a degree; all he could ask were the general – almost childish – 'but why?' It was almost as if John junior had dipped into his mind, pulled out all of his emotions and translated them succinctly and eloquently into a rational and well-valued series of semi-rhetorical thoughts.

Either that or John junior was simply thinking exactly the same thing and was a better communicator.

Well, that's what a college education does for you, he pondered.

A furtive movement from George caught John's attention; he had pulled his penis from out of his trousers and was pumping it enthusiastically with his hand. John was just about to admonish his brother-in-law when he turned to identify the object of George's self-abusing attention – Patricia had once again pulled up her skirt and was openly masturbating at her brother.

"Would you two please leave it out," John bellowed and privates were quickly stashed away again. "What has got into you both? You don't see me or the boy pulling out our plonkers and flapping them all around the room. Why the hell can't you control yourselves for ten minutes?"

George fell to the feet of his creator in shame.

"We need," he whined, and Patricia fell down next to him.

"We need," she echoed.

"Need what?" John demanded, and the two serviles paused in thought for a second.

"Satisfaction," John junior said and the three adults turned to him.

"Oh yes," Patricia groaned and slid her hands up John's leg, "we need satisfying." And she started rubbing at his crotch with one hand and at hers, through her skirt, with the other.

"Satisfy what, though?" John asked and pushed away at her amorous advances. "Is that all you want from this? All you care about now? Sex? Our potential to do things seems limitless, and all you want to do is shag."

"Not just sex," John junior interrupted, "any physical pleasure that would satisfy and take their minds off their immediate cravings; blood, violence, sex."

John was enraptured by his son's explanation and completely oblivious of the incestuous interaction taking place at his feet.

"What craving?" he asked.

"What was the first thing you did when you woke up?" John junior asked rhetorically. "You fed, didn't you? There was some sort of over-powering desire in your body that demanded sustenance. That's what they want," he indicated the two siblings gorging themselves on each other's desires, "that's what all new born-need."

"How do you know so much?" John demanded.

"Can't you feel it?" John junior enquired with a hint of frustration in his voice.

"What?"

"The power held within us."

"I know that I'm stronger," John confessed, and perhaps for the first time admired the changes of his own physique; leaner and more muscular.

"And what about that 'potential' that you mentioned?" John junior asked.

"I don't know," his father replied, "I was just thinking out loud, you know, theorising."

"Can't you feel the thoughts?"

John could feel himself becoming more and more frustrated; his son had the answers that he was after but he was not giving them to him straight. Even more ingratiating, however, was the fact that he did have the answers – along with a thousand more questions that John had never even considered. Try to work out the logic of that; he – John – was the first of this little group, and yet his son – second generation (not including the girl in the park) and underling – had been given all the answers and some sort of mystical insight to it all.

No justice in life, no justice in death.

John leapt to his feet, kicked Patricia and George apart, darted over to John junior and picked him up by his throat.

"Stop giving me riddles," he growled. "Stop playing games and tell me everything that you know."

"I'll call social services," John junior croaked.

John's eyes blazed deep crimson and he bared his fangs menacingly.

"Okay, okay," John junior conceded and his father threw him back onto the sofa.

"But I have to let you know that I don't know exactly

what's going on," he warned and rubbed at his bruised throat. "Christ, this is just like going through puberty again; all these physical changes; worrying if you're different to everyone else, if you're abnormal or not."

John's eyes had returned to their normal hue. "Just tell me," he ordered calmly.

"I know how you feel, I know what you're thinking – and I don't mean that because I understand the situation and know you well enough to have a fairly accurate presumption of how you feel – I mean I know exactly what you're thinking and how you feel. And them as well." He pointed at the middle-aged siblings who were crawling across the floor towards one another; John snarled at them and they backed away again.

"I can feel the thoughts and emotions of thousands like us," John junior continued, "all over the planet and, I swear, it's going to drive me fucking insane if I don't find a way to control it."

"Why can't I?" John asked then remembered the overpowering sensation he had felt just before he came to the house last night; the feeling of his mind being taken over by others' memories.

"See, you could at one stage but you managed to turn it off," John junior told him. "Maybe it reacts differently within different people. Why have they turned into mindless, will-less animals? Why are we able to control ourselves? Maybe it's genetic, I don't know. Who ever is fucking about with my head hasn't given me those answers yet."

Both Johns looked down at their seemingly devolved kinfolk; Patricia and George were wary of this sudden attention towards them.

"Maybe they've got the right idea," John junior said, breaking the uncomfortable silence, "who cares? Get on with it. Enjoy the power while we have it. Who hasn't, at one time in their life, ever wished to be completely devoid of morals and principles so they can go on a flurry of one-night-stands? So they could just punch that person in the face for pissing them off. So they could just ram their car into that wanker who just cut them up and gave them the finger. For doing all manner of things that would normally only come as a nagging afterthought or would prevent them because it would forever plague their conscience."

Patricia and George looked pleased with themselves for being recognised as the ones who had 'got the right idea'.

John junior looked very depressed for a moment.

"Maybe we're the unlucky ones," he mumbled," having the same strengths and weaknesses as them, but still having the weakness of strength of character; sense of morality – I don't know what to call it – but having the limitations of humanity."

Father and son – in both life and death – faced each other contemplating their own thoughts; a couple of hours ago and John had presumed the whole of life and its resources were at his beck and call – now? Well, it was all a bit pear shaped now; it was all a bit downright fucking depressing really. To think that you could not really enjoy limitless power unless you lacked of social civility in not wanting to shag your own flesh and blood. He watched his wife and brother-in-law lech at each other; he shuddered and turned away from them.

Brother and sister – in both life and death – faced each other and began copulating.

John looked back down and was mesmerised momentarily by George's hairy backside bouncing up and down. He came back to attention and said calmly, "George, I swear to god, if you don't stop FUCKING my fucking wife, I will rip out your spinal column and throttle you with it."

George withdrew and John kicked him very hard in the head.

"I'm going to college," John junior announced, stepped over his uncle's pain wracked body and left the room.

"John, wait," his father called after him, "we've got too much to sort out."

"I need some time alone," he called back from the front door. "I've got to sort out which of these thoughts and feelings inside my head are really mine."

And with that, he left the building and slammed the front door shut behind him.

A thought suddenly came to John and he dashed out through the hallway and pulled open the front door again.

"John, the sun," he screamed.

John junior turned to look at him from the bottom of the driveway. He then looked up at the sun then down at his hands for any signs of a reaction to the daylight.

None.

He returned his gaze to his father, shrugged his shoulders and went on his way.

John watched his son wander off, then noticed a few of his neighbours staring at him.

"I need him to pick up the paper," he explained. "For the bingo." He darted back inside the house and gently pushed the door up to, not wishing to draw any more attention to his household.

With his back to the door he noticed the inert body of his daughter, still lying in the hallway. She was dead. He knew that of course, she was supposed to be dead, but also still alive.

He could almost have been upset about it but figured that she was probably better off, in the long run. Better for her to be dead than have George try to shag her at the drop of a hat – he shuddered again – better for him that she was dead. Best not to think about it. Do not think about anything and you do not have any questions that need answering and that was all right by him.

Still, he did recall that her blood had tasted funny; quite tart, like an unripe orange or such.

He stepped over her body and walked back to the living room. John junior was right, he needed to simply accept what had happened. Do not ask questions; go with the flow; shed all of his mortal human morals and principles, and concentrate on being a vampire. Then, hopefully, either everything will fall into place or he would be so busy humping every bit of totty that came his way that he would just forget about all that other stuff.

He stepped back into the family room, already a great weight lifting from his mind.

"George!" he screamed. "Get the fuck off of her, you fucking putrid excrement." The weight returned and he stormed into the room closing the door firmly behind him.

John Settle Junior slouched along the street feeling like the loneliest man in the world; a stranger in a strange land, a foreigner in a foreign place; a vampire amongst men.

One of the most frustrating aspects was the loneliness. He

knew for absolute definite that he was not the only one around – all of the voices, emotions, experiences and memories that were invading his mind had told him that much – yet his first hand experience of other vampires (his family) had shown him that he was so much different. They had all changed, mentally and physically, but only he had shown any real signs of making a dramatic improvement. The others had all sort of changed laterally; none of their bodily alterations were actually improvements at all, just differences. Was he to walk amongst his own kind not being able to have them understand him or empathise with him? Let us face facts, from what he had seen to juxtapose himself against so far, he reckoned he was something pretty fucking special. All the others were just divs; he never would have dreamed of using 'juxtapose' in a sentence before today.

Okay, so he was no longer human but instead he had become an excellent vampire; a vampire above all (so far) other vampires – fair enough, that raised his spirits somewhat – the next problem he faced was what he was actually supposed to do now. The very thought of leaping on to the next passer-by and chewing into his (or her) jugular made him feel nauseous. His stomach argued with that sensation and reminded him that he had not had any breakfast before leaving the house.

He looked up and stared at the back of the neck of the man walking to work in front of him. Involuntarily, John junior's canines began to extend through his gums and his mouth became awash with saliva.

Could he do it? Was it really as simple as that?

His humanity/conscience/morals screamed 'No'; his vampire instincts and newly acquired thousand year behavioural implant screamed 'jump on his back, pull his head back AND DRINK DEEP'.

How could anyone dispute that sort of well balanced, objective and eloquently presented side of the argument?

The sound of the man's heartbeat thrummed through John junior's mind and he felt his canines pressing down into his bottom lip. He quickened his pace slightly, approached the man and reached out for his shoulder.

A powerful grip locked itself against his outstretched arm

and brought him to bay.

John junior turned in fright and guilt for being caught nearly red handed. That quickly turned to anger as he remembered who and what he was.

He looked up to the owner of the vice-like grip and he immediately recognised the face of his new god. For the first time since his dramatic change there came a peace in his mind; peace and understanding. This being had just dipped into his brain and changed the chaos into clarity. Like looking at those Magic Eye 3D pictures; at first his head was just a mush of too much imagery and stuff, then it just took a moment of relaxation, a moment for someone who knew the score to say, "Relax your eyes, look beyond the picture," and all of a sudden he could see a school of dolphins jumping out of the sea whilst being attacked by a harrier jump jet. Metaphorically speaking, of course.

"Okay," John junior muttered in response to whatever psychic instructions he was being given.

"Patience. Discretion. Control," he chanted in his semi-hypnotic state.

JUST FOR NOW, his god rumbled in response.

***

The usual form is that darkness brings forth light, or some equally profound statement. The same is obviously true if said adage was inverted; light brings forth darkness.

The light was extinguished as Cameron closed his eyes and drifted to the dreaming, a place where our unconscious is unlocked and revealed, if somewhat symbolically, to our conscious. Again, opposing poles of light and dark; the conscious where all is visible, the unconscious, a dark, secret section of the mind where one's raw emotions are kept.

Cameron's darkness brought forth light, a single spot that was too painful to stare directly at, yet impossible to draw away from. The light was life and it seemed to be dimming.

A shadow flashed before his eyes. He turned and saw he was standing in a hospital ward. The lights were flickering over his head.

He had to find his mother before they started the operation;

he needed to tell her he loved her before she went in, he needed to see her one last time.

She would not be here, in the men's ward. Quickly, find her.

He tried to run but his legs felt weighted down. He saw Gillian in bed with another man, he was fucking her so hard that she was screaming. She saw Cameron and smiled.

Her partner withdrew and walked towards him. His naked body shone in the moonlight, a body of power. His erect cock dripped blood. Gillian was still smiling even though she had been split in half.

Cameron decided that this dream was getting too sick but he could not wake himself up. The man was now standing inches from him. "Cameron," he said with his father's voice, "you will be mine."

Cameron was staring into the eyes of a god.

The god bent over Cameron, his long, damp hair flailed across Cameron's face.

The god opened his mouth wide, silver and gold teeth caught the lunar rays and shimmered like a midnight lit pool.

Someone screamed.

Darkness and light, sometimes easily confused.

Cameron sat up with a start, in the dark room strange silhouettes threatened him. A hobgoblin, a cameraman, the screaming.

He blinked a few times and the shadows focused into their correct forms and he fumbled with the alarm clock until it ceased its banshee wail.

He looked at the time. "Seven-thirty? Why seven-thirty?" he asked rhetorically and collapsed on the bed again trying to calm his breathing and racing heart.

Images flicked through his memory; Gillian smiling at him, Gillian curled up at the toilet, an argument, 'tomorrow morning', 'exam'.

"Shit!" he exclaimed and leapt out of bed. He ran into the bathroom where Gillian was still embracing the toilet.

"Gilly, wake up." He pushed her roughly. "Get up."

"Wha?" she mumbled.

"It's half seven, you've got an exam."

She tightened her hold on the bowl and curled up into a smaller foetus. "Bollocks," she groaned.

The next half-hour was spent by Cameron getting Gillian ready. This involved getting her out of her vomit scented sleeping attire (a job he did not enjoy doing, but the result was quite satisfying), getting her showered, (a job he did enjoy doing), and getting her dressed again (a job he did not get a chance to do, by this time she was awake enough to do it herself).

"I've not done any revision," she whined as she stuffed toast in her mouth.

"You'll do all right," Cameron encouraged.

She slumped in her seat and puffed out in defeat, her bottom lip protruded slightly. Cameron leant forward and kissed it. "You'll do all right," he re-emphasised.

She smiled at him. "Thanks. I bloody hope so." Gillian stood and left the house.

Cameron went back to bed.

***

She sat and stared.

***

John Settle had deemed it sensible not to tell Patricia and George about John junior's lack of reaction to the supposedly damaging sunlight. He had decided not to tell them just in case it was just a one off in vampires called John Settle, so he forced the other two to sleep during the day and rise during the night. They were to sleep in separate rooms as well.

There is one basic trouble with trying to sleep in the daytime; if you do not want to, you cannot, so George was almost relieved to have the opportunity to get up and answer the door when the knocking had begun. He trotted down the stairs to answer it. As he neared the door, his basic vampiric instincts sensed the presence on the other side – mortal.

Food, he thought, but there was also something else, a

sensation that his primal mind had not yet experienced first hand and so could not identify the signs. As he got closer, something at his core tried to hold him back; his progress was impeded with every step. Hunger and obstinacy drove him forward.

In an attempt to measure levels of emotions, one can only describe them relatively. To elaborate; Cameron's surprise to see Gillian smoking drugs was less extreme than having his door kicked down by Scottish bailiffs. Gillian was about a four, the bailiffs about seven.

George's surprise to hear of John's death would rate at a mere three on his surprise scale. To discover John's lack of death was about eight. The realisation of his own death was a borderline one/two (once a vampire, death is simply accepted). Upon answering the door and having a steel blade pierce his heart was probably what he would have considered the ten on his scale, if he had time to consider it.

George's body began shaking violently, the skin on his face blistered, the pustules popped and pin pricks of light poured from his head. He deflated as the light continued to escape.

Nutter negotiated his way past the pile of skin on the doorstep and Tracy's body. He walked up the hallway and into the living room at the end.

Patricia was sitting, naked, on a dining room chair opposite the door. Nutter walked into the room and she spread her legs allowing him a clear view of her pubic delta. "You must want some," she said.

As Nutter walked over to her she raised herself to meet him, her right hand buried itself between her thighs, her left reached out to his shoulder and she pulled him to her.

Her right hand removed itself from its self-exploration and rested on Nutter's crotch.

"You're not even hard," she said in astonishment.

"You'll never know how hard I really am," he retorted.

Her eyes widened, the corners of her mouth drew back displaying a full set of dentures from hell. She hissed malevolently and backed away from him.

Not far enough, Nutter's blade burst her heart with a precise incision. She pulled herself away from the pain; the light that streamed from her wound forced her further back until she pressed against the wall. She moved slightly and the light pushed her in the opposite direction. She was flying around the room like a balloon losing its wind.

The empty sack of skin, that was once Patricia Settle, slapped to the floor in the centre of the room.

There was an inhuman howl from behind Nutter and he silently cursed himself for getting temporarily distracted. He turned but was not quick enough.

John had rushed into Nutter, knocking him off his feet and knocking the sword from his hand.

Nutter fell onto the settee, John stood over him.

"I know you," said John.

"You all do," Nutter replied, "it's been ingrained into your collective mind since the first day."

"What first day?" John demanded.

Nutter tried to raise himself from his precarious position but John pushed him down again.

"You will answer my questions old man," John ordered.

"I take no orders from the spawn of evil," Nutter retorted and with snake like reflexes jabbed John in the eyes with two fingers.

John felt his eyes silently burst inside his skull, the pain was incredible and he lashed out at Nutter blindly, desperate for answers and revenge.

Anger raged in his mind. He wanted this man for killing his family and blinding him, but he could not get him if he could not see him. The pain eased and he felt his eye sockets filling, solidifying with something, and then he could see again.

Just in time to avoid the point of Nutter's sword aimed at his heart. John moved slightly to his right and the sword embedded itself into his left arm.

John swung a fist at Nutter's head that he managed to roll with. Nutter's movement quelled the full force of the blow, but it was still enough to propel him across the room again. Once more he hit the settee and the whole thing rolled over on top of him.

John ripped the sword from his arm and threw it to the floor. He stormed over to the upturned furniture. "Perhaps you will be more eager to answer to me after I've emptied your body of blood," he declared and pulled the settee away.

Nutter was not underneath.

John was blasted off his feet by strength usually disassociated with anything other than articulated lorries travelling at ninety miles an hour. He hurtled through the French windows and landed roughly on the patio floor.

Picking himself up, he noticed the large hole in his stomach. He turned to confront Nutter stepping through the smashed window with a large shotgun. His gut popped as all the necessary bones and organs reformed in their proper places.

Nutter fired another shot that John easily stepped out of the way of but he did not avoid the butt of the gun that Nutter swung around and smashed against his temple.

John stumbled and was once again lifted into the air by a blast from the gun. This time he landed awkwardly on his vegetable patch. Awkward in the sense that he did not really want to impale himself on his garden fork.

He writhed on the floor with the fork prongs sticking out of his stomach; the second gun shot had removed most of his right shoulder which he was now desperately trying to repair as Nutter approached carrying a spade.

"I just want to know why?" John pleaded.

"That's all anybody wants to know," Nutter replied and drove the spade through John's chest. Light gave way to darkness.

A great geyser of light erupted from the hole in John's body. It was an impressive spectacle that could be seen from ten miles away. Nutter did not stand and admire the effect, he was picking up his blade from the living room and sheathing it in his walking stick whilst pondering the whereabouts of John Settle Junior.

An hour and a half later, she was still sitting and staring.

Suddenly a wave of nausea hit her and she ran from the room. Gillian reached the toilets just as her breakfast began to make a repeat appearance. She thrust her head over the toilet bowl and coughed loudly.

Two slices of toast and a cup of tea later, she emerged from the cubicle to discover she was in the boys' toilets. She felt suddenly embarrassed as she looked at the urinals; at least no one had been in there.

The door to the cubicle next to hers opened and John Settle Junior stepped out wiping his mouth. He was momentarily startled to see Gillian.

"Was that you chucking?" he asked.

"Yeah," Gillian replied.

"Are you pregnant?"

"I should bloody think not," she snorted and started for the door.

"You're Gillian Kildress, aren't you?" Junior asked as he washed his hands.

"Yeah?" she answered suspiciously.

"I'm John Settle, from badminton."

"Oh, I remember," she said. Images that used to be him came to her memory; he had changed aesthetically and he did not appear to be as much a dorky-prat as she remembered. "Look, I'd like to stop and chat, but I'm supposed to be in an exam at the moment."

Junior shrugged his shoulders. "No problem, I might see you after."

"I shouldn't think so," she said. Just because he did not look like a prat any more did not mean that he was actually no longer one. "I've got to go straight home after."

"I'll come round sometime then?" he said/asked.

Gillian had no time for a debate with an amorously-eager-probable-prat in the men's toilets. "Whatever," she said, with a dismissive wave and left to return to the exam hall.

Junior watched her bum as she left the room. "If only I wasn't so full," he muttered to himself, "that is a meal to savour and enjoy."

Had Gillian bothered to look at the cubicle John had just vacated she might have noticed another pair of feet still in there. A pair of feet attached to a very dead student.

Gillian returned to her seat after apologising to the adjudicators and started again. She stared.

Danny and Cassandra emerged from their room at ten a.m.; Penny had already been up for an hour. Cameron was still asleep.

"Morning," Danny said and pulled a pint of milk from the fridge. He opened it and drank it.

"Did you hear the storm last night?" Penny asked.

Cassandra shook her head and Danny belched his denial.

"Really weird," she continued, "no rain, just lots of thunder."

Danny sat next to her. "It doesn't seem to have affected this household much," he said, "apart from interrupting your beauty sleep." He aimed this last comment at Penny.

"Implying what exactly?" she asked.

"You look like shit." he replied.

"Bastard."

"Did Gillian get off for her exam all right this morning?" Cassandra asked.

"I think so," Penny answered, "her car's not outside."

"We're going in to college shortly," Cassandra said, "do you want us to take anything in for you?"

"What are you going in for?" Penny asked.

"I've got a couple of essays to hand in and Cass has to pay a library fine," Danny answered.

Penny leapt from her seat. "Oh yeah, library books," she said, and dashed from the room.

"You were really restless last night Danny," Cassandra commented.

"Yeah? I was having some weird dreams," he said. "Lots of blood and stuff."

Cassandra grimaced. "Sounds delightful."

"And I dreamt of my Gramps as well," he added.

"He's been dead for ages hasn't he?"

"Yeah, I've not thought about him for a while." Danny looked decidedly upset. "I just realised that I miss him."

Penny bounced back into the room with her arms weighed down with half a dozen large books; she immediately noticed the morbid air in the kitchen. "Have I interrupted something?"

"No, it's all right," Danny said and took the books from her. "Let's go," he said to Cassandra, and left the kitchen.

Cassandra stood. "It looks like we're going," she told Penny and hurried after Danny.

Just as the door slammed, Cameron shuffled into the room,

past Penny and sat down. He looked up at Penny. "You're looking worse than I feel."

"Thanks," she said sarcastically. "Good morning to you too."

Cameron rubbed his eyes. "Sorry, didn't sleep too well last night. Had some really odd dreams."

"You and every one else." She walked over to the kettle and switched it on. "Tea? Coffee?" she asked.

"Er, tea please," he answered. "For some reason I dreamt about my mum."

"Bless," Penny said sweetly.

"Not really," Cameron explained, "'she's been dead for nearly five years."

Penny sat down. "God, I'm sorry. I didn't mean..."

He waved off her apologies. "S'okay, not your fault. I'm over it, or thought I was."

"Dreams have a nasty habit of bringing hidden memories back to the surface. Do you want to talk about it?" She rested her hand on his arm.

He smiled weakly. "Not at the moment. Thanks anyway."

"How was Gillian this morning?" Penny asked and returned to the kettle.

"Not looking forward to it," Cameron laughed.

"Did she do any work last night? Sugar?"

"I don't think so, honey," he replied.

"No, I mean," she saw him smirking at her. "Very clever."

"Just one please."

Penny put the mug of tea in front of him and she sat down again. "Do you ever get that feeling that something really bad is going to happen?"

He shrugged his shoulders. "Every day of my life," he said in all seriousness.

Cassandra parked her lime-green Beetle and they walked the short way to the library.

They joined a long queue and Danny began shuffling his feet impatiently.

"Go and hand your essays in and I'll meet you back here," Cassandra suggested.

"You're sure?" Danny asked, and piled Penny's books into her arms.

"You think I might get raped or something while I'm waiting?"

"See you later," Danny said, and walked out.

After a further five minutes her arms began to ache so she put the books on the floor. As she bent over her bum knocked into the young man standing behind her.

"Sorry," she said.

"My pleasure," he replied.

She turned to look at him and saw that the dirty, slimy shit was actually grinning at her. She sneered back at him and pushed the pile of books forward with her feet.

Another five minutes passed and she felt the man behind standing far too close to her, closer than was comfortable.

"Do you think you could stand any closer?" she asked sarcastically.

"Any closer and I'll be inside you," he whispered in her ear.

"Any closer and you'll be on the floor," she retorted and pushed him back with her shoulder.

The rest of the wait went without incident. She handed the books in, paid her fine and went outside to wait for Danny; the man was standing outside as well.

"Don't you think that was a bit impolite?" he asked. "I was only trying to be friendly."

"You were only trying it on," she corrected. "Now why don't you just fuck off and leave me alone?"

He sidled closer to her. "I could show you a really amazing time."

"Fucking loser," she announced to people outside. "This guy is trying to pick me up by telling me he could show me a good time."

He grabbed her roughly by the wrist; his voice had changed into a hellish growl. "Why don't you just shut the fuck up and put out."

His eyes had turned a distinct shade of blood red and Cassandra suddenly did not feel so cocky. She was very scared.

His mouth opened to display a pair of extended canines.

He was close to biting into her when Danny pulled him off.

"Hey man, let her..." His sentence was cut short because of the nightmare that stood facing him.

"You wanna die too, huh?" the vampire said and lifted Danny off the floor.

"Cass," he called.

Cassandra had come to her senses and leapt onto the vampire's back. He dropped Danny to the floor and threw Cassandra on top of him.

"This guy's for real isn't he," Danny said.

Cassandra nodded.

"I thought sunlight was supposed to kill these suckers."

"You shouldn't believe everything you read," the vampire said and picked up Cassandra again.

"Put her down man," Danny warned, and got to his feet.

"I'm so hungry," the vampire moaned, "and you look so tasty."

Cassandra head-butted him squarely on the nose causing him to drop her and stagger backwards. She followed through swiftly with a kick to his groin; he inhaled sharply and doubled over. She brought her knee up to his face and he fell to the floor unsure of which pain to hold.

Cassandra stepped back, watching the writhing undead on the floor. "What do we do now?" she asked.

The vampire shot upright. "Once I hurt, but now I'm cured," he announced. "It's a miracle. Praise the Prince of Darkness."

"Shit," Danny and Cassandra said in unison.

"Do you two want to die? Or do you want to live forever?" the vampire asked them.

"They'll die in their own time," a voice behind him said.

The vampire turned to face Nutter who was standing with his sword at his side.

The vampire suddenly convulsed, a hissing noise emitted from the back of his throat, a sharp crack came from his chest and he looked down to his left breast that was getting larger.

He jerked again as Danny pushed the fence post further through his back.

"Stand away from him," Nutter said.

"Why?" Danny asked, stepping back. "Hasn't that done it

then?"

The vampire exploded with the intensity of a super nova. Then there was darkness.

Danny heard a voice. "Are you all right?" Nutter asked.

"I can't see," he whimpered.

"I'm not surprised, you stared directly into the heart of evil."

"Is it permanent?" he stuttered.

"It never has been before," Nutter replied and escorted Danny towards the Students' Union building. Cassandra composed herself and chased after the two men.

"There maybe some side effects though," he continued. "I remember one young man who was actually locked in an emotional embrace with his undead sweetheart when I pierced her heart with my blade."

"What? They were snogging?" Cassandra asked.

"Snogging? No, no." Nutter shook his head. "I shall reiterate the 'locked in' part of my description."

Cassandra looked bemused.

"Cool," Danny enthused. "Was she on top?"

"No," Nutter replied.

"How did you not get him then? Were they doing it doggy?"

"Oh I see. No, I was under the bed and didn't actually pierce the blade through her rib cage," Nutter explained.

The creases in Cassandra's forehead cleared as her brain caught up with the conversation. "Oh, they were shagging."

"Crudely put, but quite," Nutter confirmed.

"Bullet," Danny chided.

"Piss off," Cassandra retorted.

"Anyway," interrupted Nutter, "the young man was obviously somewhat distressed by the explosive nature of his carnal partner and so I took him into my care for a while. His blindness eventually healed and he became quite adept at identifying the presence of vampires."

"Could he see them differently to ordinary people?" Cassandra asked.

"Erm, that as well," Nutter remarked and looked a bit embarrassed.

"As well as what?" Danny asked.

"He would become," Nutter searched his head for an appropriate word, "aroused when in the company of undead."

"You mean he got a stiffy at the sight of a vampire?" Cassandra laughed.

"It was no laughing matter," Nutter chastised. "The young man became so frustrated at his inability to control his libido during a confrontation that he sacrificed his life by facing a Prince of Darkness and actually ejaculated to death."

"Don't you dare turn out like that," Cassandra warned Danny.

"Cool," he enthused.

Gillian walked out of the girls' toilets rubbing her neck and swearing under her breath. All she could think about was how she just wasted three years of her life at university and for what? Because some bastard man – the bastard man that she was in love with – had just decided to turn up, out of the blue, again, and fuck her head up.

Last night's actions were completely against her nature, she would never smoke drugs and lie around on a carpet seething with pornography. Well, not on a school night. Not usually. But definitely not the night before an important exam.

She looked at her watch and was surprised to see that she had been wandering around college for over two hours. She was equally surprised to think that one-and-a-half of those hours had been spent in the lavatory. She thought she had only closed her eyes for a couple of seconds but must have actually fallen asleep on the toilet. At least that explained why her feet were tingling; the seat must have cut off the circulation to her legs, but as for her aching neck...

She suddenly felt very hungry.

A rhythmic bass thumping rang in her ears. It became louder as she walked down the corridor, and it gave her a headache.

She walked past the Entertainments Hall where a band were practising for that evening's gig. The drummer ceased his bass drum pounding as the guitarist swore at him to shut up. Gillian's headache eased slightly and she turned in to the canteen.

The ladies' toilets exploded with light. The light died and John Settle Junior crashed through the door and ran up the corridor shouting, "You killed my family, you bastard. I know you now and I'll get you later."

Nutter stepped through the wreckage and into the corridor; he looked around for Junior who was long gone. Another adolescent vampire had been laid to rest in the toilets but there were so many being created so quickly. He was going to have to swallow his pride and get some help from someone. He knew exactly who that someone was but did not know where that someone would be.

He also needed to find a stiff drink.

Danny finished his pint and slammed the glass on to the table.

"Careful, you could have smashed that one," said Cassandra. "How are your eyes?"

"Still can't see shit," he replied.

"I still don't think I understand what went on," she mused. "Was that guy really a vampire?"

"Apparently so," Danny said.

"You were so brave back there," she commented.

"In what way?" he asked. "You was the one kicking seven shades of shit out of him."

"You were the one that killed him. What if he wasn't a vampire and you had killed a normal person?"

"It seemed pretty obvious that he was trying to kill us as well."

Cassandra looked momentarily shocked. "Is it as simple as that?"

"How do you mean?"

"Kill or be killed."

"Under those circumstances, yeah."

Cassandra huffed her disapproval.

Danny frowned and shook his head trying to sort his thought processes. "Can I have a second please? You were calling me a hero a second ago, and now you're trying to give me the death sentence?"

"You're being so flippant about it. You just stopped

somebody's existence and there doesn't appear to be a trace of conscience." She looked down at her feet, almost ashamed of what she was about to say. It was an action that was completely wasted on Danny what with him being blind at the moment. "I thought I knew everything about you. That guy isn't alive any more because of you and that doesn't bother you at all, that bothers me about you."

"As far as I'm concerned," Danny announced as he began drinking another pint of beer, "he was already physically dead in the first place, and secondly I never actually knew the guy so it doesn't matter."

"I don't believe you just said that," Cassandra spat. "Are you seriously saying that if someone dies, it doesn't bother you at all unless you know them?"

"Don't spout hypocritical morality at me Cass," Danny retorted. "How many times have you been cut up about someone's death on the news?"

"It upsets me."

"How many times have you relished the death of a bad guy on the telly or cinema? How many times have you laughed at a sick joke that involves a human disaster?"

"That's completely different," she argued. "When someone gets killed on the screen, I know it's not real, and I know that the actor's going to get up again as soon as the camera has panned off him. There are no cameras here and that guy is not going to get up again. What about the people that did know him? What about his family? How are his parents going to deal with the death of their child? Not even that, there's no body, they're probably going to wonder if he's dead or alive for the rest of their lives and they'll never be given the opportunity to properly mourn for him."

Danny stood up abruptly and attempted to glare at her – he managed to stare reproachfully at the bench a foot to her left. It was more disconcerting to Cassandra than direct eye contact.

"Oh, and all that's my fault is it?" he shouted at her. "Because I saved our lives, I'm going to have to carry the guilt of his death around with me, huh? Is that what you're saying? And I would like to point out to you that it was our lives that were on the line. If he had killed us then we wouldn't be getting up again as soon as we were out of camera shot, unless of course it meant we were going to get up looking like him."

Cassandra was quiet and Danny tried to listen for any indication as to any response from her, whether it be verbal or physical. He heard her sob quietly and he fell to his knees and held her tightly, after scrabbling around the bench for a few seconds trying to find her.

"I'm sorry," she whispered. "I got scared."

"Me too," Danny said.

"I love you," they said together.

"I know," Cameron said and looked at his watch, "she should have been finished hours ago."

"Well, it doesn't actually mean anything," Penny encouraged. "Or rather it could mean one of two things: a) she did really well and is presently getting very drunk in the Union; or b) she did very badly and is presently getting very drunk in the Union."

"Or a) she did really well, started coming home and got killed; or b) did really badly and topped herself," Cameron added.

"Ah! Discovered at last," Penny cried, jumped out of her seat and pointed a finger at him causing him to choke on his tea, "the eternal optimist."

"The potential realist," he coughed in his defence.

Penny sat down again and returned her attention to her magazine. Cameron composed himself and wiped the tea and saliva from his chin and from down the front of his tee shirt. He leaned back and sighed loudly. Penny looked up for a second and caught his eye, she looked down again and he sighed again.

"Problem?" she asked.

"Bored," he replied.

Penny threw her magazine onto the table. "Sorry, should I strip off and dance naked across the kitchen surfaces for your entertainment?" she enquired sarcastically.

Cameron's eyebrows shot up as he pictured the whole affair. "Well..."

"Piss off," Penny suggested. "Go and root through Gillian's underwear drawer or something."

"I did that before I got up," he said.

"Well, go and watch telly then you aggravating git," she ordered.

He stood up and slouched off into the living room. Penny went to reach for her magazine and her eye caught a headline from the local newspaper: "Multiple 'vampire' attacks shock community". She picked up the paper and read more closely.

Cameron turned on the television and the local news was on. A young woman that looked like a dozen other local news presenters sat behind a desk. She had number three of the six 'reporters facial expressions' on her face; she looked serious.

"...have not released exact details of the incident, but it is believed that the bodies of the family that were found were brutally slaughtered in various rooms around the house..." He flipped channels whilst looking through the pile of videos that lay next to the TV.

He selected one, slipped the cassette into the recorder, then spent the next few minutes trying to find which channel the video was tuned to. Eventually the screen flicked to the image of a very young Peter Cook and Dudley Moore sitting in the middle of a sound studio. "You stupid fucker," said Peter, and Cameron laughed.

"Oh yes, very clever," Penny commented from the doorway. She walked over to him and threw the paper onto his lap. The shock of it landing sharply on his genitalia made him jump slightly; the pair of them blushed. Penny blushed because she knew what had caused him to jump and she could hardly apologise and offer to rub it better. Cameron blushed because he knew that she knew.

That uneasy silence that seemed to follow Cameron and Penny around made its presence known again.

"I've dropped me figs," shouted Dudley.

"What have I got this for?" Cameron asked.

"That item," Penny pointed vaguely at the paper but, under no circumstances whatsoever, anywhere near his crotch. At all.

Cameron scanned the page trying to guess what sort of article might attract a person like Penny's attention; a surgeon's sex scandal? Local kebab owner's machete nightmare? Ah...

"My god," he said.

"I thought you might say something like that," Penny affirmed.

"The new edition of the Oxford dictionary huh?"

"What?" Penny squealed and took the paper.

"You're so fucking stupid," shouted Peter.

"This one," she said, stabbing at the slaughterhouse story.

He was mildly shocked and Penny took a step up in his estimations of her. "Bit of a closet goth are you?" he asked.

"Fuck off," said Dudley.

"No," Penny replied. "I thought you might be interested in it," she said without a hint of sarcasm, humour or derision in her voice. There may have been a subtle hue of irony if you knew what you were listening for.

"Did you?"

"Well, aren't you?"

"Was this your Tuesday a.m. wank?" Dudley enquired.

"Can you please turn that off, Cameron?" she pleaded.

Cameron fumbled with the remote and the image changed to an ancient Australian hospital soap opera.

"Why would I be interested in this?" Cameron asked her whilst reading quickly over the report.

"...because Doug said he'd rather sleep with a rabid dingo long before he'd ever consider kissing her on the lips," the Nurse on the ancient Australian soap announced.

"I... It... Er."

"I never thought he'd do it though," the nurse continued.

"Good lord, no end of reasons I see." He looked up at her with an enquiring glance, the same sort of look that headmasters manage to perfect when disciplining a disruptive student, one that says, "We both know what is going on, but I still want you to tell me. Oh and by the way, you will squirm in the process".

The doorbell rang.

"I'll get it," Penny said and dashed out of the room.

Cameron frowned in confusion and stared at the headline again. "Weird," he muttered and turned on the video again.

"No, my Tuesday p.m. wank," Peter replied.

Penny opened the door to a young man she had never seen before in her life but had a nagging suspicion that she sort of knew him from somewhere.

"Can I help?" she asked.

"Is Gillian in?" he asked.

"No, she's not back from college yet," Penny informed him. "Can I give her a message?"

"She shouldn't be long though, should she," he replied.

"Er, I don't know," she turned her head slightly towards the living room, keeping one eye on the stranger but calling into the hallway. "Cameron?"

"What?" came the distant reply.

"Could you come here?"

A brief spurt of indistinguishable expletives preceded Cameron trudging out into the hall still carrying the newspaper. "What?" he huffed.

"Was Gillian having only the one exam today?" she asked him and her eyes fell on the headline of extreme importance. They widened with sudden realisation and fear.

"Yeah, just a three hour this morn... What's wrong with you?"

Penny turned just in time to see John Settle Junior lunge a hand towards her throat. She was remarkably fast and threw herself backward taking Cameron by surprise and off his feet. They both landed on their backsides facing the enemy.

"You can't come in without being invited," Penny shouted at him.

"Gillian has already invited me," Junior said and stepped onto the doormat.

"How rude," Cameron commented.

"Cameron, run," Penny said and leapt to her feet.

Junior came closer. "I know of you," he said.

"What sort of grammar is that?" Cameron asked and lifted himself up to his feet.

"Cameron, run!" Penny insisted more fervently.

"I don't run," he answered. "Except from oncoming, speeding cars."

"This is much worse," she muttered and placed a well positioned fast foot on Junior's nose, breaking it and sending him sprawling backwards.

"Wow!" Cameron gasped. "Power Rangers."

"Cameron! Go now!"

Junior rose to his feet wiggling his deformed nose. He wiped a couple of tears from his eyes and squinted in concentration; it popped back into shape.

Cameron stood and stared. "What the fu..?"

"You're both going to hell," Junior growled, as eyes turned crimson and canines extended.

"Well, I'm taking you with me then," retorted Penny, and prepared to strike.

Cameron suddenly felt very useless and left out of the proceedings; he felt that a rational, calm voice was required to ease the situation.

"Fuck this," he swore, grabbed Penny by the arm and dragged her through the living room with the interest of seeking the back door. He ran straight into Junior who swiped him to the side and over the back of an armchair.

The wind was blasted from his lungs as he lay on the floor, dazed and breathless, patiently waiting for composure or unconsciousness.

Penny threw a dragon punch directly at Junior's eyes but he caught her hand easily, inches from his face. He tutted, wagged his index finger at her and shook his head, then twisted her arm swiftly popping it out of its shoulder socket. She screamed and kicked him in the kidneys.

He lost his grip on her and fell against a wall. "I smelt your blood earlier," he said, "you put up a better fight then though."

Penny gritted her teeth and cradled her shoulder. Junior was preparing himself for the final strike; she had seen it a thousand times before and in her present condition there was nothing she could do about it.

Junior leapt, hands outstretched, teeth bared.

His head jerked back, his body twisted forward and he fell to the floor. Behind him Cameron stood holding the pointy end of the previously unusable umbrella. The hooked handle was round and digging in to Junior's neck. It pierced through the skin; he gurgled in pain and coughed up a steady flow of blood that poured out his mouth, nose and in the hole in his neck.

"Was I supposed to do that?" he asked, and grimaced at their apparently haemorrhaging assailant.

"Yes, it'll do for now," Penny gasped, then indicated to the umbrella, "Throw it to me."

Cameron unhooked it from Junior's neck with a sickening 'shlup' and threw it to Penny. She reached out to get it but had her arm snatched by Junior.

"Fucking hell," she sighed, and kicked him across the side of the head. He sprawled across the floor taking Penny with him. She landed on her dislocated shoulder, squealed and passed out.

Junior sat upright and tried clearing his throat, neck skin flapping as air whistled through it. It healed.

His head snapped at ninety degrees as Cameron swung the cricket bat at it. Junior fell face down moaning in agony. Cameron started lifting Penny to her feet and discovered that hauling unconscious women around really was not one of his latent talents.

With arms under her shoulders and linked across her breasts he began dragging her out of the room backwards. He heard an unpleasant crunching noise, like the ones that particularly eager sound effects people dub over the top of lions eating wildebeest on nature programmes and the like.

There was a pop and Cameron backed into something still. Something very still, but something breathing heavily.

"Arse," he screamed as he discovered that, once again, he was airborne.

The television reacted badly to the sudden contact with Cameron's speeding form. "You stupid fucking cu-" it said and smashed noisily. Cameron lay prostrate on his back on top of the broken screen, his head dangled loosely.

"I... I... hurt," he groaned.

"I'll put an end to that," Junior said and walked over to him.

Cameron watched him approach upside down. *Just a bit closer,* he thought.

Just as Junior was almost close enough to reach out his hands to really hurt him, Cameron attempted an overhead kick and failed miserably. He toppled over backwards, landing awkwardly on his head, there was a sharp snap and Cameron slumped to the floor.

Junior was slightly bemused by the incident but knew enough about the dead as not to touch Cameron. He returned his attention to Penny.

Nutter slumped into the seat next to Danny. Cassandra looked at the old man who seemed to look slightly different, older and more pathetic than before. She also noticed a bleeding gash on his forehead.

"You're hurt," she pointed out.

"Yes," he conceded.

"Here," she said and proffered a napkin to him. He took it and placed it to his brow.

"How did you do it?" she asked.

"I had another confrontation," he replied. "With two of them. One had just been born and was dealt with easily, the other is relatively old now and is strong."

"They get stronger the longer they live?" asked Danny. "Or rather don't live," he corrected himself.

"Yes," Nutter affirmed and sighed heavily. "I am too old and must ask for help." He bowed his head in self pity.

Cassandra looked expectantly at Danny who stared over her right shoulder at an emergency exit. She gave up.

"Who?" she asked fearing the answer.

"Someone to whom I haven't spoken for a very long time," he answered.

Cassandra sighed with relief.

There was silence for a while. Danny put his fourth finished pint down. "We'll help you," he said and Cassandra glared at him. "Won't we, Cass?"

She replied silently by flicking Danny a couple of 'V's and said, "I don't know Danny, we'll probably only get in the way. It's probably best that we don't get involved."

Nutter looked up at her. "I'm afraid you have already gone and got yourselves involved. An army of undead has a single consciousness,"

"Like Borgs?" Danny interrupted but was ignored.

"And when one is defeated the face of the victor is firmly implanted in the minds of all of them. To truly free yourselves, all must be destroyed."

"Oh wow," said Danny.

"Oh fuck it," agreed Cassandra (sort of).

"I must see to this wound and rest a while," Nutter said and went to stand but toppled slightly. Cassandra leapt to her feet but was too far away, Danny caught him easily.

She stared at him. "You can see? You bastard."

"Oops," Danny apologised. "We'd better take him home and clean his head."

"Don't think I'm going to forget about this Daniel," Cassandra spat and marched out of the bar.

"I have a feeling you're in trouble," suggested Nutter.

Danny shook his head. "No problem. I know how to bring her round." He winked at the supported Nutter as they followed after her back to the lime Beetle.

"Nice car," Nutter admired and was bundled in the back. "How degrading," he mumbled under his breath.

Gillian finished her plate of chips and snapped to attention. She had to go home. Now. Something was wrong.

The lime Beetle pulled up outside the house, all three in the car noticed the open front door but only two of them presumed that something was wrong.

"Cameron's probably nipped up to the shops," Danny said, Cassandra and Nutter stared at him in disbelief. He caught their looks and shrugged. "He hasn't got a key."

Nutter leapt out of the car and ran up to the open door, Cassandra had to drive around the corner before she found a parking space.

The young couple got out of the car and made their way back around to the front of the house and rejoined Nutter; all was quiet.

"Too quiet," said Danny.

Cassandra told him to shut up with a fierce glare.

"Sorry," he mouthed.

Nutter motioned his inexperienced helpers to wait outside while he went inside to see if it was safe, and if it was then he would call them in.

He stepped inside and walked down the hall. Danny started to follow until Cassandra grabbed his arm and pulled him back.

"I thought he wanted us to follow him in and back him up,"

he explained in hushed tones.

Nutter peered into the living room. There had been a fight, he could tell. He looked at the puddle of damp blood in the doorway and the crumpled body in the corner by the mangled television set. He drew his blade and advanced cautiously, the point leading the way.

"Oh my god, it's Cameron," gasped Cassandra from the door.

Nutter jumped and turned to glare at her, Danny tried to hide behind her.

"I told her we should..." he started but was motioned into silence.

Nutter kneeled next to the inert form and prodded it.

No reaction.

He rolled Cameron's body over and noticed his shallow breathing.

"He's alive."

"Alive alive, or dead alive?" asked Cassandra.

"Alive alive."

"Oh," added Danny and was elbowed harshly in the ribs.

Nutter noticed a broken picture frame that Cameron had been lying on. The photograph was of all the members of the house dressed as members of the Addams Family; Danny was Gomez, Cassandra was Cousin It (he presumed although obviously it was difficult to say because of the hair), Gillian was Lurch and Penny was Wednesday. He paused at the image of Penny...

"Is he okay?" Cassandra's voice brought him back to reality.

"Just unconscious. Where are the other people in this photo?" he asked.

"They should both be here," she said. "Penny had the day off and Gillian would have finished her exam this morning; she should have been back by now."

"Was it vampires?" Danny asked staring into the corners of the room for a reason unknown to everyone but himself.

"Yes."

"And Gillian and Penny?" Cassandra asked not really wanting an answer.

"If they were here," Nutter began, "then they are probably both dead."

Silence filled the room as each of the conscious members in it tried to come to terms with different aspects of the possible events that had occurred.

"What the hell's been going on here?" Gillian shouted.

Cassandra grabbed Danny and they both screamed. Nutter span on his heels rolled and brought his blade up to Gillian's left breast.

"I only asked," she whimpered. "Cass?"

"How are you feeling?" Cassandra asked.

"Scared?" Gillian hoped it was the right answer.

"Do you want to suck my blood?" Danny asked.

"Fuck off you pervert," Gillian replied.

That was the right answer.

She noticed Cameron on the floor and rushed to his side. "What did you do to him?"

"Us?" the three asked.

"We didn't do it," Danny started, "it was the vamp AARGH!" Danny stopped.

Cassandra glared at him and lifted her heel off his foot.

Gillian brushed Cameron's forehead and he started coming to. The amazing healing powers of a gentle caress.

"Penny?" Cameron mumbled.

Gillian frowned and smacked him one.

"Ow," he corrected himself. "Gillian?" then noticed the audience. "Cass? Danny? and... you?"

"You know him?" Cassandra enquired.

"A chance meeting," Nutter tried to explain.

"Bollocks," Cameron suggested.

Gillian was looking around the room in a state of bewilderment. Upturned chairs, smashed television, the red stain on the carpet.

"Where is Penny by the way?" she asked.

The three standing looked at each other in embarrassment and Cameron came to his senses.

"Shit," he shouted and leapt to his feet. "Fuckinhellshitfire. Blokecameinwentapeshit. Fuckingvampirenearlyfuckingkilledme."

"Wow," said Danny.

"Vampire?" Gillian asked.
"Us too," said Cassandra.
"Vampires?" she repeated.
"It's all rather complicated and a very old story," Nutter said sadly.
"So where's Penny?" Gillian screamed, near hysteria.
"I think she's dead," said Cameron. "We fought it but... I guess I was lucky."
"Ohmygodohmygodohmygod."
"Gill, calm down darling," Cameron soothed, or rather soothed as best as he thought he knew.
"Is that her blood?" she cried.
"Everything's a bit hazy," Cameron said.
"But probably though," Nutter informed.
"I knew you were bad luck you stupid bastard," she sobbed and pushed Cameron around, beating his chest with each burst of abuse, adding injury to insult.
"But..."
"I, fail my degree, wasted three years of my life and my parents' money, I don't see you for a year, and you come back just like that expecting sex at the drop of a hat."

He looked wildly around for some support from the spectators, or perhaps a brick to smack her in the face with.

"You get my best friend kidnapped, or even probably killed by some sort of vampire killer and you won't even try something on with me, you bastard. What is the matter with you? Don't you love me or something?"

She collapsed on his chest and sobbed quietly. He stroked her hair and hoped his gentle caresses would have the same restorative powers that had been so effective on him.

He looked up at the three stooges. Danny was holding onto Cassandra as if their very lives depended on it; Cassandra's shoulders jerked rhythmically as silent tears poured from her distraught body; Danny was just staring.

Different people deal with grief differently. Cameron had always known that, he had seen a fair deal of it in various forms throughout his life thus far. It was always his belief that nothing really happened as long as you did not accept it. If you just kept it bottled up somewhere then you did not get hurt; be strong for the weak and all that. Just what Danny was doing.

He had tried that after his mother had died and funnily enough it had not worked.

Oh, sure it had worked for a little while, but then everything he saw, heard or thought of, brought back memories of unresolved comments that had been made, of all the good times that had gone on and how much he really loved and missed her.

And then he had mourned.

Cameron looked over from Danny to see what Nutter was doing, whether he was drinking sour milk, sniffing his armpits or perhaps muttering "Rabbits, rabbits" under his breath. He was mildly surprised to see Nutter was sitting in silence on the upturned chair, sedate. A special type of grief.

Cameron filed this moment to come back to it at a more appropriate time.

***

Penny could see darkness. From it came a light and a voice.

OLD ENEMY. DO YOU KNOW US?

"No," she stuttered.

THIS IS NOT RIGHT. SHE IS OF THE BLOOD BUT NOT THE FLESH.

"Sorry," came the voice of Junior from the darkness. "I smelt her."

SHE WILL DO FOR NOW.

The light faded and Penny could see darkness again.

"That is such a cool voice," said Junior. "How do you do it?"

***

The room had been tidied to a certain degree, wounds had been tended, and Penny had not been mentioned.

Tea had been cooked, eaten, small talk had been exchanged and Penny had not been mentioned.

It had been agreed that the day, for everyone concerned, had been a mentally and physically draining one and an early night was required if they were to pit their forces against the legions of undead. Only Cameron had disputed this plan of action for reasons of personal attachment to his immortal soul and so on, but no one had really taken any notice. Gillian went to her room, Danny and Cassandra moped off, hand in hand, Nutter and Cameron were left in the mildly wrecked living room.

Nutter was staring at the wall while Cameron just watched him.

"I'll just sleep down here on the sofa then will I?" Nutter sort of asked but really told Cameron.

"Er, yes I suppose," Cameron sort of told but agreed. "But then again there is a spare room n-" he stopped as he remembered.

Nutter stared despondently at him. "I did warn you," he said.

Cameron suddenly came to attention. "No you didn't, you gave me some sort of cryptic hocus pocus bullshit about belief. Are you trying to tell me all of this is my fault?"

"Not directly. Not purposely."

"I think it's about time you came clean about everything," Cameron ordered.

"I am," Nutter started and his eyes glazed over whilst old memories flooded back to him, "very old. I have made it my responsibility to battle against and attempt to eradicate the threat of the evil dead."

"A good film," Cameron interrupted but was ignored.

"I am attracted to areas and times of outbreaks of vampiric activity. I am attracted to those who are intricately interwoven with the events that are to occur." His attention was drawn away from the flowered wallpaper and aimed directly at Cameron.

Cameron jumped after Nutter's last words sank in. "You fancy me?"

Nutter grimaced in mental pain. "Not physically attracted. Just as metal is attracted to a magnet."

"Or flies to shit," Cameron added.

"Yes," Nutter agreed dubiously, trying to work out which half of the metaphor he was supposed to be.

"Oh. No," Cameron said. "That would make me the shit wouldn't it."

"Obviously. Condemned by your own words."

"But why me?" Cameron asked.

"Why not? It's got to be someone."

"Has it? Why?"

"I don't know," Nutter said with some resignation, as if trying to explain to a five-year-old the concepts and equations of nuclear fission. "As is the way with any life-threatening disaster, there has to be one person who is supposed to be the saviour."

"I am the chosen one?" Cameron asked to no one in particular.

"You are an unfortunate accident in the games of fate and destiny," Nutter mumbled to himself.

"Is that a good thing?" Cameron asked warily.

"Not for the human race I would surmise."

"Oh. You don't think I'm up to the job then?"

Nutter scanned the room and returned his stare to Cameron. "I think more to the point is, do you?"

"Oh."

There came a silence. One of those silences that means both of the men had something they wanted to say which may be a bit personal, perhaps insulting. It really needed saying, but the longer the silence continued it became more difficult to say. A bit like trying to split up with someone after specifically meeting with them to tell them this but obviously not being able to say it straight away because that would be really heartless, but then again not being able to say it later because you have been pretending all this time that everything was fine and dandy.

Cameron, not being a man who recognised the words 'tact' or 'subtlety' very often, broke the spell.

"What was it about you and Penny then?"

Nutter looked genuinely shocked and speechless.

"I mean," Cameron decided to explain, "when you found out that she was, you know, perhaps, er, whatever, you was well choked. Over-choked for someone who had heard that a complete stranger was doing the long lonely walk to oblivion."

Nutter suddenly stared at him, wide eyed. "She was my daughter."

"Daughter? That's a bit of a Star Wars twist. Danny's not your son is he?"

Nutter was still staring.

Recollection of a tactless description of death. "Ah. Oh. Sorry."

He then started to recall public house conversations. "You hadn't seen each other in a while I understand."

"A very long while," Nutter said, returning his attention to the wallpaper. "So long I can't remember the exact number of years; well over fifty for definite."

Cameron nodded. "That is a long... Eh?"

Nutter shook his head wearily. "Explanations another time. We both need our rest."

Cameron stood and left the room. "G'night then." He said and trudged up the stairs towards Gillian's room. He passed the open door to Penny's bedroom; something was not right about this, he decided. He was not overly upset and so knew, somehow, that perhaps she was not actually dead. Not dead dead, or alive dead.

He crept into Gillian's room and closed the door as quietly as he could. Not quietly enough.

Gillian sat bolt upright. As was expressed earlier, shadows can deceive the sleep-affected eyes and brain.

"You can't take any more," Gillian shouted at him, "not tonight, not ever."

"Gill, it's me, Cameron," he whispered.

"Huh?" she uttered.

"You're still dreaming, darling." He sat on the bed next to her and stroked her hair.

"I saw someone come for Cassandra," she said.

"Not while I'm here sweetheart," he soothed.

"But you were here earlier."

"Er."

Gillian began sobbing again. "Is she really dead Cam? I can't believe that she's really gone."

"I don't think she is," he told her.

"Do you really believe that?"

"Yes. It's true. I promise." And he did not even have his fingers crossed.

"Hold me," she whimpered and he put his arm around her shoulders and pulled her in close.

She looked deeply into his eyes and whispered softly, "Properly."

Her eyes sparkled from the severe tear bath they had been receiving; they were wide with fear, expectation and anticipation. She did not know which was the worst sensation or to which predicament they were associated to. Little bits from everything seemed to make her head spin slightly and she had to shut her eyes tight, tuck her head into his neck and fight off the giddiness and nausea.

He wrapped his arms around her and for the first time since he met her she felt so fragile. Such a tall girl had always emanated such strength, which usually put the majority of blokes off, but Cameron had loved it. Now he was the strength and it felt very strange indeed. How on earth could he sit there and pretend he could protect her and prevent her from coming to harm if he could not have prevented it earlier? He felt hypocritical and pathetic. He realised he was crying.

"I love you so much," he sobbed quietly.

She trembled in his arms and he felt her tears drench his neck and shoulders. "I love you too," she whispered. "Don't ever die, please."

"I promise."

They held each other silently for a very long time, arms protecting, hands caressing and soothing.

One pair of fingers on one hand had been crossed.

Nutter stirred as he slept on the sofa. Trouble was coming and he was going to have to be more alert than ever before.

Cassandra and Danny did not sleep well. Or rather Cassandra did not sleep well because Danny did not sleep well. He kept 'seeing things' in his sleep. Really *bad* things. *Really* bad things.

The Beginning was about to begin...

Arms moved, hands rubbed, fingers touched. Eyes looked openly in anticipation into eyes. Mouths kissed, sucked, bit.

Clothes shed around them. The moonlight gave skin a bluish tint, made it look smoother, purer. Tearstains, reflected tracks of sorrow, were washed over with tears of pleasure and joy. They never let go, throughout the whole ecstatic experience, they never let go.

She felt a slight pain at first, but she wanted this so much that it subsided as if it was just a distant memory.

This was better than it could have been, should have been. Something was wrong, nothing could be this good and not be fatal.

Nails scratched down backs, sweat glistened on brows.

Colours burst behind his eyelids, his head went dizzy as blood drained from his brain and concentrated on more important areas.

Mouths bit, chewed, sucked.

Hands grabbed at flesh and held tight, trying to keep control. Not now, too soon, make it last.

A brief moment of composure, steady the breathing, eyes stared into eyes trying to comprehend the magnitude of the event.

Two shy, embarrassed smiles, then lips locked once more and their bodies squeezed together, shut out everything around them. This was only them – pure and simple selfish pleasure. Then, even the other person was not important as climactic ecstasy took over, completely. Bodies, thoughts and motion ran on automatic; this was basic, primal instinct. All voluntary processes had shut down; their passion was as natural and uncontrollable as their heartbeats.

His heartbeat drummed in his ears, pounded in his brain, blinded him. He could not breathe, his body hurt because of the intense pleasure, and just as it seemed it cannot feel any better or hurt more, the senses heightened, the feelings became more intense as he reached the very peak of euphoria, utopia, nirvana, heaven.

Oh god.

***

In the Beginning...

There was a brief sensation of falling then Cameron was

awake.

It was not that he had just awoken, or even that he was awake because he had not managed to fall to sleep. It was simply that he had not been awake, and now he was.

He realised that he was very short of breath and sucked in a huge lung full of air. His lungs ached at the over burden and he exhaled just as sharply. He concentrated for a moment on regulating his respiration.

He became confused as to where he was. Not Edinburgh, he did not have a lampshade like that. He did not have a lampshade. Memories slowly compiled in his head: bailiffs, Leeds, Gillian, bed, floor. Oh yeah. He smiled and admired the foetal form of Gillian next to him. She glowed slightly from the moonlight that streamed through the window and reflected off the sheet she was wrapped in; it had an almost metallic sheen to it in this light.

He fumbled around for his watch and located it under the bedside cupboard. He activated the light on it and discovered it was almost four a.m. He lay back down and tested himself. Not tired in any sense of the word and with no inclination to sleep at all. He put it down to one of the ironies of waking before the alarm went off – not that he could remember the last time he had set his alarm for anything.

He decided to get up and started to pull the bed sheet off him but found it was sticking quite severely to his body. It was still soaking from their journey into the unknown.

Oh yeah. He smiled again at the recollections of various images and sensations filtering through his mind. He had the notion to wake Gillian for another session, but pushed that thought away as he saw her sleeping soundly. She had been through a lot recently and would probably go through a lot later; she would need all the sleep she could get. He peeled the clinging cloth from his sticky body, stood up and stretched. Joints popped into place and muscles creaked from over-use.

He stepped over Gillian's recumbent body, passed the window and headed for the bedroom door. If he had turned his head at that moment he would have noticed his reflection in the full-length mirror on Gillian's wardrobe; he would have noticed that his naked body, too, had the same eerie, metallic radiance in the moonlight.

He hadn't, wouldn't, so couldn't.

He left the bedroom and tiptoed down the hall towards the bathroom. He strained his hearing, listening for movement from any of the other residents else they might discover him and his genitalia, but there was no sound. That shocked him into stopping. Normally he would cringe and wince at the night-time amplification of creeping noises, but this morning he was actually making no noise at all, even his breathing had... stopped? He gasped a breath and dashed (silently) to the bathroom, closing the door (silently) behind him.

He searched for the light switch and flicked it on. The light flashed red pain in his head and it went off quickly.

"Ow."

The pain subsided and he opened his eyes again, the room was pitch so he waited a moment for his vision to adjust once more to the gloom. Outlines appeared which turned into shapes which then became recognisable objects.

He turned the shower on and urinated whilst waiting for the water to heat up.

He stepped into the spray and let the water wash across his head and over his body. The warmth spread down the nape of neck. He lifted his head back and thrilled at the jets tickling his face. The water poured down his throat and he gasped in pain, then coughed out the water he just inhaled. Automatically his hand went to the ache and rubbed. It was really hurting.

Major love bites, he thought. *Vicious bitch*.

He rubbed the sore area to spread the pain and it faded slightly. *Polo necks for a month*, he contemplated and turned his attention back to the revitalising ministrations of the shower.

With eyes clamped shut to prevent the water getting in them, he fumbled for the temperature dial and turned it up. After a slight delay a burst of extra warmth erupted from the head; it washed over his body and sent a shiver down it; goose bumps appeared over his arms and legs.

He did it again with the same results.

Seven times he did it. It never occurred to him that the water was absolutely scalding. As he breathed slowly the steam entered his mouth and warmed his lungs. It reminded him of the sensation of a sauna, enclosed and claustrophobic so he turned the dial in the opposite direction until the water returned to a reasonable warmth. Then he continued turning. The sudden bursts of cold were more refreshing and vitalising than the heat and the goose bumps returned with reinforcements.

The dial could not turn any further. No hot water was coming through at all and Cameron wondered why cold showers were presumed to remedy sexual ardour, he himself could just go for another quick one with Gillian straight after this, but decided to let her sleep and also spurned the advances of his right hand.

He returned the temperature to a happy medium and reached for the soap. He scrubbed vigorously at his body and cleaned everywhere, even his feet – which he never used to bother with because the water and soap always went down that way anyway. He massaged his scalp forcefully with shampoo and conditioned afterwards, he had decided that if he was going to pit his self against the legions of the dead then, by god, he was going to smell good doing it.

Clean and refreshed he turned the shower off, stepped out and dried himself. He felt good. He had never felt this good in his life so he put it down to the sex. He should have done that a long time ago.

Suddenly he felt very, *very*, hungry.

She could see Penny, but she was not moving, just lying there in a puddle. She tried to call out but could not open her mouth properly because something was stuck in it. Instead she reached out to Penny, to shake her awake, to make her aware of her presence. She tapped her on the shoulder but received no reaction. She shook her a bit harder, nothing. She rolled her over and Penny's body slumped onto its back, her head rolled in the opposite direction to the movement of its usual attachment. The puddle was Penny's blood.

Movement caught her attention from the corner of her eye and she turned to see Danny and Gillian walk out of the shadows towards her and the body. They looked accusingly at her and she tried to tell them that it was not her doing, it was not her fault. They did not say anything, just passed her and knelt at Penny's headless corpse and pool of life, they bent and began to drink the blood, lapping it up.

Cassandra's hands went to her face in horror, trying to block the inhuman sight from her eyes but she felt something funny about her mouth, her teeth were sharp, razor sharp. She saw herself and saw that she had become a vampire. She too knelt and buried her face in the warm blood...

***

She awoke with a start, pulling her face out of the pillow. She panted rapidly, blinking in confusion, trying to clear the ghastly images and feelings from her unconscious.

She looked around the room; sunlight streamed through a gap in the curtains. Something had made her wake and she searched for it, for Danny. Her arm automatically reached for the space next to her. It was still warm and the images of the dream resurfaced then sank again.

She heard a noise outside the room and the door opened, she became irrationally scared, pulling the bed covers up to her chin.

Danny wandered in, dressed only in his briefs and started as he saw Cassandra sitting up staring at him with eyes wide.

"What's up?" he asked.

"You scared me," she puffed.

"I only went for a pee," he explained.

She dropped the sheets and slumped back on to the bed. "I had a nightmare," she said.

Danny crawled onto the bed and stroked her forehead gently. "Are you okay now?"

"I think so. Is anybody else up yet?"

"I'm not sure, I think I heard someone moving around in the kitchen."

Cassandra sat up straight again. "What if it's...?" she started.

"I think that if it was a vampire, then it wouldn't be looking for the cornflakes and coffee," he rationalised. "You're going to have to try to calm down. It's either Cameron or the old bloke fixing themselves breakfast."

"Could you go and check?" she implored.

"Jesus Cass, why won't you..." he stopped and looked at her, she was genuinely scared, not roller coaster scared, or horror film scared, this was real life scared, deep in the pit of your stomach stuff. Not the sort of scared that pumped adrenaline around your body and got you excited, but the sort of scared that turned you impotent and pathetic. The kind of scared that made you realise you are only human and life is not forever, and that there are certain things out there that you cannot do anything about.

"Okay," he said and pulled on his dressing gown. He stepped to the bedroom door and looked at Cassandra from over his shoulder as he walked out.

"I love you," she whimpered inaudibly and tried desperately to remove the sensation that she was never going to see him again.

Danny walked along the corridor to the top of the stairs that he then began to creep down. He caught himself doing it halfway down and mentally shook himself for being so paranoid and stupid. He could not tell Cassandra that everything was all right and then not believe it himself. But fear is a contagious thing. He had truly believed that everything was fine and that nothing suspect was making the noises in the kitchen until Cassandra had put the thought into his head.

He continued to creep until he reached the foot of the stairs and there he reached for a strip of broken door that could be used as a handy impaling device if one should so require it.

He paused outside the kitchen door; whoever it was in there, they were making a lot of noise for someone just making a bowl of cornflakes. He pushed the door open, slowly.

Cassandra felt the scream rip through her body like shards of glass against her soul. It was definitely Danny's voice she heard and he was definitely in serious pain.

Instead of it making her cower further under the sheets, the cry of anguish had caused her to leap across the room, grab her dressing gown and dart down the corridor and stairs before she had time to think about what was happening.

Earlier, she had been concerned for her own personal safety and probably would not have been able to raise a finger against a blood-sucking fiend even if her life depended on it. And it would of. But now, the thought of said blood sucking fiend hurting one corpuscle in the body of the man she loved, well, by god, that mother-fucking spawn of Satan was going to be in for it.

She burst through the kitchen door to see Danny curled on the floor, Cameron was kneeling over him with...

"Oh, my god," she whispered, – that looked like blood all over Cameron's face.

Nutter was startled awake by the second scream, a girl's scream. The first he had presumed to be a part of the addled images that flittered through his disturbed, dreaming mind, but he now realised it had been genuine and cursed himself for his lack of attentiveness.

He jumped off the couch, picked up his sword and ran to the kitchen. He burst through, trod on something wet on the linoleum floor and slid past the commotion and into the open refrigerator. He fell to the floor with frozen peas and milk toppling on top of him. He looked up to see a red - faced Cameron and a frowning Cassandra staring at him in alarm. He saw Danny holding his eyes in the palms of his hands rubbing gently.

"What...?" everyone asked in unison.

Cameron decided that since he was 'The Chosen One' then he should get to go first.

"I was eating pizza," he said, "Danny walked in, screamed and fell to the floor clutching his head. Cassandra ran in as I went to see what was up, and she screamed. Then you ran in, did a Torville and Dean and broke the 'fridge."

Nutter stood up and brushed himself off, Cassandra and Cameron lifted Danny to his feet.

"What happened, Daniel?" Nutter asked.

"I'm not sure," he spluttered, obviously in some severe pain. "I came downstairs and relapsed; I can't see again."

"Why has this happened?" Cassandra asked Nutter.

"I don't know," Danny replied.

"I had a feeling this might occur," Nutter interrupted. "As was the case with my previous apprentice, Daniel has attained vampiric detecting powers from his incident earlier."

"So am I going to go blind every time I see a vampire?"

Danny asked despondently.

"I think you'll probably find that you're not actually blind, just the aura from the demon is dazzling your vision," Nutter explained.

"So I just need a pair of good sunglasses then," Danny surmised.

Nutter nodded, realised that the action was wasted on Danny so added, "Yes, that should work in dampening the effects."

"There's a pair in one of these drawers," Cassandra said and went searching.

Cameron looked at the three of them in bewilderment. "Excuse me? Am I the only one that has realised the implications of Danny's reaction?"

"That we've got an excellent vampire detector," Danny announced with pride.

"That there's a fucking vampire here, now," Cameron shouted.

They all looked at each other in horror, except Danny who looked at the cooker in horror.

"Gillian," Cameron muttered and ran out and up the stairs.

"Wait," Nutter shouted after him and went to follow but slipped on the peas and milk mess around his feet.

Cameron leapt the steps three at a time and rushed to Gillian's room, bursting through without any thought as to the horrors that might be waiting within. Nothing prepared him for what he saw.

Gillian was still lying in the foetal position in which he had left her, the sheet was still pulled up to her head, she still looked as peaceful as ever. The white sheet that they had made love under that very night had been stained crimson red, the carpet that they had rolled around on in passion had been unmistakably darkened by the persistent flooding of a body emptying itself of life. Gillian's hair was matted and tangled, her face masked in her own blood.

He was going to be sick. He would have been as well, if he could have dragged his eyes away from the nightmarish vision before him. The sheet was so soaked with blood that it stuck to her body like a second skin; it moulded over her shoulder, under her arm and just touched the underside of her breast. It slinked its way down her side, to her waist and over her hip then echoed the curvature of her buttocks, thighs and calves. He suddenly shocked himself by realising he was almost getting turned on whilst staring at the butchered body of his lover, and was then suddenly shocked back to life by the remembrance that the body of his lover had been butchered.

He wanted to be sick again and would have as well had Nutter and Cassandra not disturbed him when they dashed in, arguing.

"Stay with Daniel," Nutter said.

"I need to know," Cassandra replied and ran back out of the room almost faster than when she had entered, but on the way out she was screaming.

Nutter rested a hand on Cameron's shoulder.

"How...?" was all Cameron managed.

Nutter moved forward and inspected the area, the diameter of darkness on the carpet, the girl's position. "This isn't right," he said.

"Huh?" Cameron grunted.

"I've never seen a death like this before," Nutter explained. "No signs of struggle, all this blood."

Cameron lost it. "She's been fucking opened up, what do you expect to come out? Candy floss?"

Nutter turned to him as calm as ever. "Think about it Cameron, what do vampires do?"

Cameron could not believe it; he was being given hell demon lectures over the drained, lifeless form of the woman he loves. Loved.

"They kill virgi..." he stopped after remembering last night's performance.

"Not the story stuff Cameron, the real stuff," Nutter said.

"They drink blood," Cameron finally said.

"Exactly," Nutter nodded.

Cameron waited as if there was going to be more. There was not.

"Exactly what?" he asked.

"Look!" Nutter gesticulated at blood everywhere. "None of it has been drunk, has it? It's all here. Too much in fact for just one person."

Cameron's head was spinning. "I don't understand. Are you saying that she hasn't been vampirised, just brutally slain?"

"I don't know, it's all very confusing. The blood's not even warm, implying that this must have happened-"

"What's going on?" Gillian mumbled.

"Aaargh!" the two men replied.

"Huh?" she asked.

Nutter pulled his sword up to a striking position, ready to skewer her.

"No!" Cameron yelled and shot across the room with more speed than he ever would have admitted to having. Nutter was knocked off his feet and flung to the bed. He sat up, startled but alert, then sagged as he realised that his sword had been taken from him.

"Cameron," he said, "I think this proves that she has been turned."

"Wait," Cameron said and crouched at Gillian's side, brushing the sticky tangled hair from her face. "You okay darling?" he asked.

"Hmmm," was her reply and she grinned as a memory of the night before came back to her.

She stretched and made a purring noise as consciousness returned to her body. She smacked her lips and grimaced. "I've got to brush my teeth, Cam, I've got a really bad taste in my mouth."

She opened her eyes and looked at him and her surroundings. His face showed distinct confusion and fear, and the sheets that were once white were now red. Very red. Blood red.

She jumped up, knocking Cameron over, and stared in horror at the covers, and then at her blood covered, naked body. "Whathefuckhashappened?" she screamed.

Cameron stood quickly, grabbed a dressing gown and wrapped it around her. "It's all right," he soothed.

"It's not fucking all right," she shouted back. "I look like an overused tammy for fuck's sake."

"Let's go and get cleaned off and I'll try to explain in the process," Cameron suggested.

Gillian then noticed Nutter on her bed and jumped again. "How long has he been there?"

"Er, not long," Cameron replied.

Gillian pulled the gown tighter round her as she became conscious of her nudity, then she and Cameron left the room, leaving a very confused Nutter reeling to himself.

"It was never like this in the old days," he muttered.

Gillian went and got cleaned off whilst Cameron explained absolutely nothing. He watched her intently scrubbing the blood from her body, and kept a hand surreptitiously on Nutter's sword.

Upon removing all traces of haemoglobin from her nubile form (Cameron could not watch her and not think of sex no matter what the situation), she dried and dressed.

Cameron had never been what may be described as a 'vampire expert', but did consider her movements not to be normally associated with those of the Prince of Darkness' minions of evil. That is to say that Cameron never would have presumed one of the many rituals of the night stalkers, before they prepared themselves for an evening of arterial orgies, would be to check one's cuticles and file one's immaculate nails. Still, he was as new to this as was his recently made undead girlfriend. Perhaps she did not know that she was supposed to bay at the moon, or perform some sort of necromantic rite. Maybe you were supposed to get a manual or something; "Lestat's Complete Guide to Immortality and Jugular Rending". He relaxed slightly and wondered briefly if making love to her now would be considered to be necrophilia.

The pair of them walked downstairs to the kitchen where Danny, Cassandra and Nutter all stood on the opposite side of the table facing the way they came in. Gillian entered first followed by Cameron. Still armed.

Danny's jaw dropped and his eyes widened behind his sunglasses. "Cool," he said.

Cassandra looked decidedly uneasy. She had momentarily witnessed one of her friends lying in more than just a pool of blood, a lido more like, and now here she was, alive. Or not as the case probably was.

"What's cool?" Cassandra asked Danny.

"She's fucking glowing man. All over, like an angel," he replied, a little too passionately for Cassandra's liking but she left it for the moment.

"I'm what?" Gillian asked and sat down in front of them, Cameron remained where he was.

Nutter decided to set the record straight. "Young lady," he started.

"Gillian," she corrected.

"Gillian'," he continued, and smiled nervously at her apparent lack of realisation of the seriousness of the situation. "I am to be the bearer of bad tidings, since it is apparent that Cameron has failed to 'explain' anything."

Gillian turned her head to him and he shrugged his shoulders.

"Go on then," she urged.

"At some point this morning, you have been..." he searched for the right words. This had never happened to him before – to actually sit in conference with a vampire – normally he would encounter, fight and dispense. This was all too strange.

"Killed," Danny continued.

"Thank you, Daniel," Nutter acknowledged.

"What?" she asked incredulously.

"You've been killed, Gillian," Cassandra affirmed.

"Don't be so bloody ridiculous, Cass. Look at me."

"I saw you," she stammered, "in all that blood."

"If this is some sort of joke, it's in bloody poor taste," Gillian shouted.

Cameron put his hand on her shoulder to calm her down.

"It's no joke," Nutter continued. "I'm afraid it does seem as if you have been turned."

"To the Dark Side," Danny boomed in his best Darth Vader.

"Cam?" Gillian needed more confirmation.

"I think you're dead, sweetheart," he said.

"I can't be, look," she implored.

"Try holding your breath," Cameron suggested.

Ten minutes later...

"You can stop now," Cameron said.

Gillian suddenly looked very worried. "I don't feel dead," she said. "I feel great, I've never felt better."

Cameron suddenly thought of how good he had felt when he first got up.

"That's because all of your mortal impurities have been destroyed," Nutter explained. "Daniel was not far wrong when he described you as an angel, but you must remember, Lucifer was an angel too."

"I don't feel evil," Gillian protested.

"I must say that this is very peculiar," Nutter agreed, "normally a newly turned body requires sustenance."

"You mean food?" Danny asked.

"Yes, do you not feel the pangs of hunger?" Nutter asked Gillian.

Cameron remembered his hunger this morning.

"Well, now that you mention it," Gillian said, "I could murder a cup of coffee."

"That wasn't quite what I meant," Nutter said. "Do you not feel the blood lust?"

"The what?" four voices asked.

"The blood lust is an incurable condition of the vampiric state, especially prevalent in the new born. It is a hunger for blood, human blood; a vampire cannot survive on any other. When the body needs to eat, the mind is taken over by the scent of blood, the sound of a heart beat, the lack of your own. I understand the sensation is almost maddening, it sends the body into an uncontrollable rage that only rests when the beating has stopped and the lust has been sated.

"The four of us here should turn you into a wild animal."

They all looked at Gillian with awe, fear and expectation; Cameron gripped the sword tighter.

"A cup of coffee and some toast would be fine," she said at last. "Really."

Four young faces looked for guidance from the eldest, more experienced face which showed severe signs of confusion. Nutter shrugged and muttered, "I suppose so."

Cameron turned and made his way to the kettle. Only Danny took his eyes from Gillian and followed his path.

"Oh, fucking shit," Danny said.

Cameron spun around with the sword. "What is it?" he asked in alarm.

"You," Danny said. "You're one too."

Cameron dropped the sword to his side. "Fuck off," he said in disbelief.

"I mean it man, you've got the same glow all around you. I couldn't see it before because you was standing so close to her," Danny pointed at Gillian.

"I am not a vampire, okay?" Cameron shouted, obviously getting annoyed, and returned his attention to the kettle.

"Listen pal," Danny shouted back, "I should fucking know, all right? I am the vampire detector around here."

"You couldn't detect your own arse," Cameron told him. "Even if it farted to give you a clue."

"I could too," Danny argued, "even with both hands tied behind my back."

"That probably would help you a bit," Cameron muttered.

"He's a fucking vampire," Danny told everyone else, "that's why I was blinded earlier."

Cameron turned back to face his friend – the word 'friend' being the furthest from his mind at that moment – his eyes glowed red. "I AM NOT A FUCKING VAMPIRE."

There was a shocked, frightened silence.

"Cool," Danny said.

"Fuck," Cameron said.

"I concur completely," Nutter agreed and made a movement forwards for his sword whilst Cameron was distracted in his state of shock.

Cameron came to and jumped back, brandishing the confiscated weapon at Nutter.

"Don't try it pal," Cameron warned. "I'm not going to cause trouble, so you had better not."

"Why not prove your good intentions by returning my weapon then?" Nutter countered. "You see before you three unprotected mortals, two of whom are your friends. If you are still in control of your mortal senses then prove it to them. Put their fears at ease, make them comfortable."

"I don't want to die," Cameron told him.

"And I shall not kill you as long as you don't threaten us, and until you prove we can trust you."

"Cam," Gillian said. He heard her but did not turn his attention from the old man. "Give him the sword."

Cameron stood staring at Nutter for a moment, weighing the possibilities, the possible escape routes and the future implications. Finally, he threw the sword across the work surface, at which Nutter picked it up deftly and returned it to his walking stick scabbard.

"I'm glad we understand each other," Nutter said. "I had a feeling about you, Cameron; I'm glad that it was right."

Cameron turned his back on Nutter and flicked the kettle on, Nutter had to resist his primal inclinations to re-draw his sword and plunge it through Cameron's heart. He had to see how all this was going to turn out, and possibly find out how it happened.

Breakfast had been partaken by all; the potentially evil undead over one side of the table; defenders of all things good over the other. Small talk had not been made.

Cassandra broke the silence. "So can anyone become a vampire?"

"Technically yes," Nutter replied, "although the individual does have to be sexually mature."

Gillian and Cameron threw a quick, secretive glance at one another.

"Why sexually mature?" Cassandra enquired.

"It has to do with desire and craving," Nutter explained. "It is a basic human trait to want sexual gratification, if one is not in the position of enjoying sex, one does not desire it."

"You can't want what you've never had," Danny cited.

"No, that's not true Daniel," Nutter corrected. "Sex and reproduction is a natural action of all living organisms. Creatures do not question the 'whats' and 'wherefores' of their motivations, they simply know that it is something they need to do at certain times in their lives. Humans crave sex nearly all the time, and mainly for pleasure rather than reproductive purposes. Granted, the drive of men and women is of different intensities, but the craving is there as soon as the body is capable of accepting and enjoying the act.

"The turning of a body is very much like copulation and reproduction. The vampire that attacks the body – instead of giving the potential for life – removes that potential and kills the body but the craving, the desire, the lust lives on in the shell and the vampire is born.

"What we have here," he indicated the two undead at the breakfast table, "is an anachronism. These two have not been 'raped' in the usual fashion of vampiric activity. I would hazard a guess that, somehow, they turned themselves."

The three mortals stared at the two possible 'exceptions that prove the rule'. The two undead felt extremely self-conscious about their private lives under such scrutiny.

"They shagged," Danny announced.

Considering the lack of blood that was contained within their now immortal frames, they both managed to turn a most remarkable shade of red.

"They bloody did as well."

"Interesting," Nutter mumbled to himself. "Yes it would seem that they willingly gave in to each other, volunteered their mortality to each other for the sake of eternal love."

Gillian and Cameron looked at each other.

"That is so sweet," Cassandra simpered and ran around the table to hug her friend. "I'm so happy for you Gill."

"Yeah, righteous, Cam," Danny agreed, "but you only had to lose your cherry, not every pint in your body."

Cameron's embarrassment turned into 'laddish' arrogance. "Yeah, well Danny, you know what it's like, when she keeps begging for more, what can you do? Ow!"

Gillian soothed the ache from her now sore knuckles. Cameron grimaced and rubbed his dead, dead shoulder.

"Don't you turn into a lager drinking football lad now, Cameron," Gillian warned then turned to Nutter, "or is this part of the 'turning' process that you mentioned?"

"Not quite," Nutter replied. "I am intrigued as to the conditions of your transformation to immortality."

"Eh?" four voices asked.

"You were both virgins were you?"

Again, blood-drained faces managed to redden heatedly, Danny and Cassandra felt for them, but it did not stop them smirking as well.

Gillian's blush of embarrassment turned to one of anger. "Look, just leave us alone will you. We don't know what's happened, or how it happened, it just has. This is so humiliating having you prod and poke at our private lives. It's none of your sodding business. We shouldn't be treated like this."

"Yeah, we're human too," Cameron supported. "'Prick us and do we not bleed?'"

"No," Danny answered.

"Oh yeah," Cameron remembered.

"Shut up Cam," Gillian ordered, "you're not helping."

"Sorry," he apologised.

"I too must offer my apologies young lady, I was getting carried away with the science of the subject." Nutter explained. "You must understand from my point of view that this is all very strange and interesting."

The tune from 'The Twilight Zone' drifted around the kitchen, but was stopped with a harsh look from Cassandra.

"Anyway," Nutter continued, "if we feel that we can all trust each other's conditions and motivations, I shall shower and freshen up, ready for the day's battle."

"Oh yeah, I forgot about that," Cameron moaned.

"At least you don't have to worry about dying now," Danny consoled.

Cameron looked up and smiled. "Oh yeah."

Danny suddenly leapt to his feet. "What time is it?"

Gillian looked at her watch. "Nine thirty."

"Animaniacs," Danny said and ran into the living room. The other four watched him dash out. "Hey!" he shouted from the other room, "the telly's been... oh yeah."

A collective, 'Oh yeah,' spread around the kitchen.

"We must ready ourselves," Nutter declared and left the room.

"How are we going to do this?" Gillian asked no one in particular.

"I suppose he knows all the classic places to look," Cameron suggested.

"And Danny would be able to spot them a mile away as well," Cassandra added.

"I know all that," Gillian said, "but do we go out dressed like Rambo and armed to the teeth with stakes, garlic and silver bullets?"

"That's werewolves," Danny told her as he came back into the kitchen.

"I know," Gillian retorted sharply, "but if there are vampires, why not werewolves?"

This brought an awed silence over the youths.

"Frankenstein," Cameron suggested.

"Don't be so bloody stupid Cameron," Gillian chided.

"Oh and 'werewolves' isn't stupid?"

"'Aren't'," Cassandra corrected.

"I meant 'werewolves' as an individual, collective subject."

"This really isn't the time or place to have a grammar debate," Gillian said.

"Where is?" Cameron asked.

"In English class," Danny told them. "I'm going to fill my college bag with stakes." He left the room once more and headed towards the garden.

Cameron stood and followed him. "Why can't you just take a packed lunch like everyone else?"

Cassandra sat in Cameron's vacant seat. "How was it?"

Gillian smiled. "I never could have imagined," she said.

"That good?"

"Amazing."

"Blimey."

"I mean," Gillian hypothesised, "it may have been that good because of the draining of blood from one's circulatory system perhaps."

"True."

"Perhaps next time it'll be really crap, you know?"

"Perhaps."

Gillian's grin spread across her face again. "But probably not though, eh?"

Cassandra grinned with empathy. "Probably."

In the garden the boys were searching for suitable stake shaped branches.

"Holy water's supposed to be a good deterrent isn't it?" Danny asked.

"So I've heard."

"Well, doesn't the mere mention of the words instil dread into your very being?"

"No," Cameron told him.

Danny quickly lifted two sticks he was holding into a cross shape, Cameron convulsed and fell to the floor.

"Shit," Danny spat and dropped his offensive stance. "I was only testing. Sorry, man."

"'S' okay," Cameron replied and got to his feet, "I was only joking."

"Oh," Danny thought for a second. "What about garlic?"

"I never really know how much to put in, you know? You can't taste it while you're cooking, and you only know you've used too much when you stink for three weeks after the meal. I tend to use two cloves for whatever."

"That's not what I meant."

"But I think you got the answer you deserved."

Danny shrugged and continued his search, then suddenly thought of something. "Can you do that thing that Gary Oldman did, like slide along the floor without moving your feet?"

"I don't know," Cameron pondered then came to a conclusion. "I can 'moon-walk' though."

Danny shook his head. "I never managed to get the hang of that, I used to be able to do the 'caterpillar' though."

The girls had finished their chat and went to see what their partners were up to. Looking through the back door window they could see Cameron making the motions of walking forwards, but sliding backwards. Danny was lying on the grass on his front sending a wave down the length of his body and wiggling backwards.

Cassandra buried her face in her hands and Gillian merely shook her head in amazement.

"Saviours of the human race, huh?" Gillian said to no one.

Cameron and Danny were standing next to each other at arm's length and with their hands linked. Cameron started a wave in his free arm that passed through his body, down the other arm and into Danny's. He then passed the wave through his body, down his free arm where it bounced back and returned to its original position down Cameron's free arm.

Danny convulsed in laughter. "No soldier of Satan would be able to break dance. You're still cool man."

"Thanks," Cameron said and proceeded to do his impression of a human beat box by spitting everywhere and dribbling down his chin. This sent Danny into a bigger fit of hysterics.

The girls resigned the fate of the human race to perpetual slavery to the evils of the Dark Lord and returned to the kitchen.

Danny calmed himself and Cameron wiped the saliva from his chin.

"So how'd you happen then?" Danny asked. "Or how do you think you happened?"

"I really don't know. The Nutter..."

"The who?" Danny interrupted.

"Nutter. The old bloke."

"Is that what you call him?"

"Well, he is, or rather I thought he was when I first met him," Cameron explained.

"Does he know?"

"I shouldn't think so. Not unless he's psychic as well."

"Anyway, 'the Nutter'...." Danny prompted.

"Oh yeah, the Nutter said it was all about belief. I believed in vampires and that meant they would come looking for me."

Danny thought about this for a second with a frown across his face. "So from the dawn of time, vampires have existed because you believe in them now?"

"Not just me. Everyone."

"But I don't believe in vampires," Danny said to him.

"So?" Cameron shrugged.

"Well you said they only exist if you believe in them and I don't."

Cameron paused, his brow furrowed whilst his brain searched for an answer. "Well I don't know exactly how it works, I'm only telling you what he told me," he eventually admitted. "Just because I am one doesn't mean I know the whys, hows and whats. All I know is I believed and lo, they were there."

"But I don't believe and they're still there. Are you trying to tell me your beliefs are stronger than mine?"

"No. Maybe you did believe, just a little bit, but didn't know it."

"What? A subconscious belief in vampires?"

"Why not?"

"Bollocks."

"Probably," Cameron finally agreed. "But you do believe now though don't you?" he added.

"Yeah, but that's a bit Rene des Cartes isn't it?"

"In what sense has 'I think therefore I am' any relevance to this?"

"Well," Danny was thinking about this carefully; existentialism had never been a strong subject of his. Not while he was sober anyway.

"Well," he repeated, "it doesn't actually explain why you are here in front of me as a vampire. You're telling me to accept it simply because you are. My initial beliefs have been shunned and contradicted simply on the basis that you exist because you believe that you do. And because you exist because of your belief, you are standing before me. I, therefore, have to believe in you, therefore you do exist because of my belief."

"Yeah?" Cameron asked dubiously.

"You came prior to my belief in vampires. You can't say that vampires exist because I believe in them after I've seen them when I didn't believe in them before."

"From Dougie Fresh to debating philosophical theories of self determination and existence. I'm impressed," said Nutter from the doorway.

Cameron and Danny looked at him in amazement; standing behind him were the girls, staring with equal wonderment. He was cleanly shaven, washed, brushed and sparkly clean. His blonde hair had been tied back into a serious ponytail completely exposing his 'new' face. The crystal blue eyes shone even more now and said, 'Really, you don't want to mess with me'. His shabby clothes had gone and he had obviously decided to raid Danny's wardrobe (what with him being roughly the same size), he was decked in black shirt, trousers and trainers. The shirt was perhaps a size too small, or could it be that he really did have a rather impressive physique.

Danny broke the silence. "How do you know about Dougie

Fresh?"

"He was probably one of the worst examples of 'Hip Hop' to infect the British music industry during the eighties."

"Damn straight," the boys voiced in mutual, and new, respect for this man.

"Oh by the way," Nutter said, "the bathroom faces this garden and I managed to hear every word you two said. The name will do for now." He directed the last comment at Cameron who suddenly became a bit self-conscious.

"I've had worse," Nutter added and returned into the house.

"What did you call him?" Gillian asked.

"Later," Cameron stalled.

"Nutter," Danny announced.

"That's a bit rude isn't it?" Cassandra commented.

"That's terrible, Cam," Gillian said.

"Cheers, pal," Cameron turned on Danny. "But anyway, it's not as if he's introduced himself or anything is it? I mean, who is he? He's hardly the social type, is he? We don't know anything about him apart from being Penny's Dad and all."

The conversation stopped.

"He's what?" Cassandra asked.

"Bullshit," Danny declared.

"Well, that's what he said," Cameron told them.

"I don't like it," Gillian announced, "it is all rather sus' isn't it?"

"What? You think he's dodgy?" Danny asked.

"Well, we've all accepted this a little too easily, haven't we?"

"True," Cassandra agreed.

"You think maybe he's involved in this a little deeper than he's making out?" Danny suggested.

"How can a guy who tells us he's a professional vampire hunter be involved any deeper than that?" Cameron asked him.

"He could be the Dark Lord of the Sith himself," Danny replied.

"I trust him," Cameron declared.

"Yeah, well, maybe you would," Danny said.

"What's that mean?" Cameron inquired.

"You could be a henchman of the Duke of Darkness."

"And what about me?" Gillian asked.

Cassandra took a step away from her. "It does sort of make semi-sense, Gill."

"Oh thanks."

"Does it make any sense at all," Cameron started asking, "that three of the hordes of hell should be sharing breakfast and making polite conversation with those one would normally presume to be the prey of their insatiable appetites?"

The two with a full complement of platelets, haemoglobin, and red blood cells thought about this for a second.

"I suppose," admitted Cassandra.

"Double bluff?" suggested Danny.

"Grow up," the other three replied and went back into the house.

"You've got to be prepared to face all of the possibilities," Danny shouted at a closed door and ran after them.

**

It was very dark. It seemed to be lighter when Penny closed her eyes than it did when she was looking around. She did not know how long she had slept for, but did know that it had been for a very long time. She yawned loudly and startled herself with the sound in the stillness of... well, where ever it was that she was. She rubbed her shoulder, it was still sore from the little fracas she had been involved in, but it was usable again. She wondered how the others were and immediately pushed them from her mind. If they were okay, then fine, they did not need any help, if they were in trouble then she could not offer any help anyway. And if they had been turned then they were past help. She needed to concentrate on her own predicament and problems. She wondered why they had not turned her yet.

WE ARE WAITING. HE WILL COME FOR YOU.

This made her jump slightly, but comforted her as well. At least she now knew roughly where she stood; she was being constantly watched.

"They probably think I'm dead," she told the voice.

PERHAPS, BUT HE WILL STILL COME FOR YOU.

"Who?" she demanded. "Who's 'he'?"

HE IS OF YOUR FLESH.
"Oh no," she moaned, "not him. Anyone but him."

She suddenly felt a presence, very close to her. Something made of paper was pushed into her arms. It was a bag of some kind with something radiating a moist warmth from inside.

"Take it," said John Settle Junior's voice.

"What is it?" Penny stammered.

"MacDonalds," he replied, "I thought you might be hungry."

"Thanks," she said. "Did you get a drink as well?"

***

The five defenders of humanity, in their various forms of mortality, sat in the living room trying to make plans.

"Okay," Cassandra stood up and wished to surmise the ridiculous arrangements thus far. "You," she indicated Nutter, "think you know where their hide-out is – or rather think you'll be able to sense where their hide-out is – and think that we should follow you ambling around Yorkshire sniffing at the air."

"Something like that," Nutter conceded.

"Whereas you," she pointed at Danny, "think we should just walk around Yorkshire letting you identify who is and who isn't a vampire and then systematically wipe them out."

"Absolutely," Danny confirmed and held aloft a nicely pointed branch that he had been whittling onto the carpet (much to the complaints of Gillian until she was reminded of the state of the rest of the house. "I think you could say goodbye to our deposit then," she had suggested).

"Now Gillian, you think we should go looking for Penny."

Gillian nodded.

"But I have already said that Penelope is more than likely being held captive at their 'hide-out'," Nutter reiterated.

"Okay, so that's two to you," Cassandra told him. "I reckon the best way to find out where they are is to catch one and torture the bastard until it squeals and I vote for Danny's plan. Two all. Cameron?"

"Well," Cameron started and paused. A serious look spread across his features as he made sure he had everyone's attention.

"Nutter has already expressed his opinion that things are going to happen whether we go looking for them or not, so I suggest we wait here for a couple of hours until 'The Dragon' opens, go down there, have a few beers and wait."

"Can I change my vote?" Danny asked and received a kick in the shin.

"Are you serious?" Gillian enquired.

"Sort of," Cameron replied, "maybe not so much about the pub, but generally yes."

Nutter rubbed his chin. "He does actually have quite a valid plan. Fate has a way of playing its pieces whether one takes active participation or not."

"What about Penny?" Cassandra reminded. "She might be in trouble."

"Well, Penelope's situation is not as precarious as one might imagine. Firstly, if anything drastic were to have happened, then I think from the evidence of this room it would be reasonable to deduce that it has already happened. Secondly, believe it or not, she is very capable of looking after herself."

"And then some," agreed Cameron.

"Quite," Nutter continued unabated, "thirdly, I am of the opinion that she is actually being used as bait."

This last comment shocked the troops to an even higher degree of attentiveness.

"They know I am in the game," Nutter said, "and the Prince will be eager for a rematch."

"So she is your daughter," Danny blurted.

"Yes she is."

"But Danny's still not your son," Cameron stated, and Nutter merely sighed wearily.

"But you kicked her out of the family," Danny continued digging his hole.

"Yes, I did. It was a very long time ago during a period of very different moral values and disciplinary punishments."

"You told me last night you hadn't seen her for over fifty years," Cameron reminded him.

"Yes, I did," Nutter admitted. "It has actually been even longer than that."

"Eh?" the other three queried.

"It is quite a complicated story, but during my earlier years of vampiric studies I foolishly experimented with genetic testing, blood transfusions and such the like, to see if the turn was reversible."

"And?" Cameron interrupted.

"I found no cure for it. But in the process I did, somehow, give myself longevity. My ageing slowed.

"I did not actually realise this until close into what should have been my fourth decade. My wife then, had aged considerably, but I had merely assigned this to the rigours of childbirth and poor health. My younger brother by ten years came calling as to her well-being and looked very much older than me.

"Eventually, my wife died, my brother died, my entire collection of family and friends passed on and I became unable to carry the emotional burden of friendship or love because of the inevitable pain it would eventually cause me.

"Foolishly – or perhaps simply humanly – I searched for love again and remarried. By this time the hazards to the mother during childbirth had been cut drastically and I was to be a father again, this time to Penelope.

"It became apparent that my curse had been passed on to her, when in her fourth year, although she was walking and talking as is the norm for infants at that age, she had not actually grown very much since birth. My wife assumed she was to become a midget or such like, but on her death bed some twenty years later Penny had grown to the stature of perhaps a six year old.

"I took it as my sole responsibility to raise her and train her to survive in my world. I had firmly been embedded in the vampire culture; they all knew me because of my earlier crusades to defeat them; to keep Penelope near would have meant that she would eventually have become as involved as me. Perhaps because she was part of my flesh and blood, she already was involved and personally training her was the only way to protect her. So we became a partnership, and a very effective one at that."

For a moment, lost in the mists of time and remembrance, his eyes sparkled with pride and satisfaction.

"And then there was her minor infraction of my moral codes and I caused our paths to split."

He looked at his junior apprentices, perhaps looking for forgiveness, perhaps looking for the retribution that he felt that he deserved. Neither came.

"But all of this is perhaps an example of why Cameron's plan is possibly the best one because, as is the way with destiny, our paths are converging again."

Everyone was silent for a while, contemplating the magnitude of Nutter's words – Cameron was right? That had to be the strangest thing they had heard so far.

"So what?" Danny enquired. "Are we just to sit here and wait for one of them to turn up and invite us back to his place for a cup of Penny?"

"Once again Daniel, you have managed to grasp the situation, but word it somewhat tactlessly. But basically yes."

"Sod that," Danny continued. "I still think we should go out there and kick some blood-sucking bastard's arse."

"Yeah," Cassandra enthused.

Nutter thought about this for a second, then nodded. "I concur. I believe the best plan will be to gain some field experience with some of the lower drones before we embark on conflict with the Dukes of Darkness."

"Excellent," Danny yelled and jumped to his feet waving his double-ended stake like an enthusiastic, extrovert Ninja overdosing on tartrazine and orange 'Smarties'.

"Perhaps somewhat more subtly than that, Daniel."

"I'll get my bag to put them in," he suggested, and ran out of the room.

"So, do we go out in a huge group and attack on mass or what?" Cameron asked.

"I think we will cover more ground by splitting up. Mortals and undead," Nutter told him.

"But you know what a vampire looks like, and Danny can spot them a mile off. What are we going to do about it?" Cameron complained.

"I believe you two will be able to identify them through your innate oneness with all walking dead," Nutter replied and stood up as Danny thundered back down the stairs stuffing an assortment of sharp objects into a shoulder bag.

"Let's do it," he said and the three humans proceeded to leave.

"Wait," Gillian called out. "What if we need to meet up or something?"

"Oh yeah!" Danny shouted and ran back up stairs. Seconds later he returned with two walkie-talkies, one of which he threw to Gillian. "You'll have to get batteries but they should be okay."

Then there were two; two bemused, confused vampires, standing in a bomb struck living room holding a dead walkie-talkie wondering how to combat the forces of darkness.

Cameron seemed to have an idea and he turned sheepishly to Gillian. "We could always just go and do it, you know?"

"Not after what happened last time," she replied. "God knows what state I'll come out in if I let you go near me with that thing again." She prodded at his crotch with the radio antenna.

They left the house, went to the corner shop and bought a set of batteries for their radio and switched it on.

"Hello? Hello?" Gillian called into it.

"Scrshhhhhhhhhhh," it replied.

"Are you pressing the button on the side?" Cameron asked.

"Yes, I'm pressing the bloody button," she snapped back. "I do know how to work one of these. Hello, hello?" she called into it and showed Cameron that she was 'pressing the button'.

"Scrshhhhhhhhhhh," it replied.

"Something's wrong," she deduced.

"Oh, and you speak fluent static do you? I suppose you can read television 'snow' as well, can you?"

"Don't get sarcastic. Why aren't they answering?"

There came a long 'beep' back at them followed by a series of intermittent long and shorter 'beeps'. It stopped.

"Hello?" Gillian said.

"Sorry about that," Danny's voice transmitted. "Cass wanted to do it but couldn't."

"What was all that 'beeping'?" Gillian asked.

"Morse code," Danny replied.

"Why?"

"I thought it might make the atmosphere more exciting and secretive."

"And the conversations very long and boring," Cameron said out of earshot.

"Well don't," Gillian told Danny.

"...tom of the radio," Danny said.

"What?" Gillian demanded.

"What?" Danny echoed.

"What did you just say?"

"That the Morse code alphabet is at the bottom of the radio."

"Well, don't talk while I am," Gillian ordered.

"But I hadn't finished," Danny explained.

"I didn't know that."

"Get him to say 'over' when he finishes," Cameron suggested.

"Oh, yeah. Say 'over' when you've finished speaking," she transmitted. Adding, "Over," for emphasis.

"Cool," Danny said. "Over."

"Where are you now? Over," Gillian asked.

"Down the bottom of the road. Over," he replied.

Gillian and Cameron looked up the street and saw nothing. They turned around and looked down the other way. About five hundred yards away they saw their three associates, two were waving at them.

"Oh Jesus," Cameron sighed in exasperation.

"We'll go this way then, towards town. Over," Gillian told them.

"Okay. Over," Danny said. "See you later. Oops, sorry."

"Over," he added. "That was the last 'over'. Over. Bye."

"Be careful, Gill," came Cassandra's voice.

"You've got to say 'over' after," Danny's voice informed her in the background.

"Over after," Cassandra informed them.

"No, just 'over'," Danny ordered.

"Don't talk to me like that, Daniel, I'm not stupid," she told him. "Over," she said down the radio.

"Come on," Cameron said and started walking away. "We could be like this for hours. Don't look back."

They walked for a few streets, hand in hand, and simply enjoyed the silence that they could generate between them. Both of them dealt with their own respective thoughts.

"How do you feel about all of this, Gill?" Cameron asked.

"I don't know," she replied honestly. "Physically I feel great; everything looks better, I can see everything a lot clearer, hear so much more. My thoughts seem to be clearer as well. I'm not bothered about my overdraft, university, what my parents are going to say, anything."

"I know what you mean," he acknowledged. "I suppose it could be something to do with us being dead, you know? Nothing really matters any more. Or perhaps all the other stuff that's going on is just a little bit more important."

"But why don't we have this 'blood lust' business?"

"I really don't know," he admitted, "maybe it's because of our motivations and the way we 'turned' each other rather than being infected by another vampire."

"What about all that stuff about 'eternal love'?" Gillian queried and Cameron shrugged his shoulders.

Cameron suddenly stopped in his tracks. "You feel that?" he asked. "Did you just get a sinking feeling?"

"Yes," she answered. "There's one in that house isn't there?"

"I think so. Well?"

"I suppose we'd better go check."

"I suppose."

The house that their attentions were now focused on was at the very end of the road. It stood alone on the corner of two streets. A driveway led up to the side and to the back of the two-storey building. A red Sierra was parked at the very end of the drive between two hedges; one was the border of the house's back garden and the other blocked the street that ran parallel to the drive.

They walked slowly up the path, warily eyeing the house, the windows and the car.

A curtain twitched slightly in one of the upstairs windows and Gillian stopped, clutching her stomach.

"What's wrong?" Cameron asked concerned.

"I feel really sick, she groaned, "there's something in there that makes me want to puke."

"Wait here, I'll go see," Cameron told her and jogged up to the front door then rang the doorbell.

An oppressive feeling came over him as the door opened and an elderly woman put her head through the gap. "Yes?" she asked.

Cameron was shocked, he presumed the door would open to a red-eyed, fang-toothed, drooling mutant from the darker recesses of Clive Barker's repressed nightmares, not this wizened, slack - jawed biddy from the darker recesses of the Post Office queue.

"My girlfriend is in pain, and I need to use your phone," he told her and pushed the door to enter. He was surprised to discover the door would not budge, yet it seemed that it was only being held in place by the old woman's twig-like arm.

"I'm afraid I don't have a phone, dear," she wheezed at him and began to push the door shut. Behind him he heard Gillian groan loudly and turned to see if she was still standing.

She was stretching her eyelids, clearing her pain-wracked head.

"I'm okay," she told him. "I'm all right now."

Cameron smiled at her and then remembered his original intent. He turned back to the woman just in time to see her lunge at his neck; her pearl white razors glinted in her mouth. He was paralysed with fear as her teeth got closer.

The woman looked as if she had been struck by lightning as she flew backwards into her house, screaming and convulsing fitfully.

Cameron came to his senses and saw Gillian standing next to him rubbing her knuckles. "I knew all that time punching you would come to good use one day," she muttered.

"Let's finish this," Cameron said, "quickly."

They both started into the house. The old woman had got to her feet by now and was warding them off like a territorial protective tomcat; she hissed evilly.

"They never did make a 'Grandmother of Dracula' did they?" Cameron asked rhetorically. "Now you know why."

"Who are you?" she growled. "You aren't one of the One."

"I am not a number," Cameron told her, "I am a free man."

"And you can call me 'Buffy'," Gillian added.

"That's very good," Cameron complimented.

With a final hiss, the old woman shot up the stairs. She did not run up the stairs very quickly, she actually leapt, straight up to the next floor.

The two attackers were momentarily startled. Gillian was the first to move as, what appeared to Cameron to be a fright train, crashed through the wall of an adjoining room, collided with her and carried her through the next wall and outside.

"Fucking Jesus H. shit!" he commented and ran through the hole in the outside wall. He stepped across the rubble of bricks, breeze blocks and wall insulation to see that Gillian had the situation well under control.

"You okay, hon?" he asked.

She had a determined expression in her eyes and was holding the male protagonist of her sudden departure off the floor at arm's length by the throat.

"Don't worry about me, lover," she told him, and body-slammed her captive onto the drive with the force of an industrial pile driver.

"I'll just go and deal with Super Gran then, shall I?" he asked.

"Yep. I think I can manage things this end," she replied, whilst repeatedly pounding her opponent's head with a breeze block that had come to hand.

Cameron stepped back through the hole in the wall, amazed at how well she was dealing with the situation, and the sheer brutality with which she was dispensing with her first henchman of Hades. He was also thinking of how humiliating the situation could end up if he was to require assistance whilst battling the mother of the mother of all vampires.

He proceeded up the stairs and came face to face with what could be simply described as a hell hound. It was not an actual hell hound, of course, it is absolutely impossible for them to grow quite that big without cross breeding them with a Shire horse. And their mouths cannot hold that many teeth. Oh, and they do have a certain degree of self-esteem not to drool that much.

"Nice doggy?" Cameron asked but knew the answer before

he had asked the question.

With its teeth firmly clamped around Cameron's head, they both tumbled down the few steps Cameron had managed to advance. They crashed to the floor and Cameron, in his attempt to relieve his face of the unpleasant sight of canine tonsils, discovered the animal was female. He swore silently through the pain and redirected his punches to where he hoped its kidneys were.

The bitch yelped as much as it could without releasing its grip.

The pressure started increasing around his temples and he discovered that he really had no choice in the matter but to...

The beast squealed in major pain this time and leapt away from Cameron's body. Blood spurted from the animal's mouth and Cameron spat the chunk of its tongue out of his mouth as he got to his feet.

"Walkies," he said, in a manner that would have had Barbara Woodhouse fetching a lead.

The dog pulled itself together, in the sense that, yes, its tongue did slide across the floor and slip back into its mouth. Cameron was ready to concede there and then but the creature from beyond the pit lunged again.

This time Cameron was ready, or rather, presumed he was ready. He brought his fist forward to make contact with the beast's muzzle but missed. The dog continued forward whilst Cameron's arm slid down its throat and into its stomach. Both parties seemed mildly surprised by this turn of events and it was probably only due to Cameron's reaction of revulsion that saved his arm from being bitten off. He moved first, swinging his arm in a tight arc, tossing the dog through a nearby window.

As he mindlessly wiped the various fluids of the dog's digestive tracts off his arm and on to his top he left the house to try to finish the animal off.

It was not where it should have been but had noticed that one of its masters was in dire need of help so had leapt on to Gillian, snapping at the back of her head. She was trying to push the animal away whilst still sitting astride the distraught demon that was currently having the other half of its face beaten away by her bare fists.

The two of them overpowered her and she fell backwards, vulnerable to the mercies (that is to say none) of the devil's guard dog's guard dog. The vampire she had been methodically pulverising had got to its feet and proceeded to kick her in the ribs. It seemed to Cameron that its face was slowly filling out and piecing itself back together.

Cameron rushed over to the scene, grabbed the vampire by a shoulder and hurled it straight into the air. He then grabbed the dog by the scruff of the neck and lifted it off his girlfriend. He did the same wrestling move to the dog that Gillian had done to her vampire at the onset of her fight. The dog's back snapped viciously and it howled in agony, then it wailed and began to change. Bones rotated in sockets, fur sank into skin, legs and arms straightened, and its head rounded. The old woman lay there naked on the ground, groaning in pain.

Cameron fetched a sliver of broken glass from the front lawn and plunged it into the woman's chest. She sat up and screamed a banshee wail.

"Just like 'Pulp Fiction,' huh?" he commented to Gillian.

The woman began to effervesce, skin bubbled and popped, white light dribbled through the holes. Her skin poured to the floor in one final brilliant blaze of super nova.

They stared at the pool of pink and grey and grimaced.

"Uma Thurman did not react like that," Gillian noted.

They heard an extremely loud thud and looked up to the roof of the building; the vampire had landed on the very apex of the house and had begun sliding down towards the rear garden.

"Do you want to finish it or shall I?" Cameron asked.

"I'll do it," Gillian informed him, "you look like shit." She got to her feet and ran through the house to the back.

"Oh right," he shouted after her, "so I've got to have a complete Richard and Judy make-over before I can do battle with the legions of the lord of flies?"

But his complaints were lost because Gillian was already crashing through the back door, ready to face the onslaught of... an empty back garden.

"Where are you?" she shouted, but did not really expect an answer, or the answer she got.

He dropped on her head from the roof. "In your face," he

replied.

He picked her up roughly and stared at her. "You're pretty," he told her and added, "for now."

With speeds associated with professional tennis, he 'served' her across the garden and into the shed that sat at the bottom. The building collapsed on her impact and indeed on her.

Cans of paint, garden tools and planks of wood bounced off her already severely bruised head. She felt something grab her ankle and begin pulling her out. She wrapped her fingers around something hard and heavy, ready for her release.

She was pulled clear of the wreckage and she swung the object she had salvaged towards the being that had pulled her out. Cameron was most surprised to be struck full in the face with a petrol-powered lawn mower, he rather expected, at most, a kiss for pulling Gillian free.

He was propelled across the garden and into a compost heap in the opposite corner. Meanwhile, the vampire he had struck down whilst coming out to the back garden to offer assistance had got to his feet and had observed the accidental conflict with some amusement. He watched Gillian discard the mower and run to her boyfriend's assistance. He had a very evil idea.

Cameron was dazed, his eyes rolled around stupidly in their sockets. Gillian tried slapping his cheeks like they do in the films but it did not work. She was just considering the practicality of fetching a glass of water when she heard the mower start. She turned and saw the blades churning towards her at a great speed.

"Cam, we're moving," she ordered as she lifted him up and started running. Looking briefly behind her to see how far away the blades were now, she noticed the vampire was no longer chasing them... sorry, chasing her. Cameron had fallen flat on his face and the Qualcast-wielding nightmare was bearing down on him with much glee. She saw Cameron lift his face to the operating end of the grass cutter and then watched him, presumably through delirium, actually put his arm into the blades.

"No!" she screamed and hid her face in her hands, not wanting to witness the rending of her lover's flesh or hear his screams of anguish. Oh yeah, hear. She covered her ears just a bit too late.

The steady sound of air whipping blades ground to a halt as Cameron clutched one of the rotating steel razors of death. The machine groaned with the exertion of sudden inactivity and then blew up with the effort of trying to continue with its primal reason for being.

The vampire was thrown to the floor, ever so slightly on fire. Cameron and the remainder of the mower were thrown into the compost heap once more. Gillian opened her eyes and became passionately enraged at the mincing of the man she loved. She was going to tear that mother fucking spawn of Satan's scrotum off and make him eat it.

Hey, I'm only telling you how it was.

Faster than a speeding copyright clause, she raced across to the vampire who was patting out the flames that threatened to engulf him. He was unaware of her approach until it was too late. She hit him hard and they both lifted off the floor and across the garden, crashing through the hedgerow and into the driveway. They fell onto the Sierra that was minding its own business. Its roof buckled under their forceful collision and its suspension attempted to withstand the exertion with futility. They bounced off, through the next hedge and out into the road. The chassis of the Sierra remained touching the floor.

Out in the road, Gillian was once again continuously flattening the vampire's nose. Every now and then he managed to get a stomach punch or a head butt to make contact but Gillian did not seem to notice.

They bounced once and rolled to the opposite side of the road; two cars collided in an attempt to avoid the two bodies in their paths.

The vampire managed to get on top and was unceremoniously cracking Gillian's skull on the road. He probably would have been able to continue in this fashion for quite a while if it had not been for a motorcyclist, who – whilst swerving to avoid the motor car mayhem – drove right between Gillian's legs, bounced off her crotch and slammed into the back of the undead who had the offensive advantage. The driver fell from the bike which continued its journey with its new involuntary passed-on passenger crossed into the path of the oncoming traffic. A car steered to avoid but was not quick enough. Its wheels made a mash of his legs and dragged him back down the road from where he had come.

Gillian sat up rubbing the pain in her most private of privates and was pleased to see that her attacker was being brought back towards her, in what appeared to be an extreme amount of pain.

His slide stopped just by her feet. "Hurts, huh?" she asked with a hint of maliciousness. She got to her feet and picked up a discarded bumper. She crunched the end of it into a point with her hand and plunged it into her opponent's heart. His scream intensified in pitch and decibels.

Occupiers of the cars within the vicinity, and any pedestrians that had at first found the show interesting, had long since vacated the area to what they presumed to be a safe distance.

The bumper that protruded from his chest began to glow and continued to get brighter. Gillian decided not to hang around to admire the conclusion, but to hurry back to her possibly dead, dead boyfriend; she jumped onto the car as the bumper-stake had reached an intensity as bright as the sun, it was impossible to stare directly at it. The vampire thrashed wildly as he approached the end. The bumper touched the car and cut through the metal like modelling glue cuts through polystyrene. It sliced into the petrol tank.

It was an interesting explosion involving four of the cars that had collected in the action; each one went up in a chain reaction. Witnesses later said that they could still see the bumper shining through the eruption. As for the girl that had been responsible for the carnage, well, she must have been killed; she was, after all, directly on top of the car when it went up. She *had* to have been killed.

***

Cassandra was still arguing with Danny as to how to use the radio when Nutter informed them that Gillian and Cameron had turned the corner and that they, too should get on with what they had set out to achieve. He took charge of the walkie-talkie.

"The first thing to do," he instructed them, "is to get on the offensive. As soon as you recognise one of them you must take them by surprise and strike. Don't allow them to realise that you know what they are, otherwise your identities go into the collective memory forever until they are all destroyed."

"Well, it's a bit late for that now then, isn't it?" Danny mentioned.

"True," Nutter agreed, "but you must realise that for a vampire who has never actually seen you first hand, to be able recognise you, it must do a sort of search through the collective database, which will then give you valuable seconds before it realises who you are and strikes."

"Ask questions later," Danny finished.

"If your first hit doesn't do the job right, you won't have a chance to ask any questions later," Nutter warned.

Cassandra held tightly onto Danny's arm; she was obviously apprehensive about their 'mission'. Their first encounter had happened completely out of the blue and she had reacted instinctively and without thought. But now? Now they were actually going in, what was the word? Premeditated? This was stupid. All the battles so far: theirs, Nutter's, Cameron and Penny's, then Cameron and Gillian – whatever that was – at the end. Four 'involvements'. Then she remembered some hackneyed cliché; 'To be four warned is to be four armed' or something. They had had their four warnings but she was not sure how the number of arms you had was going to help in a battle with beings with the strength of Hercules and the teeth and appetite of Jaws. Perhaps it was something to do with having more fists to hit with. None-the-less, the adage should really read, 'To be four warned and still go looking for trouble is to be down right fucking stupid'. Yeah, that was better.

She wished she had voted for Cameron's plan.

"We are close," Nutter said and broke the silence like a fast moving mallet would break your skull.

"I don't see anything," Danny commented.

"What if they're inside a building? Would you see them through the wall?" Nutter asked.

"Good point," he conceded.

"So what then?" Cassandra queried. "We play 'Knock Down Ginger' until one of the doors is answered by Nosferatu?"

"No," Nutter said, "we go to that house there," and pointed to the building on the opposite side of the road.

"Shit," Cassandra muttered.

Nutter strode across the street towards the house. Danny followed and Cassandra hesitated. Danny turned half-way.

"What's up?"

"I don't know if I can go in there."

"Why?"

"I can't do anything Danny," she confessed. "You can see them, he knows how to kill them. Even Gill and Cameron are in a better condition to fight them and they're dead. I can't do anything."

"Do you want to wait here?" he asked.

"Of course not. I don't want to leave you to go in there alone."

"I have had an idea," Nutter announced. "Daniel and I will enter this building. I will look out for him, have no fear. You, Cassandra, will wait out here as back up. If there is more trouble than we can handle, we will need someone in reserve."

"Okay," she said and suppressed a sigh of relief.

Danny and Nutter continued on towards the house, pausing once to check that Cassandra was ready. *For what?* she thought.

Nutter rapped on the door; he could smell the stench of death that lay just behind it. It is not a smell that is instantly recognisable; it is something that you learn to identify. It does not smell of rotting flesh, or musty, stale crypts; death smells of death just like bananas smell like bananas. Not that death smells like bananas; but like bananas, it has its own personal, distinctive odour and anything that it comes in close contact with carries the smell around with it forever.

His nose wrinkled involuntarily because a waft of 'death' air suffused his olfactory senses as the door opened and a young man, perhaps about Danny's age, looked out. He had obviously only just got out of bed.

"Yeah? What is it?" he mumbled, scratching his tousled hair.

"Nyaaargh," said Danny, and stepped back in revulsion.

The vampire realised he had been rumbled and pushed the two males back down the path they had travelled, perhaps slightly harder than was necessary since they landed in the road, but then vampires are not a species known for their consideration for others.

The two men landed hard and rolled clutching their chests, Cassandra was running faster than she ever had before (except for earlier that morning) and passed between her falling comrades before they had hit the dirt.

The vampire was momentarily confused by the approach of this undersized assailant and it was this lapse in concentration that gave Cassandra the first notch on her belt. She lifted her body into the air, thrusting her left leg out towards her target and tucking her right leg under her bum. Her shoe struck solidly onto the vampire's chest, the rapier-like heel pierced his breastplate and plunged into his heart. The two of them fell into the house, him onto his back and her rolling neatly further down the corridor.

A door opened in front of her and the head of another dishevelled young man poked out. She leapt to her feet and kicked the door shut again. Nearly shut if it was not for the boy's head wedging it open; he screamed and withdrew.

The hallway flashed bright white behind her.

She pulled the door open to see her second target clutching his squished cranium.

Taking a moment to ascertain his life/death combination she decided, "Undead by association," and brought the pointed toe of her right shoe up into his heart region. This merely resulted in the possible-but-probable vampire being hurled backwards into a wardrobe. He fell back out in a tangle of clothes and coat hangers and lay very still. Too still. Kind of like 'dead' still.

Cassandra suddenly thought that she might have killed another mortal and, without thinking, ran forward to roll him over and see what his condition was.

Having not seen the 'Evil Dead' films enough, she was most surprised when the now-supposed-to-be-human seemed to instantly leap to his feet and throw her across the room. She bounced across the bed and collided with the bedside cabinet.

She struggled to get her bearings and get to her feet but she simply wrapped herself up more in the sheets and entangled herself in the cord of a bedside lamp that she had inadvertently brought down with her.

Her face came out from the swaddling to see the vampire looming over her. Her hand found hold of something solid and heavy which she thrust at her imminent death bringer.

The bulb shattered as it hit his chest, the glass sheared through his already weakened chest. The light fitting cracked against his breastplate, his downward motion and her arm's upward motion allowed the plastic to splinter through the bone and plunge into his heart. He squealed his displeasure at this turn of events and evaporated; his light was sucked down the lamp, through the cable and into the electric socket.

Cassandra lay there, wide eyed, wrapped and wrecked. Danny burst into the room, his eyes searching around everywhere but where they needed to be looking.

He left the room at which point Cassandra shouted at him and he came back in and spotted her.

"Sorry, Cass," he apologised, "I thought you was some sort of Roman statue or something."

She struggled out of her bindings and muttered unintelligibly under her breath. Danny presumed that what she was saying was not something that he really wanted to be able to hear.

"Where's Nutter?" she finally demanded audibly.

A muffled scream from upstairs answered her inquiry, a subtle lighting effect briefly shone through the door.

"I thought you said you couldn't do anything?" Danny asked her.

"Yeah, well," she replied noncommittally. "What happened to you two anyway?"

"I blew it big time, darling," he confessed. "I didn't expect to 'see' what I did."

"What was it?"

"Well, it certainly wasn't anything like the way Cameron and Gillian look," he explained. "These guys have serious darkness, Cass. They suck the light out from around them and they are real fucking hideous to look at, you know? Like, an anorexic Freddy Krueger."

They walked out into the hall as Nutter descended the stairs. "There were only the three of them," he said, "and I just vanquished the third."

"Oh, man," Danny moaned, "I'm losing already."

"You got the first one, darling," Cassandra reminded him.

"Oh, yeah, one-all, Nutter."

"I have destroyed a few more than that in my time, Daniel."

"Okay," Daniel thought for a moment. "One-all on the day."

"You got yours yesterday, Danny."

"So I am losing then?"

"Yes," Cassandra and Nutter voiced in unison, eager to end this conversation.

If their sharp reply had not ended the topic of debate, then the explosion that resounded from across the city would have.

"I wonder how Gill and Cameron are doing?" Cassandra pondered.

Gillian's body fell into the centre of the garden in a crumpled, smoking heap. She groaned.

Her body 'popped' in various places as she straightened and stretched her smouldering limbs. Her scorched blackened scalp paled to a soft pink and started sprouting auburn curls. As she lifted her aching body, flesh slowly crept over her arms, across her back and down her legs.

She got up on to her newly refreshed, reflashed feet and stumbled over to the compost pile that contained the wreckage of the mower and boyfriend combination. She dreaded to see what mangled mess lay underneath the bulk of scrap metal but threw it to one side anyway.

She was more surprised to see Cameron lying there almost untouched. Not counting the few shredded garments he was adorned in, physically, he looked undamaged.

"Cameron?" she whispered.

His eyes flickered slightly as consciousness returned. He turned his head to her and his eyes sprung open so quickly Gillian actually jumped.

"Oh my..." he said.

"What?"

"You've got no clothes on, darling."

She frowned at him then looked down at herself and discovered that, yes indeed, she was as naked as the day she was born. But unfortunately, when she was born she was not so amply endowed and socially conscious about her nudity. She ran into the house.

"Don't get dressed on account of me," Cameron shouted to her, dragged himself to his feet and staggered after her. Entering the house he could hear her swearing and rummaging around upstairs.

"Watcha doing?" Cameron called up.

"Don't come up here," she yelled down.

"Why not?"

"I told you you're not to come near my body again after what happened last time."

"But darling," he pleaded, "it is in my trousers."

"I'm coming down now anyway."

And did she? And then some. She poured down the stairs like a vision from a fifties high-class movie. That point when the heroin enters the ballroom in a glittering white gown, and floats down a crystal staircase.

No, hang on.

She padded down the stairs like a boyfriend's nightmare. She was barefoot and dressed in some of the clothes that the granny from hell no longer required, a pretty grey and pink floral dress that was too small length-ways and bust-wise. She had compensated her obvious breast problem by trying to cover them with a loose knitted olive green cardigan.

"Oh, Jesus," Cameron mumbled.

"Fuck off," Gillian told him, "it's all she had."

"Didn't he have anything?"

"It looks like she was living alone."

"Then what was he...?" Cameron started to ask and then Nutter's words of 'sexual desire' came back to his mind and visions of that naked frame in action soon took over.

"Can we leave now and possibly get you into some more suitable attire?" he requested as a cold shiver passed through his spine.

"With pleasure," she agreed.

They left the house and noted with relief that the burning cars had been extinguished. The area was being closed off; police were setting up metal fences to stop people getting too close to the extinguished crime scene. The road was an abundance of fire engines, ambulances, police cars and their associated passengers and operators. Police were questioning eyewitnesses; reporters were trying to find out what had happened – and having been refused interviews with the officials – began asking the people who had only just shown up wanting to know what all the fuss was about. A couple of lawyers were seeing if there was anyone to sue.

A police officer was questioning one of the original car drivers.

"Sorry, sir, could you repeat that?" the PC asked.

"I said 'at about a hundred miles an hour'," the increasingly agitated witness repeated.

"Figuratively, of course," the PC prompted.

"Of course bloody figuratively," the man spat, "I've never seen a human move as fast as that. I don't exactly know how fast it was, I just know that it was too bloody fast."

"For?"

"For a normal human being."

"What is your point, sir?" the PC asked, put down his notebook and pen and considered fetching the breathalyser from his car.

"You've seen 'Superman', like that."

"Superman, sir?"

"Look, I know how ridiculous this all sounds. I know it might seem that I'm either drunk or in shock but I swear, two bodies flew into the road directly in front of me, a damn sight faster than a living human body should be able to."

At that point, a WPC entered into the confused questioning. "I've got a bit of a problem, Dave," she said to her colleague.

"Yeah, I know the feeling. What is it?"

"The other driver reckons that the two bodies were flying."

"There, see," interrupted the driver.

"Yes, all right, sir," the PC calmed, "it could be that you're both in shock. What do you mean, flying?"

The WPC shrugged her shoulders. "'Flying'. They flew from over there," she pointed at the hedge, "and landed in the road."

All three turned their attention to the supposed direction of the flying bodies and saw a young couple walk down the driveway. The young man looked as if he had been sleeping on the streets for a few years and the girl must have been a student. Students seem to be the only stage of humanity without the dignity or self-awareness not to wear clothes that look like they had once belonged to your grandmother. *And* she was not wearing any shoes or socks.

"Excuse me," the PC called to the couple.

At that, a lot more attention was directed towards the youthful duo.

Cameron and Gillian turned to the direction of the call to see about fifty-plus civilians, reporters and various public servants staring at them. One police officer was approaching them.

"What do we do?" Gillian mumbled.

"Leg it?" Cameron suggested.

Too late, decided the bobby's well trained pace.

"Would you mind coming with me for a moment?" he asked them.

They looked at each other for support, but none came from the glance of either so they just went with the flow.

Following the policeman back to the mayhem and confusion, he turned to them again and pulled out his notebook. "Now, can I have your names and addresses please."

They gave them.

"Do you know anything about this little lot?" He indicated to the burnt out wrecks with his pencil over his shoulder.

They both shook their heads.

"So are you telling me that although you were both in that house, you didn't hear the explosion which has actually been reported to us from the other side of the city?"

"Er," Cameron said.

"That's her," said a voice.

"Eh?" said Gillian and turned to look into a crowd of television cameras and the witness who had said that she had to have died in the explosion.

"She's the girl who was fighting," the witness reiterated.

"It bloody is as well," confirmed the driver.

The PC called Dave had been commended many a time for his quick reactions and instinctive actions that had led to a number of successful arrests. Today was going to be his last day on the force. He grabbed Gillian's wrist and was about to say, "If you wouldn't mind accompanying me down to the station," but got as far as, "I-". He realised that he was no longer holding the young lady who had been successfully identified by two reliable witnesses; he realised that his feet were no longer actually on the floor; he realised what a strange sensation it is to actually fly through the air. He had fallen great distances before, but nothing really life-threatening; this was something different altogether; he could see the entire incident scene below with perfect clarity. He was upside down, going round again. He thought of his wife and... apple pie? He was coming down now. Oh dear, the strange sensation had now become absolute mortal terror. He peed himself as the concrete floor came up towards him very quickly. Then there was a blur and he was sitting on the pavement, he looked up towards the way he had just come from and noticed the young man patting his shoulders and moving his mouth.

"Are you all right?" Cameron asked again, patting the PC's shoulders, trying to wake him.

"Is he okay?" Gillian asked, genuinely shocked by her reaction to the grab, and to the policeman's reaction to her reaction.

"I think so," Cameron reported back, "just shocked."

Gillian was amazed. When she had been fighting the other vampire, all of her extra abilities had been in proportion to his and seemed quite natural, but now that she had asserted them against a normal person, she was in awe of herself.

Two bigger policemen approached her from behind and also approached the option of either early retirement or desk jobs.

Again Gillian had reacted the same as anyone would have if they had been grabbed roughly from behind and had their arms forced up their back painfully. The two officers clutched at their broken bones and Gillian stood over them apologising profusely. An army of officers prepared to bear down on her; one was radioing in for back-up and the possibility of armed officers.

"Gillian, go careful with them," Cameron shouted at her and then realised what he had said; 'them'? Is it really a case of 'us and them' now? He sounded like a parent who had just caught his child squeezing the life out of a pet hamster because it loved the animal sooooo much. These were not little animals, they were human beings, but they were as precious and fragile to them as the metaphorical crushed rodent was to the child. He noticed the television cameras.

"Oh no," he groaned.

"What?" Gillian asked whilst keeping an eye on all the approaching uniformed officials.

"I think we're about to appear on the local news," he pointed at the reporters.

"Can't we grab the cameras and destroy the film?" she asked.

"You'll probably find that it's being recorded somewhere else anyway," he said.

"Ow," Gillian muttered and folded on the ground. This paused the approach of the wary officers so Cameron took the opportunity to drop to her side.

"What?"

"That pain again," she forced between clenched teeth.

"Oh no, not now," he said and scanned the on looking crowd. "There's three of them Gill. Snap out of it, darling, I, won't be able to take them on my own."

Gillian had apparently passed out.

He looked up at the policemen approaching slightly faster now. They were trying to make sure he stayed calm and make sure he knew that if he resisted arrest the consequences would be dire (not actually specifying, or realising, whom it would be 'dire' for). One was reading him his rights.

Cameron needed a bit of time. He needed a diversion. His eyes caught sight of an ambulance and the onlooking paramedics whose attentions had been distracted from the fallen officers towards this new turn of events. He leapt up to his feet, causing a couple of officers to dive backwards.

"Police brutality!" he shouted at the cameras. "They've killed my girlfriend!"

This caused a fair amount of confusion as to how she might have died and how it could possibly have been the fault of the injured officers.

"Probably ruptured herself by throwing that first copper fifty feet into the air," hypothesised one onlooker.

An officer rushed forward and grabbed Gillian's wrist. Nothing. Shit. He then felt for a pulse in her neck. Nothing. Shit shit. He then placed his ear on her chest. Still nothing. He checked her breathing. Shit shit shit shit shit.

"Quickly," he called to one of the paramedics who then dropped her damaged patient and ran to the scene. The officer had began administering CPR to the girl; the ambulance driver took over when she got there.

More officers and paramedics approached and wanted to help, no one was watching Cameron. He was free to change into his super identity and strike terror into the undead that prowled his streets and fed upon his civilians.

Actually he sneaked off into the increasingly dense crowd and circumnavigated the voyeurs until he got to the position of the three targets he had spotted earlier. Once again he had forgotten that if he could 'feel' them, they could 'feel' him.

The four demons of darkness exploded through the audience into the mass of official vehicles. Onlookers were thrown in every direction and would put many a doctor on overtime today.

A police car rocked violently on its suspension as the three newly identified harbingers of doom tried to persuade Cameron's head that flat would be a much more agreeable shape for it.

Cameron tried to think of something witty and off the cuff to say but kept getting a mouthful of metal each time he attempted negotiations.

They pulled him back out of the head-shaped dent in the car door and thought their remodelling of the motor's exterior was quite fetching, so they put another head-shaped dent further down the side followed by another two.

By this time, the crowd had separated into the screaming,

running, 'I've just remembered something more urgent to do', fleeing members of the public and uniformed professionals, against the remaining hard core; slightly mentally unbalanced voyeurs; the 'I've got a job to do and it's my duty' public servants; and the more eagerness-for-a-story-than-sense reporters.

Cameron's assailants pulled him from the car once more to check his physical condition. Cameron was sure his neck was broken as it lolled limply from side to side. He was right, it was.

Drastic times called for drastic measures so he decided to pass out. This seemed to please the vampires even more as they tossed his lifeless body up in the air to have it smash down onto the roof of the car. They then decided that they were hungry so turned their attention to the crowd of onlookers.

Gillian's first taste of consciousness was in her mouth and it was of stale cigarettes. Someone was blowing fetid smelly breath down her throat. Next she realised that someone was roughly pounding at her left tit. She was horrified to think that Cameron had started smoking. She opened her eyes carefully to discover a paramedic's ear in her vision.

The pressure on her breast ceased, her dress was ripped completely open and two slimy, cold metal rings were placed over her heart. Somebody shouted, "Clear," the mouth stopped inflating her and her view was filled with blue skies and her mind filled with the realisation of what was happening.

"Wait!" she shouted, but it was too late.

Her body convulsed drastically at the charge passing through her chest, the young woman doing the deed was accidentally head-butted as Gillian doubled up from the shock. The officers and reporters who were surrounding her spread outwards quickly. One brave paramedic reached out for her wrist. Gillian started at the contact but was too dazed to react any more violently than just stare at him.

The nurse fumbled for a second with a frown across his forehead. Then, with curiosity overriding fear, he moved forward and pressed his fingers into her neck. Nothing. Shit.

"You're dead," he told her. "She's dead," he said, passing the information on to the surrounding watchers.

"I'm beginning to wish I was," Gillian retorted.

The crowd backed off again and the cameras zoomed in.

"Where's Cameron?" she asked anyone as she remembered the reason why she had fainted.

"Who?" someone asked.

"My boyfriend."

The officers and reporters remembered the young man and realised that he was no longer present. A commotion further down the road caught their attention and they were just in time to avoid being pounced on by one of the hunters. They moved quickly, leaving the hungry in a space with the bemused.

This was a new feeling to the freshly turned, former business studies student; this girl was sort of one of them, but at the same time different, like that guy they had just trashed – they did not share the conscience. She was gorgeous and she had her tits out. Another hunger surge coursed through his body and he threw her back to a lying position, spread her legs and knelt between them. He fumbled with his belt and trousers, preparing himself for sexual indulgence. She seemed to go for the idea because she started moving her body further towards him, eventually sitting upright and helping him with his zipper with her right hand and pulling the back of his jeans down with her left. They dropped, and his swollen cock sprung bolt upright into the air. Gillian moved her body further forward until her face was almost touching his, then she lay back again in a pose that, to him, indicated 'get on with it'. The pose was actually so she could get in a better position to place the de-fibrillator around his free hanging testicles and press the buttons.

"Clear!" she declared to it.

It does not matter who the victim is, or how evil his motivations are, when an attack on a pair of gonads is successfully carried out someone will always empathise. A sympathetic, 'Ooooh,' a sharp sucking-in of breath and a collective padded slap of many thighs clenching together could be heard from various positions around the scene.

It felt to the vampire as if his balls had exploded up inside his body. He did not so much as jump away from the pain but propelled himself away as a bullet would from a gun. Gillian calmly stood up, covered herself and walked over to the pain-wracked wraith. With nothing better to use, she punched her fist down through the vampire's chest, and applied so much force to the blow that she actually cracked the concrete underneath him.

His face contorted as existential pain transcended testicular agony. Gillian gave him an extra bit of testicular and kicked him in his overtly swollen bollocks. That did the trick. His skin folded as a solid body shaped lump of bright light shot out of his head in reaction to the kick. It dissipated.

She turned her attention to screams coming from behind her; the other two – a girl and a boy – were sating their desires of various kinds on the innocents in the crowd. The boy was aggressively raping a young woman he had indiscriminately plucked from the fleeing crowd; the girl had given up with trying to rape her captive since she could not get him to get it up, so contented herself with ripping his throat out.

Gillian was about to dive into the fray when she passed the crumpled police car and noticed Cameron's limp arm dangling over the lip of the bowl shaped roof. She hopped up to see what his condition was and was mildly shocked to see his head twisted nearly a hundred and eighty degrees from its normal position. She gingerly lifted the wobbly noggin and returned it to its more aesthetic and practical point of origin. It cracked as bones slid back into place and slowly consciousness returned to him.

"You keep falling asleep on me," she told him.

"What? Were we doing it?"

She tutted, pushed him off the roof then jumped down after him and lifted him to his unsteady feet.

"Let's do this quickly and get out of here," she proposed.

"Let's fuck it and get out of here," he suggested but she was already advancing on the feeding girl. Cameron trotted after her, stopped and ran towards the boy.

Again, these two appeared to be of the heroes' ages and were probably students at the university.

"Soon they're going to be dog meat," Cameron muttered.

He slapped his hand on the rapist's shoulder and pulled him away. The woman stopped screaming for a moment and stared at Cameron.

"Run," he said, and she did.

The vampire came at him, knob flailing wildly in the attack.

Cameron stepped to the side at the last moment, grabbed at the protruding weapon and ripped it off.

"Oooooh," somebody said.

Cameron tossed the dismembered member to one side, wiped his hand on his jeans, then went after the neutered blood sucker who was running around, holding his groin in agony. He picked up one of the fences and tried to rip out one of the bars but the whole thing just buckled under his ministrations.

"Arse," he said, picked up another fence and continued his pursuit of the de-phallussed one.

Something was wrong, for some reason the vampire had slowed his running and was not screaming in agony quite as much as he had been or should have been. Cameron looked down at his target's clasped hands and definitely saw them swell out as if a balloon was being inflated within them.

The vampire stopped running and screaming altogether now and turned triumphantly to face Cameron, proudly displaying the return of his genitalia.

"How the fuck did you do that?" Cameron asked in amazement.

"It's all part and parcel of the glory of being immortal," the vampire replied.

"So you can regrow any lost bits?"

"Any form of self-repair," he told him, "you did your neck."

Cameron rubbed it unconsciously, his neck had been broken and now it was not.

"So you can replace any limb – or whatever – that comes off?" Cameron pressed.

"Uh-huh," the vampire replied, tucking himself away.

"Why doesn't the limb grow a new you?"

This caused the evil dead to pause in thought and gentle refilling of assets. "I don't know. Maybe 'cos it's whatever part is attached to your head," he supposed then added, "or heart."

"But what if you're cleaved right down the middle?" Cameron asked.

The vampire was obviously getting irritated and his eyes glowed. "I don't..." he started and then noticed the fence Cameron was now swinging down at his skull.

There was a mixture of noises involving metal buckling, bones cracking, flesh tearing and a vampire squealing as he was neatly split in two. Cameron watched with interest as the two halves twitched and wriggled, neither side seeming to be able to regroup. Tendons and sinews slithered across the gap, trying to pull his body back together; skin started forming over the exposed innards, attempting to grow another half-a-body until everything just seemed to give up. The vampire's body slumped and the light burst upwards from the bisected beast from the Netherworlds.

Gillian's attempts to separate the female from her prey had proved futile thus far; each time she tried to grab the vampire it turned to keep the screaming man firmly between the two of them.

"Hey, bitch queen! Leave him the fuck alone and come get some from me!" Gillian dared.

Either Gillian had discovered the magic words, or the vampire had finished its meal – whichever – the evil one lifted its head and smiled at Gillian. Its pointed canines poked out of her mouth slightly, blood oozed down its chin. It dropped the body of the man and gave Gillian the full attention that she had so succinctly requested.

It moved quickly, very quickly. Gillian had not even noticed the bloodthirsty female make any preparatory motion; one instant the vampire had been standing in front of her, and in the next it was standing beside her, punching her in the head.

Gillian went down and rolled away from the attack. She leapt to her feet and saw her opponent just standing still. Just smiling at her.

It was gone again. This time Gillian noticed a slight blur at the initial point of movement. She was about to move before the vampire got to her position but the vampire got to her position and put its knee in Gillian's back. This time she did not have the opportunity to get up as quickly; the vampire jumped on her head then flipped off to stand a couple of metres away ready to strike.

Gillian got up and tried to clear the grogginess from her squished head by rattling her brain around.

The vampire moved. Blur. Gillian concentrated. Out of the

corner of her eye, blur.

Gillian swung round a hundred and eighty degrees and her fist followed suit in a tight arc. There, the vampire seemingly appeared again out of nowhere and was most surprised when Gillian clocked it one across the chin. It went sprawling across the road and Gillian followed, diving on top of it and pinning its back to the ground.

The vampire appeared as if it was beginning to choke. It became apparent that it was actually retching. A geyser of warm blood spewed up into Gillian's face. She turned her head to avoid it but all that achieved was that the liquid seeped into her ear and then gently trickled down her cheek when she looked back down at her captive.

Gillian was most distressed by this event whilst the vampire seemed most amused. "Taste it," it urged, "then you'll know why."

That was all it would take, all she had to do was lick her lips and find out what the attraction to human blood was. She wiped away the warm regurgitated offering that was trickling round to her mouth and punched the girl a couple of times for good measure, knocking her unconscious. She knew it would be for but a brief moment before she would awaken again and start zipping around the place once more. She needed to find something long, sharp and pointy. Her eyes fell upon a dried-up discarded willy.

How careless, she thought, *I hope it's not Cam's.*

A camera tripod had been left at the side of the road, she picked it up and turned to go back to her prey but her prey suddenly appeared on the end of the tripod slightly more surprised than Gillian. She flashed white like a single blank frame in a film reel and was gone.

Gillian looked around somewhat confused expecting to see the slight blur that indicated her enemy's arrival, but it did not come. Instead, the man who had recently been drained attacked her from behind. He jumped on her back, wrapped his legs around her waist and repeatedly punched her on the head and in the face. She became disorientated, trying to get a hold of him, trying to hit him with the tripod and failing in all instances.

She staggered around hoping to bump into something that

might help her but all she found was a car. This was getting stupid; so far she had battled with four experienced vampires and vanquished them but for a few minor problems, and now this freshly raised from the dead idiot was taking her (a registered vampire killer) on and causing her the most amount of aggravation and annoyance thus far. He was not hurting her, or damaging her, he was simply pissing her off.

"GET OFF OF ME!" she growled, grabbing one of his legs and prising it free. She then pulled it very hard and swung him round onto the road. Next she picked up the car she was standing next to and used it as a stake.

The car crushed down on the trainee bloodsucker and remained upright as if it were growing from the road. There was a muffled dispelling of light from under its bonnet.

Gillian stood there for a couple of seconds and dared the car to move or for any sign of life to enter her field of vision. Eventually she calmed down.

"Excuse me," a woman's voice called from behind her, "I wonder if you wouldn't mind answering a few questions."

Gillian turned to identify the owner of the voice and saw her. Then her microphone, then her television camera and its operator.

"Ack," she replied.

The reporter realised that she was the attention of an individual who had just slam-dunked a Mercedes on top of a man and remembered that she, herself, was only human.

Something that every journalist should do at certain times in their careers.

"I wondered if you could spare me a couple of minutes to explain who you are and what is going on?" she asked in a more soothing voice. "Please?"

"Who are you?" Gillian asked, which was the first mistake upon being caught in the media eye, which is to stop ignoring their presence.

"My name's Linda Greaves, and I'm a reporter for ITN."

"Uh huh."

"And you are?"

"Gillian. Gillian Kildress," she said rather warily, searching each question for any hidden inference that might appear on the headlines tomorrow as STUDENT SUCKS COCKS. Gillian was another person that had fallen for the journalistic myth that all reporters were truth-twisting leeches. She had fallen for the journalistic myth, which was a good thing, because it was not a myth.

"But what are you?" Linda pressed.

"I don't understand," Gillian replied.

"We just filmed you picking up that car and crushing another human being underneath it. No normal person could do that."

"Oh, he wasn't human," she indicated to the vertical vehicle, "he was a vampire."

The cameraman suppressed a snigger. Linda's mouth curled up at the edges but quickly straightened when Gillian glared menacingly at her.

"A vampire?"

"Yes," Gillian confirmed.

"An undead being that feeds on human blood?"

"Yes."

"So what are you? A super-hero or something?" Again the cameraman tried not to laugh but failed miserably. Gillian was getting really angry now.

"I'M A FUCKING VAMPIRE TOO," she growled with eyes aglowing and fangs a-showing. "I ALSO FEED ON BLOOD AND I'M FEELING A BIT PECKISH RIGHT NOW."

Gillian turned away and stormed over to where Cameron was standing watching the proceedings. The two reporters stood stock - still, eyes wide, skin white.

"I think I just pissed myself," Linda confessed.

"I did worse," admitted her partner.

***

"I'M A [BEEP] VAMPIRE TOO," she growled with eyes aglowing and fangs a-showing. The television picture changed to the face of Linda standing in front of the wreckage of cars and bodies.

"So there you have it. Has Leeds been overrun by the

demonic forces of evil and these two youths are here to save the day? Or is this all some elaborate hoax to try and boost the attendance figures of the local cinema multiplex which is showing a horror special this coming weekend. We asked George Walker, multiplex manager."

The picture changed to a well-dressed man leaving his house. "Don't be so stupid," he said.

John Settle Junior switched the TV set off and pondered over this new turn of events and this new attractive quality about the girl of his dreams.

"She's been turned," he said to his master but remained facing the screen.

"No, not quite," came the reply.

Junior turned at this. "But you saw her, heard what she said and how she said it?" He practised again the guttural growl at the back of his throat.

"Yes."

"Then what's the problem?"

"Did you see what she was doing? She was destroying my children, your brothers and sisters."

"They aren't any brothers or sisters of mine. They're a bunch of simple-minded idiots to let themselves get killed," Junior muttered.

"I know that you have adapted to your turn more positively than most of the others," his master praised.

"'Most'?"

"Very well, all of the others," his master conceded, "but that does not mean you turn your back on them in a time of trouble. I feel the new birth of a child and I feel their death ten fold. They hurt me as much as they hurt them. Go out, bring her to me."

"Can I have her?" Junior pleaded.

"If she does not desire me."

"Huh?"

"She is as you are, in control."

"Bloody women's lib," Junior spat.

His master's eyes rolled skyward and he suppressed a sigh.

"What about the other one?" Junior asked.

"Kill him." Did his master's voice tremble slightly?

"But if they're not ours, where did they come from?"

"They are self-generated, spawned from love rather than lust."

"Bleurgh," Junior commented.

"Quite," his master agreed.

"What about the girl?" Junior asked.

"I'm still waiting," his master replied.

"Are you sure he will come?" Junior asked sceptically.

"I have... felt it."

"Hmmm," Junior mumbled and left.

"And bring me back my lunch," his master shouted after him.

***

"The cemetery?" Danny suggested. "In a huge crypt or something."

"I shouldn't think so, Daniel."

"How about a huge castle at the top of a hill at the end of a deserted track."

"Are there any around here?"

"None that I know of," Cassandra answered.

"Then no."

Cassandra and Nutter were leaning over a large map of the area trying to locate a suitable location for a vampire hold. Danny stood in the background making unhelpful suggestions.

"Whitby Abbey," Danny said.

This caused a serious second of contemplation from Nutter, but only a second. "I shouldn't think so."

"I bit too obvious perhaps," Danny said.

"Perhaps," Nutter agreed.

Cassandra rested her head in her hands, supported herself on her elbows in the centre of the map. "Well, where have they always stayed in the past?" she asked.

Nutter turned his gaze to the mists of time. "One time I recall they stayed in a Franciscan Monastery, then another time in a cemetery."

"A-ha," Danny declared.

"Then there was that time in the castle in Belgravia," he

continued undaunted.

"A-ha!" Danny declared twice as loud.

Nutter's eyes seemed to mist over and a smile spread across his lips. "Then there was that time in the French brothel."

"Yeah but we want to know where vampires hide, not where you spent your holidays," Danny said and received a severe glare from the master vampire slayer.

"When and where was the last time?" Cassandra inquired.

"I was drawn to Canada. It was almost twenty years ago now and up until then they had tended to settle for the kind of Gothic habitations that Daniel keeps suggesting. However, this time they had actually managed to purchase a five star hotel in one of the more exclusive areas of Montreux."

"A hotel?"

"Yes, Daniel. Because of all the people they had turned, they managed to simply pool their financial resources. It was very simple."

"So they might just be at a hotel now then," Cassandra suggested.

"It is very likely," Nutter pondered, "it is quite easy just to turn the hotel manager and staff, take over the place and hence have enough space for all of your minions of evil incarnate."

"Shall we go then?" Cassandra asked.

"It's as good a place as any to begin searching," Nutter agreed.

"We'd better tell Gillian and Cameron then," said Danny, "they could meet up with us and help."

He picked up the radio, pressed the button and spoke into it. "Breaker, breaker, this is Stoker One calling Stoker Two, come in, good buddy."

There was a moment of contemplative silence before the reply of, "Eh?"

"This is Stoker One calling Stoker Two come in," Danny repeated.

"Is that you, Danny?" Gillian's voice asked, adding "Over."

"That's a big ten-four."

"Eh?" her voice enquired.

"We've been clashing with some smokies up our end, come back," Danny told her.

"You've had what up your end?" she 'came back'.

"Oh for Christ's sake Gill, haven't you seen 'Smokie and the Bandit'? Don't you recognise CB talk when you hear it?"

"I recognise a stupid prat when I hear one," she informed him, "now let me speak to Cass."

Cassandra snatched the radio from Danny before he could complain. "I'm here, over," she said.

"Is everything all right?" Gillian asked.

"Uh-huh," Cassandra confirmed. "We had a little fight which we won and we're now going to try and find their base. How are you? Over."

"We had a minor inconvenience but we're both fine," Gillian said not too convincingly. "Do you want us to meet up with you? Over."

"Where are you now? Over."

"On the high street, heading into town. Over."

Cassandra thought for a second. "Wait for us by the chip shop," she said, "and we'll be there in about half an hour. Over."

"Okay," Gillian agreed, "but I've got to get some clothes on first. Over."

"Eh?" Danny questioned.

The two dishevelled, badly attired undead entered the supermarket under the severe scrutiny of the store security and other customers.

"What are we in here for?" Cameron asked Gillian, whilst throwing a few cursory glances back at his oppressive starers.

"This place has got a clothing department," she told him. "Have you got your credit card?"

"Hmmm," he answered without conviction, not wanting to let her know that all of his cards had been cancelled and that he had been planning to nick whatever it was that they wanted.

Gillian led the way expertly around parallel shelves of beans, toilet rolls, and CDs until they were suddenly suffused by women's garments of every shape, colour and type. Cameron became suddenly self-conscious of his male presence amongst this feminine jungle of silk and lace. He tried desperately not to be too obvious when ogling the models in the underwear adverts.

"Stop it, you perv," Gillian scolded.

"I'm going to look in the men's section," he told her and wandered off.

"Don't you dare buy anything until I've checked it first," she shouted after him.

Cameron scowled moodily as the delicate pastel shades changed to garish primaries, jeans and granddad jumpers.

"I bloody live by myself, support myself," he mumbled under his breath, "don't need nothing off no-one. I'm a self-reliant vampire and I'm not even allowed to pick my own clothes."

He looked down at his shredded blue shirt, blue jeans and dirty blue trainers. He mentally shrugged his shoulders. *So what? So I like blue, so bloody what? You don't have to worry about clashing colours if you wear all the same. So blue isn't a cool colour, I'll show her.*

He roamed around the shelves, picking items of clothing with a specific 'look' in mind; he then went to the changing rooms.

Gillian entered the area that the store had put aside for what they assumed was men's requirements of fashion and searched for Cameron, dreading what sort of 'blue' items of clothing he might have deemed worthy of wearing. She might as well just let him have a free shop around 'Top Man'. You can take the man out of the 'eighties, but you can not take the 'eighties out of the man. Cameron actually still owned a 'Pringle' jumper, and he could not even use the excuse that he played golf because he did not play any sport. And he did not play golf either.

She had discarded her 'granny' wear and was walking around in clothes not too dissimilar to those she lost in the explosion. She kept the labels with her to be able to pay at the tills.

"Can I have your autograph?" said a familiar voice behind her.

She turned and saw John Settle Junior proffering a pen and piece of paper. "I saw you on telly, I was very impressed."

"Thanks," she said and automatically took the pen and paper from him, then realised what she was doing and blushed.

"Are we still on for that drink?" he asked.

"I'm waiting for my boyfriend," she told him.

"Ah, that explains who that guy was who was with you on the news," he deduced. "Are there really vampires around then?"

"Yeah," she said, and searched desperately for Cameron to come and save her. "I've already killed about half a dozen of them."

"My, how endearing."

They stood in silence for a moment, Junior stared unashamedly at her whilst Gillian looked everywhere else but at him, she became more and more agitated the longer he continued to stare at her.

"Look, I don't mean to be rude," she finally blurted out, "but would you mind just fucking off. I really don't like you very much and would appreciate it if you didn't keep hanging around me all the time."

"ARE YOU GOING TO KILL ME TOO?" he growled.

Gillian stumbled backwards from his oral attack, tripping over a rack of shirts and falling to the floor. She looked up at him, his eyes glowed red. His fangs bared for striking, he smiled evilly.

"You're..." she stuttered.

"So are you," he pointed out.

"So am I," Cameron announced from behind Junior.

John turned to see the new and improved Cameron stood in 'Super Hero' pose and decked in black; black roll-neck, jeans, trainers and trench coat that seemed to billow out behind him. A younger, new improved version of Nutter.

Recognition crossed Cameron's face. "You son of a bitch."

It then passed over to Junior. "You broke your neck, didn't you?"

"Where's Penny, you fuck?" Cameron demanded and struck out at Junior's face, soon discovering his head was no longer where his fist was heading. Junior had ducked without effort beneath the blow and body-charged Cameron into the racks of clothing and into the customers who were standing innocently behind him.

The two crashed into a tangle of clothing and screaming bodies. Cameron kicked out and struck Junior in the stomach sending him flying back the way he had come.

Cameron cleared himself from the chaos of clothes to see

Junior ripping the arms off a couple of security guards who had erroneously grabbed him in an attempt to contain this violent outburst. The two men fell to the ground; one died instantly of shock, the other a little while later as the blood spurted from his open wound.

Gillian had regained her senses and charged into Junior's back sending him flying forward again. Cameron grabbed a piece of shelving and swatted the incoming target towards the far wall. He collided against it with a crunch and a groan. He fell down amongst a couple of racks of suits.

Gillian and Cameron met up, eyeing Junior's landing site with caution. All around them customers and staff ran about in a frenzied chaos.

"Is he the one that came into the house?" Gillian asked.

"Yeah, he's the one that took Penny."

"I'm going to rip his fucking head off," she promised.

"I'll hold him down," he offered.

The pile that Junior had fallen into began to stir and he rose from amidst the middle of it; he did not look happy. "You're going to pay dearly for that," he growled. "You," he pointed at Gillian, "will kneel before me in total subservience, and you," he indicated Cameron, "will die very painfully."

"Well, I've died once in total ecstasy, so why not?" Cameron shrugged. "I'll try anything once."

"Cam?" was all the warning Gillian could provide him as Junior became a blur and Cameron had disappeared within it. Stacks of shelving from one side of the building to the next appeared to disintegrate in swift succession as the blur moved from one end to the other. Unfortunately a few innocents in their path also appeared to disintegrate, but into a fine crimson mist.

The two high-speed rivals arrived in the warehouse after a half-metre concrete wall had proved to be no opposition. The two stood in the middle of thousands of boxes and crates of various consumer goods. Then one of them fell to the ground bereft of consciousness.

Junior smiled down at his lifeless enemy, he scanned his immediate vicinity for something to kill him with, ah, there, that broom.

He snapped the head off leaving a rough sharp point at the

end. He poised it in a striking position above Cameron's chest and drove it down. The staff entered Cameron's body and he awoke to the pain. It cracked through his breastplate and in a fraction of a second the point pressed against his heart and he thought he was going to die.

Gillian bust a shopping trolley across the side of Junior's face and once again he was airborne, but this time tangled in a web of metal and casters.

She looked down at the body of her boyfriend with the pierced left breast, his eyes were wide, his mouth was open and he was gripping the staff.

"Cam?"

"Pull it out, please," he groaned.

The broom handle plopped out of his chest and he breathed heavily with the relief of pressure from his cardial muscle. He rubbed at the already closing hole, trying to spread the pain.

"Why...?" she started.

"It didn't go all the way in," he answered without needing to hear the question.

"What do we do about him?" she indicated to the now vacant mangle of trolley. "Oh," she added a bit disappointedly.

Cameron got to his feet and dusted himself off. He was mildly untarnished considering the intensive beating he had just endured. The entire episode had taken less than a couple of minutes and about a dozen fatalities, but the pair walked away with a brand new outfit each and it cost them nothing but a couple of bruises and a nearly punctured heart. At least they had discovered who part of their enemy was.

They met up with their associates and the appraisals of Cameron's new uniform were all favourable. As they walked towards the city centre they swapped the stories of their recent battles. The younger two of the three humans were most impressed when they were told that their immortal friends had actually been responsible for the explosion that they had heard earlier and were looking forward to catching the news story later, perhaps taping it for future posterity and stories for future grandchildren.

If they lived that long, Nutter reminded them.

Upon entering the town centre they noticed that there was

not a shopper in sight, the high street was empty. There did however, appear to be an unusual proliferation of armoured vehicles and soldier-type individuals.

"The armed forces have been called in," Nutter observed.

"Why?" Danny asked.

"I think the news report was probably enough to send panic through the city and cause an exodus of citizens to evacuate the immediate area. As for the soldiers, I should imagine the government has been waiting for something like this to happen around here."

"Huh?" the four youths inquired.

"Vampiric infestations have occurred all over the world; most countries have successfully prevented the media broadcasting the news across the globe."

"You mean, the government probably knew that this was going to happen?" Cassandra asked.

"I should think so," Nutter said.

"Then why haven't they organised any form of deterrent?" she urged.

Danny nudged her. "Cass, look around, what do you think this is?"

She looked at the armoured trucks that blocked their path and the dozens of guns that were pointed at them. "Oh," she said.

They saw one of the soldiers step in front of the centre truck and raise a loud hailer to his mouth. "Attention. You will all lie face down on the ground with your arms and legs spread away from your bodies. You will do this now and do it quickly. If you do not follow my orders without resistance, we have been instructed to open fire and have been given the directive of shoot to kill." He put the megaphone down and stepped behind the wall of barrels and cross hairs undoubtedly aimed over important points of the heroes' anatomy.

Young trainees looked up to their experienced comrade for guidance and it appeared as if he was looking to them for the same reason.

"I've never had to deal with automatic weapons before," Nutter confessed.

"Great," Cameron groaned and flapped his arms against his

sides in exasperation. This caused a multitude of fingers to tighten slightly on their respective triggers.

Nutter appeared to lose it. "Well I'm sorry, okay? I'm sorry I don't have an answer for everything, I'm sorry I haven't encountered every single eventuality under the fucking sun. I'm sorry."

The young sergeant that handled the megaphone calmed his troops. "Steady," he said. He was slightly confused with this confrontation. He had been told that they were to converge on a group of extremely dangerous individuals, and all that had turned the corner was some old man and four dishevelled looking student types. Now to top it all, after he had delivered his well-practised 'do or die' orders, instead of instantly dropping to their bellies in the shapes of stars they seemed to be arguing amongst themselves. He now doubted their innocence and was quite prepared to mow them all down in a searing shower of hot lead.

The four young adults still had not recovered from Nutter's outburst; it was the first time that they had heard him swear.

"Will they kill us?" Gillian asked Cameron at last.

"How do you mean? I don't think they'll give much thought to shooting us, no."

"No I mean will it kill us though?" she reiterated.

"I don't know," he said and turned to Nutter.

"Another instance that I don't have an answer for."

"They're only bullets," Danny pointed out.

"Yes but are bullets just miniature metal stakes?" Gillian theorised.

"Hmmm," Cameron mused.

"Look," Cassandra chipped in, "you two might survive but I know for definite that Danny and I wouldn't."

"Nor will I," Nutter added.

"Danny, lie down," Cassandra instructed and eased herself to her knees.

This has gone far enough, the sergeant thought. "Fire a round above their heads," he ordered and the soldiers obeyed.

The sound of fifty guns firing at once scared the shit out of the heroes and Danny fell to his face overtaking and beating Cassandra's fall from grace. Gillian was too shocked to move,

Cameron searched his body for holes and Nutter was trying to think of an amicable way out of this. He saw the soldier step in front of the truck again.

"That was just a warning shot."

That explains it, Cameron thought.

"The next will be aimed directly at you if you do not comply to my instructions immede..."

"What's 'immede'?" Danny's muffled voice asked from the gravel he was getting off with.

"I don't know," Nutter murmured and searched the fleets of trucks for a possible explanation for the soldier's sudden silence. He was no longer where he had been standing and indeed, the barrels of his fellow soldiers' guns were no longer trained at them or visible at all.

"I think it's time to leave," Cameron suggested.

"Yes, I'm hurting," Gillian said.

"Get up," Nutter told Cassandra and Danny and they did. The proceeding sight was something they all would rather have avoided if it was all the same to you, thank you.

Each truck had a body climb onto it, each body was brandishing a large automatic weapon, each body's eyes glowed red, their teeth shone white and sharp in the sunlight, and they howled their disgust and eternal torment at the bright skies and pure heavens. Then each body on each truck was joined by another, and another, then two more, then another until the trucks were overflowing with screaming spawn of Satan. They poured off the roofs and fell to the floor just to get up and scramble back into another space. They seeped through the gaps between and under the trucks, they spanned from one side of the street to the other, a dozen or so heads deep, they taunted the heroes, waving their weapons in the air. The bodies of the previous owners were tossed across the mob like body surfers at a rock gig, except the over enthusiastic youths at their favourite pop heroes' concerts do not usually have their limbs ripped from their sockets whilst traversing the other spectators.

"I think we should definitely be leaving this party, now," Danny said.

"Yes," the others agreed in hushed tones in case they caused the screaming hordes to start using the firearms that they had purloined; the armies of darkness had become heavily armed armies of darkness and a lot more than a wooden stake was going to be needed to send this lot on to the next life.

They slowly edged their way towards a side street, a gun fired and all hell broke loose. Literally. The hordes of Hades were engulfed in a frenzy of blood lust and gun mania. They were not specifically aiming at the five defenders of good but what the hell, they were there and good enough targets in that case, but really anything would have done. They fired at shop windows, benches, bus stops, street lights and each other. They swarmed through the city streets.

The pursued five ducked their heads and ran for cover. Why they thought ducking their heads would prevent a bullet entering their bodies they did not really know, but that was what they always did on the cinema.

Gillian felt a stinging pain sizzle through her right shoulder but continued running; Cameron was cut down by a hail of bullets stripping through his legs. He fell to the floor in pain and nearly tripped Danny who was following close behind; he paused to help him.

"Keep going," Cameron shouted at him. "I'll be okay. Go."

A bullet whistled past Danny's ear and he needed no further encouragement. He ran to catch up with the others and they did not stop until they knew for sure that they were no longer being pursued.

The four stopped to catch their breaths; Gillian searched the street from where they just ran from. "Where's Cam?"

"He got hit," Danny told her.

"No!" she yelled and started to return down the path they had just emerged from.

Nutter stood in her way and did not budge when she went to move him. "Gillian," he said in soothing tones, "if Cameron is all right, he will remain all right. If he is to die then he will already be dead. We need you and your strength. Your friends need you."

She turned to look at her obviously distressed housemates, Cassandra had grazed her forehead at some stage during the fray and Danny was not looking quite as cock-sure as usual. Even Nutter had lost a portion of his inner strength that seemed to radiate and support them all; now he just looked a bit like an old man. Was it really all left up to her? Could she hold this desperate bunch of love-lost and torn individuals together? She would have to try.

"Let's go and find somewhere to rest and recuperate," she said and they walked off. Being watched.

Cameron desperately tried to fix his legs, the bones had been fractured and huge chunks of flesh had been ripped free. Every time he fixed a bone another bullet tore into his frame and splintered another. This was getting ridiculous.

He tried crawling towards a nearby shop for cover but a bullet slammed into his shoulder and paralysed his right arm. All he could do now was roll onto his back and perhaps cry if he wanted to.

He looked down the length of his body to see an armed and uniformed night demon smiling gleefully at him. "Had enough?" the enlisted vampire asked.

"How long have you been standing there?" Cameron puffed.

"I did the twelve in your right, the fifteen in your left, and the one in your shoulder," he told him.

"I just thought they were random bullets," Cameron chuckled to himself.

This confused the newly conscripted soldier of the legions of Beelzebub. This guy had just been riddled with about thirty rounds and was on the very brink of death and he was laughing? Still he supposed it was quite amusing really, when you thought about it.

"I thought," Cameron chuckled, "that every time I tried to get up, a stray bullet was knocking me back down again. I couldn't believe my bad luck, but it was you, just standing behind me waiting for me to try to move." His laugh had intensified even more now and was even more infectious. The soldier started guffawing at his own deviousness.

Cameron's laughter eased slightly. "You're new at this aren't you?"

"Uh huh," the soldier chuckled.

Cameron stood and snatched the gun off him and said,

"Last in, first out."

Cameron swung the gun round and pointed it at the surprised soldier's heart, but instead of pulling the trigger he plunged the barrel into his chest and out through his back. "Consider yourself demobbed."

The soldier started vibrating on the gun's barrel, Cameron pulled the trigger and fired a couple of rounds off into an approaching vampire's forehead. The roof of its head lifted off and the beast fell to the ground with legs twitching.

The soldier erupted into whiteness which attracted the attention of every other vampire swarming the precinct.

The streets were deathly silent, vampire eyed vampire seeing who was going to make the first move. Cameron was briefly reminded of the multitude of westerns he had ever seen.

"Are you laughing at my mule?" he asked no one in particular and sprayed the surrounding area in short bursts of bite sized death. A few enemies attempted to fire a few rounds back at him, but the majority of them dived for cover. Cameron was interested to note a couple of bursts of white light from the corner of his eye.

"That's that question answered," he muttered to himself and fled for a side street, quickly pursued by the denizens of darkness. A couple of armoured trucks pulled off in pursuit.

Vampires seemed to pour out of everywhere, they came out of front doors and were felled by a torrent of raging bullets. Most of them flashed briefly as their candles were snuffed.

Soon enough the gun ran out of bullets and so it was used one last time as a makeshift stake and Cameron continued his flight unarmed.

As he ran past house after house, a vampire leapt through the front window, or crashed through the door. Like some sort of perverse domino effect, Cameron's movement past a building was awaking the dead within. The demon in the last house on the street erupted before he had reached it. Without slowing his pace, Cameron grabbed the monster by the throat with his left hand, ripped the beast's left arm out of its socket and plunged the bone into its chest. Flash! He smiled at his improvisation, but only for a second.

From above him came a burst of flame and shortly after,

from behind him came an explosion. The blast sent him sprawling to the floor. He looked up and saw the rooftops were lined with a gauntlet of bazooka-armed vampires.

"Shitty fuck," was a reasonable summary of his situation.

Another burst of flame, Cameron moved, another explosion on the point where he had been. He landed on the roof of a parked car, leapt to his feet and ran faster than he ever had before, straight down the line of abandoned vehicles. As his feet cleared the roof or bonnet of each car, a fraction of a second later, it exploded as another rocket missed its intended target.

Were they doing it on purpose or were they really that crap?

His trainers slipped slightly on a roof and he threw himself onto the next car as the previous one detonated.

With no time to catch the breath that he did not need any longer, he saw an incoming missile and once again managed to throw himself forward to the next automobile before the impact. He lifted himself and started running for his life again. He was not totally convinced that being caught in one of the explosions would actually kill him, but he was as sure as he was sure that Sandra Bullock was an absolute sex goddess, that it would hurt like buggery (not actually like buggery, but in the sense that 'buggery' was an indefinably huge quantity), and that meant completely and utterly.

The car behind him blew up and he thought that he was actually comfortably ahead of the barrage, then his trainers slipped again and he fell, head first, through the rear window of a silver Capri. *How embarrassing,* he briefly thought.

He tried to wrestle himself free from under the back of the front seats.

"Arsey fucking cock," he shouted at the situation.

He pulled his legs in and twisted his body round just in time to see a multitude of screaming stars shatter through every other window of this boy racer's wet dream of Cameron's destruction.

"Get out," was all he had time to say and desperately tried to.

The car catapulted a dozen metres into the air from the multiple blasts of seven well-aimed rockets. It flared brightly as the petrol tank caught and covered the surrounding street with flaming fuel. Bits flew off in various directions, smashing through house windows, denting other cars and making a general mess of the street. A suitable death for such a car; one could almost wish that its owner had been present to witness its demise. From the driver's seat.

The flanking vampires smiled down at their handiwork. Their master would be most impressed and their rewards would be great indeed.

Something caught the attention of one of the bazooka wielders. Something black, slightly smoking, hovering between the two rows of roofs.

Cameron stood on the air, level with his assailants, directly above the centre of the street.

"I," he said to the onlooking vampire, "LIVE."

"Fuck," the vampire declared and levelled his weapon at his floating target. He fired a rocket and Cameron gracefully glided out of its way.

The rocket – one of its basic values being not to stop until it hits something – continued to the opposite roof top; the vampire there was able to fire his weapon in a desperate attempt to destroy it before it ripped him to pieces. His rocket crossed back across the road and struck the original firer. He detonated in a burst of flesh, flames and light.

"Let's party!" Cameron announced to the rest of the crap commandos.

Having not learned from example, all those that could, fired straight at Cameron. He lifted himself into the air lightly and each missile passed without incident beneath him to strike at various bodies at opposing sides of the street.

Having managed to wipe out about two-thirds of his attackers without actually doing anything but quote a couple of tired old clichés, Cameron swooped through the ranks of fleeing vampires picking them off the roofs and impaling them on various spiked railings.

This was absolutely fantastic. "I can fly, I can fly, I can fly," he squealed with delight and loop-the-looped with a terrified undead grasped firmly by the leg. He let go at the highest point of his ascent and the bloodsucker propelled even higher.

Cameron pointed himself down and dive-bombed the

panicking parasites. At the last second he levelled his speeding body and cut a path directly through the deserting demons, using his own body as a stake, and his velocity to rip the undead's torsos from their legs. A path of flashing bright white mapped the route of his multiple exorcisms.

After a while the streets were quiet again and Cameron was almost upset, but he thought he had better relocate his team and show them this new turn of events. From this heightened position he could see the entire city and the complete lack of populace. At various times he noticed vampires skulking from door to door, either looking for victims or each other.

Cameron closed his eyes as he sailed over the roads below; he mentally reached out, feeling all the scabrous entities below him who also felt him scanning the land. He continued to stretch his mind out, widening the diameter of his radar until he touched her, they were all safe.

He smiled and flew out towards them. He was amazed at how well he could fly. It was like you would imagine flying to be; if he wanted to go in a particular direction, he just did. It was not like he actually had to concentrate on the movement, just more of a natural process, like walking. You do not 'think' about walking; if you want to walk, you walk.

He saw them creeping down a side street and lowered himself down to them, in front so as not to startle them.

The four of them were quite startled to see Cameron descend from the rooftops as if he was David Copperfield.

"Oh my god," Cassandra mumbled.

"If you like," Cameron allowed with as much divinity as he could muster in his intonation.

"Cool," Danny professed.

Cameron returned to his normal self. "Isn't it just?"

Gillian threw her arms around his neck and held on tightly. "I didn't think I was going to see you again," she whispered into his ear.

"Me too, darling," he replied and stroked her hair whilst returning the hug ten-fold.

An interrupting cough emitted from Nutter's mouth and the two lovers released each other. "I think we should continue on our way," he suggested.

'Up from the depths' is such an ominous and worn description, but it does fit perfectly in this instance, for indeed a deep rumbling and tremoring came up from the depths. The ground split under their feet and they were thrown in all directions. From the crater in the middle of the path a dark figure arose with the same grace that Cameron had descended them. Following this figure of dread was John Settle Junior, clambering ungracefully from the hole.

"Phoar!" Danny exclaimed. "He smells like my kit bag."

Pure evil has a smell, it is not a nice odour as one would imagine. It does not smell of brimstone or your wicked aunty's bedroom, it smells like a sweaty, stuffy sports bag; but that is unpoetic and completely eradicates any sense of horror from the proceedings. Evil smells *evil*.

"Ah, Professor, at last we meet again," the dark figure directed at Nutter with a voice that sounded like a European who had learned to speak English watching the old Ealing comedies.

"Terry Thomas anyone?" Danny whispered to his friends and the other three nodded.

"The two leading pieces have taken a long time to encounter each other this time," the Evil One continued, unaware of the side-ways conversation.

"I have been distracted," Nutter told him.

The devil from the depths surveyed Nutter's acquaintances with disgust. "What an absolute shower," was his judgement and the four youths tried not to laugh.

"What can you see, Danny?" Cassandra whispered to him.

"Nothing," he said, "just complete darkness. I can't focus my eyes on anything there, they just keep sliding off it."

"Fuck you," Cameron told the judger of human character at first glances.

"Ah, star light, star bright," the devil chanted. "First star I see tonight. I think I will, I think I might, expunge that light of yours tonight."

"Anum, anartum, anar, anus," Cameron countered somewhat pueriley but who cares.

"Rectar, rectas, recti, rectum," Danny supported.

This enraged the dark figure slightly more than perhaps was rational, but it brought a smile to Cameron's and Danny's faces, at least they knew they could wind him up.

"Impertinent fools!" he shouted at them. "Do you not know who I am?" He lifted himself a few metres higher off the ground, a movement that generated a rumble of thunder from the gathering clouds above.

"The puppet that teaches maths on Sesame Street," Danny suggested, adding, "One, one incorrect guess, HA HA HA HAR!"

"What?" the melodramatic one yelled.

"Grandpa Munster," Cameron offered.

"Two, two incorrect guesses, HA HA HAR!" Danny said.

This seemed to annoy the flying one quite a bit, for in a yell of anger he summoned a screaming gale down the alley in which they were standing and knocked all six of the pedestrians off their feet and down into the next street.

From the pile of bodies one flew up and out from the receiving end of a severe kick to the stomach. Junior rolled as he hit the ground and growled at the group of bodies untying themselves from each other.

"Left hand, red," Danny commented.

All five got to their feet and stood facing Junior and the now descending 'can't take a little joke' lord of the vampires.

"I suggest you tell them, Professor," he said.

Without taking his eyes from the two beasts in front of him, Nutter turned his head slightly to infer that he was directing his conversation to his associates. "He is Zorga, and he..."

"What?" Cameron interrupted.

"I said he is Zorga," Nutter repeated, "and he is..."

"Zorga?" Cameron questioned.

"Yes," Nutter confirmed and tried to go on, "and he..."

"Not Count Zorga?" Cameron interrupted again.

Nutter sighed. "Yes 'Count Zorga'. He is the..."

"Naaah," Cameron shook his head disbelievingly.

"What do you mean 'Naaah'?"

"Count Zorga?"

"Yes."

"Really?"

"YEESSS!"

"What?" Danny entered into the conversation.

"He's Count Zorga," Cameron told him and pointed at the cowled figure opposite.

"And he is..." Nutter started.

"What?" Danny asked again.

"Yeah. Count Zorga," Cameron repeated.

"Count Zorga?"

"Yeah."

"Why's he a Count?" Cassandra asked.

"All Princes of Darkness are 'Count'," Nutter informed her. "But he is..."

"Count Zorga," Danny puffed. "You're winding me up."

"Count Zorga," Cameron told him again.

"I think we've covered that," Nutter remarked tersely.

At the other end, the Count apparently called Zorga was once again getting somewhat distressed by the lack of respect for him and the rituals of meeting *the* dark prince. "I am Count Zorga," he announced, "and I am the -"

"Shit sucker," Danny added and Cameron spat everywhere trying to hold back his laughter.

"What?" Zorga yelled. Junior stifled a giggle.

"Count Zorga, shit sucker," Danny said.

"That's right," Cameron agreed.

"What are you two talking about?" Gillian asked.

"It's a Derek and Clive sketch, 'Count Zorga, Shit Sucker'," Cameron told her.

"It's a film that Dudley Moore went to see," Danny confirmed.

"Are you serious?" she inquired.

"Oh yeah," Cassandra remembered, "I've heard that one."

"God, how embarrassing for him," Gillian commented.

"He must have had a worst time at school than Billy Ollocks," Danny mused.

"This really isn't the time or the place, people," Nutter advised.

"How dare you!" Zorga roared. "Do you not realise that I am the Dark Lord himself?"

"Darth Vader?" Danny whispered in awe.

"Do you not feel the power of my evil?"

"I can smell it," Cassandra said.

"Do you not tremble in fear at my mere presence?"

"I wouldn't say it was a 'mere presence' would you?" Cameron added. "I think he's selling himself a little short, I'm impressed."

"I don't think we should carry on like this," Gillian advised her friends.

With a final roar of anger both Zorga and Junior dived into the quipping group. They fell like skittles and quickly jumped to their feet ready for a counter attack but one was not ensuing. They looked at each other in bemusement, then they noticed.

"Where's Gillian?" Cameron asked.

***

Zorga was sat behind an opulent oak desk that had been positioned in front of a large window that overlooked the city; the sun had already begun its descent and could no longer be seen above the highest buildings. The heavy cloud cover shone in luminescent silver as it was underlit by the dying star.

Junior entered the room.

"She's fine," he said without prompting. "I've given her her last few moments with her friend."

"How very human of you," Zorga sneered.

"Some habits are difficult to shift," Junior countered.

Zorga sighed and fell back into his seat; he stared at the boy with a concerned frown.

"What?" Junior asked.

"There is trouble amongst my heads," Zorga told him.

Being able to mind-read was an excellent gift and Junior had been using it so much now that he almost relied on it. He could not, however, see into Zorga's mind and so could not see the explanation behind this comment.

'Heads,' he thought, another talent that I wasn't aware of?

"No," Zorga spat, "I don't have interchangeable heads; and what's a 'Worzel Gummidge'?"

"It's..."

"Don't bother," Zorga interrupted, "I'm talking about the higher generations; the old boys; my next-in-commands as they would put it."

"What about them?"

"Well, why don't you hear it direct," Zorga said and motioned to a side door. It opened and a small fat man of about fifty years stepped into the room. His hair was pure white and long; an alley of baldness had crept halfway up his head. He wore matching purple velvet jacket and trousers that hugged two inches above his ankles. He wore a white shirt with a billowing ruff that made him look like he was rabid.

"Who are you?" Junior asked.

"Your senior and I demand a more respectful tone from you when you speak to me," the man replied.

"This is the Count Marchand de Puissy," Zorga introduced.

"'Pussy'?" Junior asked.

"'P'wissy'," Zorga repeated phonetically whilst the Count glared at Junior.

"This is exactly what I was talking about," the Count roared.

Zorga raised a hand to calm him down and turned to Junior. "The Count -"

"And others," the Count added which received an admonishing stare from Zorga. The Count bowed his head.

Zorga returned his glance to Junior. "The Count, and others, have expressed their concerns about you having risen so quickly in the ranks."

"But -" Junior started but stopped when Zorga raised his hand again.

"They are concerned that this sudden elevation will cause a breakdown in the lines of discipline within the extremely old and well-established hierarchy that has developed over the centuries."

There was silence.

Zorga turned to the Count. "Is that about right?"

"Yes," the Count replied. "We just want to establish that although he appears to be your," he searched for a word.

"Personal assistant?" Zorga suggested.

"Yes," the Count said. "Although he may be this personal assistant of yours he does not hold authority over us."

Zorga looked at Junior. "Your comments?"

Junior seemed genuinely mystified by this turn of events.

"But I do," he said.

"Do what?" the elders asked.

"I do have authority over you lot," he told the Count at which he nearly gagged. "I answer only to my Lord here and any others will answer to me."

Zorga roared with laughter whilst the Count turned red of face and red of eye.

"How dare you," the Count mustered, "do you have any idea what generation I am?"

"You were born in a small village in the South of France that had no name in the tenth century; you were caught and created 52 years later in Paris by our Lord here. In that sense you are second generation but you were by no means amongst the first."

"How did you know all that?" the Count demanded. "You, you're not even in the lower hundreds. You are a second generation of that whore Sister Elizabeth and we all lost count of where she stands."

"That's the problem with you old fuckers," Junior told him, "you seem to think that social standing comes from age and authority depends on social standing. Authority comes from intelligence and knowledge."

The Count stepped between the line of Junior and Zorga and turned his back on the youth.

"Zorga, I demand that he be put in his place."

Zorga's eyebrows raised. "'Demand'? Your confidence seems to have outgrown itself."

The Count physically deflated slightly as he slowly realised that the cards were not being stacked in his favour.

"Let me ask you something, Albert," Zorga said calmly. "Do you really think that I have so little control over my affairs to allow someone to attain a level of such power without knowing it?"

The Count shook his head.

"What century do you think we are in?"

The Count's jaw wobbled as he tried some mental arithmetic.

"You don't even know," Zorga told him. "You still think we're in the sixteenth when being bourgeois is fashionable and respected."

"Well, I was asleep for two centuries after," the Count tried in his defence.

"You were a pile of dust in a scuttle pan," Zorga told him. "You allowed your excesses to get the better of you.

"We are now living in an age when everyone has the mentality of the peasant but the intellect of the politician. Not many are impressed by affluence any more because it can be so easily achieved; the lowest commoner can get wealth beyond your imagining by the simple selection of six coloured balls. Times have changed and with that so have attitudes, beliefs, society and people. Humans in general are more greedy, depraved and vicious than most of the more evil Counts of the golden days.

"Do you understand what I'm telling you?"

The Count looked concerned but shook his head.

"I'm telling you that the old ways no longer apply; that new politics have to be considered to allow for the new legions; we need someone who knows the times to advise us."

The Count looked over his shoulder at Junior who just grinned back.

"Look at him, Albert," Zorga said.

"I see a child," the Count observed.

Zorga stood and slammed his hands on his desk.

"Bah! You've allowed your petty fears and jealousy to blind your eyes," he shouted and marched around the desk to face the Count. He grabbed the flinching vampire by the neck and thrust his head towards Junior.

"Look at him and tell me what you see," Zorga ordered.

The Count looked again and examined Junior with his vampire eyes. The boy had powers; most vampires are gifted in one, sometimes two, ways but he had half a dozen that he could tell. He had ambition, confidence and potential. He had the desire. The Count saw Zorga as he may have been at the start of his new existence.

"That's right," Zorga muttered and released his grasp of the cowering old man. "Now you understand."

The Count stood upright and straightened his clothes; he turned to Zorga. "Yes, Lord," he said.

"Both of you, leave," Zorga commanded. "Junior, bring me Gillian."

Junior nodded and they both turned to go.

"Albert, you're up too early, go back to sleep," Zorga suggested and made his way back to his desk seat. "And mind your manners in future."

The Count and Junior left the room and the younger male closed the doors behind them. The Count turned to him.

"I may have to answer to you from now on but I don't have to like it; nor will the others. Watch your back."

Junior smiled. "It's funny you should mention that because I do have an errand for you."

***

Penny had woken to the sensation of another presence in the darkness. "Hello?" she called.

"Penny?" replied Gillian's voice. "Is that you?"

"Oh no Gill, they've got you as well," she groaned.

"'Fraid so," Gillian conceded. "Hang on, I'm coming over."

"Wait," Penny shouted out. "You don't know where we are, there could be pits around here."

"There aren't any pits," Gillian informed her. "A pretty garish carpet, but no pits."

Penny heard the voice come closer then felt Gillian's touch on her arm. It was very comforting, but at the same time something made her tense up.

"It's okay," Gillian soothed, "it's only me."

"How could you see?" Penny asked, then nausea hit her. "They haven't done anything to my eyes have they?"

"No, no. It's just that perhaps it's not 'only me'."

"Huh?"

Gillian explained everything that had been happening in the outside world since Penny's disappearance. Everything.

"My father," she whined.

"He seems really nice," Gillian reported. "He is very sorry for cutting you off."

"That's easy for him to say when he thinks that I'm dead."

"Oh no, we all knew that you were alive."

"Thought," Penny prompted.

"No we knew. Cameron told us. He knew. So did your Dad."

"And you call him what?"

"Cameron thought of it," Gillian explained, "Nutter."

"It suits him."

"He seems to like it anyway."

The girls lapsed into a silence, both contemplating their futures.

"So how old are you anyway?" Gillian asked.

"I really don't know, to be honest, Gill," Penny confessed. "When you're in a perpetual state of infancy for long enough, you forget about the passing of time."

"Are you all right? Have they hurt you at all?"

"No," Penny admitted, "they haven't touched me since I was brought here. I think they were waiting for you lot to come and get me, then they gave up. Where are we anyway?"

"The Royal Lodge," she was told.

"The hotel?"

"Yeah. There's a bed just to your left."

"Oh, for crying out loud. I've been sitting, eating and sleeping on one of the floors of one of the nicest hotels in the city. Bastards, why did they have to make it so dark? Help me up."

Gillian lifted her friend and directed her to the four poster bed not more than two metres away from her.

"Bastards," Penny muttered again. She fell onto the bed and sighed with relief. "Sorry Gillian," she said.

"What for?" Gillian asked but received no reply except for Penny's heavy, sleepy breathing.

Through the darkness Gillian heard the door open and Junior stood in the opening.

"You're to come with me please Gillian," he requested.

"And what if I don't want to?" she asked then doubled over as her 'pain' shot through her body. It was worse than the first time, the worst than it had been so far.

"And I can make hurt it even more darling," Junior told her. "I can also stop it. So please, come with me."

"I'M GOING TO RIP YOUR FUCKING THROAT OUT," she

informed him and the pain ceased. Did it stop because she had scared him? Or was it because he felt sorry for her? Whatever the reason, the pain had stopped and she had calmed down. Relatively.

"Okay," she said. Yeah, she would go with him, only so she could find out where she stood and to be able to get in a better position to go for his jugular. "Just don't call me 'darling'."

He closed the door behind her, the hallway was lit normally, but from the room it had appeared as dark as midnight. A mystery but not one that particularly bothered her.

"The room is an extension of the Master," he told her. "He is darkness personified and he has left a part of him to watch over your friend. I have a feeling she is going to die soon though, because she's not needed as bait anymore."

"If she dies," she said calmly, "so do you."

She noticed him flinch from this. Ah yes, the cold, calm assurance of a woman is usually more effective than her base threats.

They passed through a set of large wooden double doors that opened automatically on their approach. They entered what must have been an executive suite of some kind. In the centre of the room was Zorga, naked. He looked old but he had the very firm figure of an Olympic sprinter. The desk had been moved to the side of the room and replaced by the writhing naked figures of half a dozen slaves of both sexes. They poured cups of blood to him; they performed oral sex on him; they massaged him, and he lay there and just let them get on with it.

In the corner of the room two bodies were hanging by their arms; chained to the wall. They looked pathetically at Gillian as she entered; one of them groaned in pain as one of Zorga's servants filled another goblet with his blood.

Zorga lifted his head and acknowledged their presence. "Would you care to join us?" he asked Gillian, and two naked bodies parted to make room for her. He offered his erect penis to her.

"Only if I knew that I would be giving you herpes in the process," she told him and he laughed. "You didn't seem to find our jokes so funny earlier," she said.

"That was disrespect and arrogance," he told her, "I believe you would describe this as 'spunk'."

He did not do what some people might think he would do.

Gillian felt decidedly uncomfortable as she stood and watched the nubile bodies sate their dark lord. After he was satisfied he stood and was robed in black silk; it clung to his body like the darkest shadows in the most oppressive of alleyways and Gillian could not help but shiver.

"You interest me greatly," Zorga told her and held her chin in the palm of his hand. He looked deeply into her eyes; she did nothing but return his gaze. "Yes, you interest me greatly." He turned his back on her and strolled over to a large wooden chair in the corner of the room, every where that he was not seemed to be lighter than where he was.

Gillian was getting extremely irate. "What is it that you want?"

"Want?" he asked as he placed himself in his throne. "Yes, what is it that I want? Junior?"

John Settle Junior was mildly startled by his sudden involvement in the proceedings. "Er, world domination?"

"Ha!" Zorga howled. "Junior, your vision is so narrow. If I were to turn the whole world, who would we have left to feast on?"

"Dunno," Junior shrugged. "We could have a farm or something."

Zorga seemed to ponder his words. "Not bad. How would you feel about that, Gillian? You don't mind if I call you Gillian, do you?"

"Call me anything you want," she spat. "I think it's disgusting."

"Really? Worse than a cattle farm?" Zorga asked. "A place that breeds living creatures simply for slaughter and sustenance?"

"That's different," she answered, "they're not human beings."

"They're still living creatures."

Gillian had nothing to say in her defence.

"Do not feel too disheartened," he comforted, "I have had to justify that argument more times than you could possibly imagine."

She sneered at him. "Fuck off you patronising bastard."

This got a raised eyebrow in response. "As I said, spunk. It is endearing in you Gillian, but I really can't encourage it." He gently nodded to Junior and Gillian crumpled to the floor as the pain swept through her midriff.

Eventually the mist of agony passed from her vision and she pulled herself up from the floor. She wiped the perspiration from her eyes and rubbed at the dull throb in her stomach.

Junior would never be exactly sure what hit him but he was sure it came from Gillian. His neck cracked and his body hurtled across the room slamming against the wall and into a couple of the bodies that hung there, they emitted short screams of pain then fell silent. Deathly silent.

Gillian glared with hatred at Zorga and was surprised to see him smiling with great delight. "Excellent," he cheered, "you *are* fantastic."

"You like that?" she puffed. "Come get some then, there's plenty to go 'round."

Zorga's eyes seemed to light up. "I do believe you're serious, and I do believe you could give me a run for my money, but no, not today I have other plans for you."

Gillian heard a muffled pop from the direction of Junior's discarded body and could see movement from him out of the corner of her eye. As he got up it seemed as if he ripped a limb off one of the hanging bodies, Zorga motioned for him to stay.

"Do you realise that you just killed those two mortals?" Zorga asked Gillian.

Her hatred seemed to falter for a second as her eyes flickered to the lifeless forms on the wall, but it returned in full as she returned her attention to Zorga.

"Very good," he praised, "almost no concern for human life."

"That's not true," she argued, "it's just that I'm more concerned for my own life at this present moment, and I have a feeling that they were just put out of their misery."

"Yes, perhaps, but surely you consider yourself to be better than them?"

"No," she answered a bit too quickly.

"You think of them as lesser, inferior creatures, you have

proclaimed yourself their protector so you must think you are of a higher order."

"I..." she was obviously flustered.

"You and I are of the same flesh, Gillian, we are stronger, faster, more intelligent. We are better."

Gillian was losing her moral battle. She knew that she was better but that did not mean she had to treat humans like animals, they were not there for her every whim.

"I want you to peruse my organisation here, Gillian. I want Junior to escort you around, and you can go wherever you wish to go. If you like the way we run things here, Gillian, you may sit at my side for all eternity."

"You still haven't told me what you wanted," she said.

Suddenly he was there, standing before her, his face inches from hers. "I want you," he purred.

Gillian was standing in the hotel's reception, she was looking lost and Junior just watched her for a second. "Well?" he asked. "What would you like to see?"

"I'd like to see you dead."

"Boom boom," he said.

"What is the point of all this exactly?" she demanded.

"He wants you to see what a great bloke he is darli-" he stopped when he saw the look in her eyes, "sweetheart. I think he wants you to fall for him. He does like you; I think you remind him of someone."

"It wouldn't be Winona Ryder by any chance would it?"

"Eh?"

"Doesn't matter," she said. "So what's the deal?"

"It's nothing special, nothing world threatening or anything like that," Junior said. "He runs it like a small business, only thinking of the now, of the small time gains. That world domination thing I mentioned, he'd never contemplate that because it's too forward thinking. He just wants the pleasure and gains here and now. He's blown it thousand of times before and will continue to if he carries on in this way. He pops up, gets a few followers, draws attention to himself and gets foiled by the heroes. That's not the way to run a successful business."

"I'd hardly describe this as a 'business'," Gillian

commented.

"Ah but it is," Junior corrected. "We are the producers and retailers of eternal life. The system here is run like a sales pyramid, each acquisition that you make strengthens you, then every sale that they make, you get a certain percentage of their commission."

"So what are you then? Vice President or something?" Gillian enquired.

Junior shook his head. "No, no. I'm quite a way down the corporate ladder as it were, there are loads of His first acquisitions that have more senior positions than me, but I am smart. A lot of acquisitions tend to bring out the Neanderthal in people. It affects different people differently. The blood lust can be quite crippling to some and the taste of blood is sometimes very addictive. You've seen those morons outside, running around like headless chickens: screaming, debauching, and doing whatever they like because they have the power to. I swear it only happened because he picked a student base to start with – its like the fucking rugby club have got control over the city."

Junior suddenly remembered where he was and the point of his explanation. "Anyway, because I have remained in complete control of my mental faculties and craving, I have been unofficially promoted."

"What's the pay like?" she asked sarcastically.

"What? 'The wages of sin' you mean?"

"Death."

"But we're both already dead," he pointed out.

"Are you trying to tell me that you cannot kill what doesn't live?" she demanded.

"Perhaps," he shrugged.

"Well, I think I've had quite a productive day disproving that point of view," Gillian told him.

"Hmm," Junior pondered, "I think you might be slightly disappointed to find out that you didn't actually achieve very much, relatively speaking, in terms of the size of the whole army. Those bodies that you did destroy are no more, granted, but the power we had financed in them had grown quite favourably and all you did was liquidate those assets for us. We just reaped the benefits of those short-term investments. We should be thanking you."

"I'm not sure I understand," Gillian said. "Are you saying that when you turn someone you give them a bit of your immortality?" Junior nodded. "Then that grows inside them and if they die, you claim back the 'power' you originally gave them plus the growth."

"I call it the 'infernal interest'," he said. "So, shall we begin the tour?"

"I'm not really bothered about spying on a bunch of gorging evil dead, sucking each other off," Gillian said.

Junior shook his head with despair. "You really do have a blinkered opinion of us, don't you, Gillian?" She frowned at him. "I would have thought that my description of the business so far would have indicated that this is far more than just sating our lustful desires, or at least more than just our physical lustful desires."

Junior turned and headed towards a large set of glass double doors that led into a bar and dining room. Unsure of what else to do, Gillian trotted after him. By the time she had reached the doors, Junior was already passing through the swing doors at the end of the dining room that led into the kitchens; again she followed. She pushed the doors aside and stepped through. Junior was standing in front of a large metal door that had a huge lever and bolt lock mechanism. It looked like it should belong to a bank vault or a giant freezer.

Junior lifted the heavy lever effortlessly and swung the door open, it *was* a giant freezer. The frozen, condensed air cascaded out into the kitchen, poured across the floor and swirled around their feet; she had a brief image of some big rock star stepping out through the darkness – maybe Michael Jackson; she believed he lived in conditions like these.

She peered into the gloom and could pick out only the vague shapes of clichéd carcasses hanging from the ceiling. Junior flicked on the light switch and Gillian wanted to scream.

***

It was getting dark, the four exhausted champions of evil

were returning to their home, relatively silent, 'relatively', in the sense that everyone was silent except Cameron who was whinging like a five year old.

"But why can't I?"

"Because I do not think that you should," Nutter told him.

"But why?"

"Because."

"That's no reason."

"It's a good enough reason."

Cameron rammed his hands into his trouser pockets and scuffed his feet along as he walked.

"Pick your feet up and stop slouching," Nutter ordered.

Cameron stopped walking, so did the others.

"I could just go, you know," he stated.

"Go on then," Nutter dared.

Cameron thought about this briefly. "I just want to know why you won't let me."

"It's getting dark."

This shocked Cameron for a second. "What? You don't want me to get lost? Mugged, perhaps? Or maybe it's too near to my bedtime?"

Nutter continued the procession. "If you like," he said on passing Cameron.

Cameron stared after the diminishing forms of his allies.

"Cameron, come on," Nutter shouted at him.

He lifted himself off the ground and floated after them. "But why can't I?" he whined.

"Cameron, when do vampires come out?" Nutter asked.

"Well, apparently at all times of the day," he answered.

"All right then, when are they supposed to come out?"

"At night," Cameron said.

"But only those that believe the sun will kill them," Nutter informed.

"And?" Cameron prompted.

"Those that believe the sun won't kill them are a mere fraction in comparison to those who believe that it will."

Danny and Cassandra seemed to wake up at this point. "Oh shit," they said.

"It's going to be a busy night then is it?" Cameron asked.

"Probably, since we appear to be the only mortals left in the entire city," Nutter replied. Adding, "Present company excluded of course."

"Of course," Cameron concurred. "But how long do you honestly think it would take me to find her?"

"Well, it's taken us three hours already," Danny chipped in.

"We need you to help us stay alive until morning," Nutter explained.

"But if I could sense where she was…"

"But you can't and have not been able to," Nutter reminded him. "They have probably got themselves a very nicely psychometrically protected base, hence the reason I have not been able to locate them and why you cannot locate Gillian." He abruptly turned ninety degrees and Cameron was left floating down the street by himself.

"But -" he started and noticed that he was alone and had in fact passed the house. He looked back to see Nutter staring at him from the doorway.

"Are you coming in? Or are you going to patrol the surrounding area quickly?"

"Sarky git," Cameron muttered and flew off.

"Cameron!" Nutter shouted after him with genuine concern then returned into the house shaking his head.

The carcasses were bodies; dozens of frozen bodies hanging lifelessly from the rails in the ceiling by meat hooks imbedded in the back of their necks.

"Oh, I'm impressed," Gillian managed after a moment's composure, "you don't farm your food, you freeze it."

Junior looked confused. "What? Oh I see. No, this isn't food, Gillian. You can't eat from the dead because it's not good for you. This is a reserve army, my idea actually. You see, because they're frozen, like suspended animation, they can't be sensed you know? So even if every other soldier does get defeated at some stage or another we can call in the secret cavalry. Pretty clever eh?"

Junior flicked the light off and swung the door shut.

"You're obviously not too confident as to your chances of success," Gillian stated.

"It's nothing like that, it's just an experiment really." He stopped and appeared to think for a moment. "Would you like to see my war room?"

"Slightly more original than seeing your etchings I suppose," she mumbled.

They left the kitchens the same way they had come and called for a lift from the lobby. As is usual, they suffered an embarrassed moment of silence.

"Why are you showing me all of this?" Gillian asked. "Isn't it a bit dangerous in that I might escape and thwart all of this?"

"'Thwart'? Do people actually say that? That's one of those words that I've always seen written down but never actually heard spoken. No Gillian, we're not bothered because you won't escape."

Was that a pain she felt in her stomach? It seemed to be nothing but a memory when she thought she felt it and Junior gave no indication as to inflicting it. Whether it was an intended message or not, she got it.

"And anyway," Junior continued as the lift 'pinged' its arrival, "I already told you that He has plans for you."

They stepped into the lift as the doors parted, turned and faced the lobby. "Going down?" Junior asked and the doors slid ominously and quietly shut. Gillian could not help but feel uneasy at the usage of over obvious literary symbolism and metaphor.

The lift actually ascended.

She was only mildly aware of the tinny muzak that filtered into the lift, her mind was concentrating more on what these 'plans' for her might be and if there was any possible chance for her to escape.

The lift 'pinged' at the end of its journey and the doors opened. Junior indicated for Gillian to exit first; she did so but kept a wary eye on him whilst checking the status of the floor they had arrived at. Just another floor, undifferentiated from any other corridor in the hotel. For some reason she felt sleepy.

"Come on, this way," Junior called and startled her to awareness.

"Why do I feel so... Have you drugged me or something?" she asked.

"No, no," he replied, "you're just feeling the conditions of some of the other, older tenants on this floor. Those that believe that the sun is actually dangerous."

"I never thought of that before," she said.

"Best not to as well," he warned, "we wouldn't want you turning into a hoover bag's contents come dawn would we?"

She did not really understand what he was saying and was too drowsy to bother to try to get him to explain. She felt so very tired.

"Here we are," Junior said as they reached the very end of the corridor, "the honeymoon suite."

Cameron floated above the city's rooftops thinking of all the things that he could have been doing instead. Of all the things that he should have been doing instead of battling the undead demons of the devil and trying to save the world.

This moment of musing could be described as a reality check; one of those quiet, contemplative periods of pondering during a time of chaos, a time when the brain says, "Right then, the story so far is this..."

Cameron had fallen in love, or rather, had discovered that he had fallen in love. It is a very easy thing to slip into without realising; only when the object of your adoration nips off for a while can you identify your emotions from the loss. Kind of like getting down to your last, favourite sweet, saying, "Oh no, I've only got one left because I've scoffed all the others."

And it can give you the same sort of stomach ache as well.

The woman he loved had been captured and was probably in very extreme, and very real, danger. In normal circumstances he would not hesitate for a second about dropping everything and go after her, but then again in 'normal circumstances' he would not be considering this fifty feet above the streets, and he would definitely have second thoughts about going up against a swarm of vampires if he was still mortal. But then again, in normal circumstances there would not be any vampires, Gillian would not be in trouble, his friends' lives would not be in jeopardy and he would not be faced with this dilemma. He would still be slumming it up in Edinburgh if everything were 'normal'. He would still not have realised that he was in love with Gillian and he would certainly still be a virgin. So it was all pretty much a redundant hypothesis in the first place and then he realised that he was losing track of exactly what the point was that he was trying to make ... Er.

In conclusion then, did that mean he was supposed to go after Gillian or not? Because on another hand, there were his comrades-in-arms who did need his help in the forth coming battle that was bound to take place. If he rescued Gillian – not ignoring the possibility that he could fail in that attempt – his allies would more than certainly not survive and then it would be just him against the army of ... oh whatever – he could not be bothered. What had the world ever done for him? It seemed that his existence was a never-ending crawl from one bad experience to another. Was it not about time that he looked after number one for a change?

Apart from the fact that because of his Mother's death and the resulting insurance pay-out he had not needed to work a single day of his life, he genuinely believed that he was having a rough time of it. That is not to say that not working is some sort of compensation for the demise of a member of one's family; it was just that Cameron never really took into consideration that he was a bit of a waster, a bit self-centred, a bit self-indulgent, slightly self - possessed. You know what I am getting at. He was a bit crap at dealing with his own problems. His Mother died and he ran away, tried to hide from it and from everything that would remind him of it: his home and his family. However, he did keep spending the money he had inherited which had some sort of Lady Macbethian effect on him; in the way that it was consuming him with constant guilt and remorse and he was never really aware of it. The aforementioned Scots Queen had to commit suicide to escape her overwhelming conscience; Cameron had also had to die to come to terms with his troubles. Unfortunately it seemed as if more problems had arrived with his early, and somewhat unusual demise.

Perhaps he was not paranoid about life being against him; it is only called paranoia when you can prove that nothing is really happening.

Cameron became distracted by the glare from a pair of headlights on full beam belonging to a lorry of some description. It was parked on the side of the road and seemed deserted. He sailed down to it and as his eyes became accustomed to the glare, he identified it as one of the armoured vehicles belonging to the army. There was definitely no one around so he decided to investigate. Upon looking inside the vehicle he came to an important and very necessary decision.

Gillian just wanted to lie down for a while. In retrospect it had been a very long and exhausting day. Junior's words did not seem to have any meaning, she no longer cared and all she wanted to do now was just lie down.

Junior had her arm and was leading her into the room, which would have been difficult for her to describe even if she had had the conscious will to look around and study it. It looked bigger than it physically could be; darkness and shadow seemed to stretch out for miles all around her as she dimly became aware that she was now alone. She tried to shake the sleepiness from her head and find a point of reference to focus on but there was nothing except herself, standing in an island of light surrounded by an unending ocean of cold, brooding unconsciousness.

"Your light," Zorga's voice whispered from the shadows. "I am drawn to your light like a moth to a flame."

"Bit... bit of a corny phrase... isn't it?"

"Do not fight this Gillian."

"With... my dying... breath."

"Your light is so strong, so beautiful, I do believe that if I were to touch you, you would burn me."

"I'd certainly... try." The light that surrounded her seemed smaller, the darkness was pressing in.

"For all its beauty, I must extinguish your light Gillian. We were meant to be together and as you will never willingly turn to me, I will make you mine."

The essence that was Zorga washed over her completely. She was not sure whether she had passed out, was dreaming, or if she really had been lifted off her feet and wrapped in a shroud of midnight. She felt delicate, cold fingers caressing her neck, her back, her legs. Her naked body was being sensually massaged by the night and she could not fight it, she did not have the strength, she did not have the control, and if it was a dream she was not sure that she wanted it to stop.

"Cameron," she sighed and there he was, gliding through the darkness, taking her in his arms again, kissing her neck the same way he had last time.

"I wonder what will happen this time," she whispered.

"He's been gone too long," Danny said.

"He wouldn't have gone looking for her, would he?" Cassandra asked.

"Not after I told him not to," Nutter replied, "not after I told him that we needed him."

"I don't know," Danny mused, "you did treat him like he was a bit of a kid back there, you know?"

Nutter's jaw dropped and he turned to Cassandra for support but she was nodding her head in agreement with Danny.

"Even then," Nutter said, "he's got to come back to help us, hasn't he?"

"Only from our point of view," Danny said.

The three of them sat in their respective seats in the living room in complete silence.

"What time is it?" Cassandra asked.

Nutter looked at his wristwatch. "Five minutes to midnight," he told her.

"So he's got five minutes then," Danny commented.

"Daniel," Nutter said, "you do seem to have a great amount of difficulty discerning the differences between reality and cinemagraphic clichés."

Outside the honeymoon suite, Junior was pacing and muttering obscenities under his breath. Further down the corridor, a door opened and the Count stepped out, stretched and yawned.

Junior looked at his watch then frowned at him. The Count looked blearily up and down the corridor, blinking the sleep from his eyes; he noticed Junior's concerned expression. "I always react badly from an afternoon nap," he said.

"Hurry up," Junior ordered, "or you'll be late, you've only got five minutes to get there."

The Count thought about making a snide remark but decided against it. "Plenty of time," he muttered, walked over to the lift, pressed the 'call' button and waited.

Junior stared on in disbelief. The Count glanced over his shoulder and shrugged in embarrassment.

"Use the window?" Junior suggested.

The Count thought for a second and a look of clarity passed over his face. "Ah," he said, nodded and wagged his forefinger at the ceiling. He turned, trotted down the corridor and around a corner, there was the sound of breaking glass and the diminishing scream of someone who, for some reason, could not remember how to fly.

Junior smiled at his ability to manipulate the talents of others.

The lift announced its arrival with a cheery 'ping'.

Junior smiled again then remembered where he was and returned to his muttering.

***

Danny was at the living room window, staring out into the street. "It looks like it's getting darker," he murmured.

"You're getting paranoid," Cassandra said.

"And clichéd again," Nutter added.

"No, I swear," he countered, "it's almost pitch black out there."

"Well, it is midnight, Danny," Cassandra reminded.

"What about the street lights then?" he asked.

"Maybe they haven't come on tonight," she suggested.

Nutter stood. "They were on when we came in," he said and walked over to the window to look out. "And they're still on now."

"I can't see them," Danny said. "It's pitch black. The kind of black I see when I look at one of them, but this is the whole street. Black."

Nutter looked out standing closer to the window. "Well I still can't..." The face of a red eyed demon appeared directly in front of Nutter's.

Nutter screamed loudly and threw himself back into the room; he tripped on the edge of the carpet and landed heavily on his backside.

"SON OF A BITCH!" he shouted in anger and embarrassment.

"Danny, come away from the window," Cassandra begged.

"Oh my god," he replied. "Zulus, thousands of 'em."

Nutter composed himself and got to his feet; he followed Cassandra back to the window and they looked out; there were vampires, everywhere. The bobbing heads of the undead could be seen from one end of the street to the other. It looked like the television footage of the London marathon, where you knew the people were moving but it just looked like they are bouncing up and down on the spot. Here, however, instead of running down the street they were collecting outside the house, bouncing up and down on the spot. They were crawling through the windows and doors of the houses opposite; they were climbing and flying over the rooftops.

There were vampires everywhere.

"What are they doing?" Cassandra asked.

"Waiting," Nutter replied.

"What for? Reinforcements?"

"I think I owe you an apology Daniel."

"Eh?"

The clock in the hall began its musical announcement to the imminence of the midnight hour and Nutter looked up in dread.

"It's fast," Danny told him and he sighed with relief.

There came a single sullen chime from the hallway.

"Only by twenty-four seconds," Cassandra muttered with dismay.

BONG.

"I've never seen so many before," Nutter whimpered.

BONG.

"I suppose we should be flattered then, should we?" Cassandra muttered.

BONG.

"'So much difficulty discerning,'"

BONG.

"'the differences between reality and,'"

BONG.

"'cinemagraphic cliché.'" Danny mimicked.

BONG.

"So this is it then?" Cassandra asked.
BONG.
"I don't suppose Cameron,"
BONG.
"would have been much help after all," Danny said.
BONG.
"Nutter! What do we do?" Cassandra demanded.
BONG.
"Subject them all to oblivion," Cameron said from behind them.
BONG.
There came the unearthly scream from the blood - lusting spawn of evil. The living room window shattered just as the three mortals turned away to look up at Cameron hovering in the middle of the room with a double barrelled shot gun in his hand and a pile of other assorted armaments beneath his feet. They did not wait another second before they leaped to the pile of purloined army issue death bringers. As they went down, Cameron brought the shot gun up in line with the hordes of hell as they climbed through the window, he fired off both barrels, tearing the first wave of undead invaders to shreds, they burst into their various personal light displays. He swung the barrel down to his upright knee, snapped the gun open which ejected the spent cartridges. In the same motion he had brought out another pair of cartridges from his coat pocket and slipped them into the barrel before the used ones had hit the floor, he lifted the gun at the window again, clicked the firearm whole again and fired immediately. The street flashed with the extinction of another half dozen denizens of the devil. He repeated the loading and firing sequence again.

Before Cameron could fire off his third round, Danny had armed himself with an oversized chain gun which he pointed at the door that led to the front door; a swarm of vampires had burst through and were falling over each other to get in. Danny opened up without hesitation and liberally sprayed the entrance with hot, screaming lead. The wooden doorframe disintegrated, the plaster around it disappeared, limbs were rendered asunder and heads popped open like ripe fruit; the hallway flashed and flared like an over enthusiastic fireworks display. "YEAH!"

Danny screamed as he felt the gun pushing him backward along the carpet.

Nutter had acquired himself a slightly smaller, but no less lethal, automatic rifle that he aimed at the door that led directly out to the back garden. He pulled the trigger but nothing happened. The door cracked as something very strong pushed against it from the other side. He pressed his finger against the trigger as hard as he could but again nothing happened.

"This one's not working," he shouted above the noise.

Cassandra glanced over, assessed the situation and, without fuss, flicked the safety catch off.

The door burst open and a vampire threw itself at the confused Nutter, his finger tightened instinctively and he rolled under the attacker. The bullets ripped down the length of the night beast, lifting it higher and spurring its trajectory straight towards Cameron's back. It burst into a ball of light that poured over and into him, he gasped as if someone had dropped ice down his shirt, but it did not distract him from his pattern of defence. Nutter ensured that no harm had come to him and returned his attention to the back door.

Cassandra had laid her hands on two automatic pistols that she fired alternately into a vampire that had just charged through from the kitchen. She advanced on it, constantly ploughing the shots into its convulsing body. When she got close enough she kicked it in its crotch, it doubled slightly and she brought the butts of both guns hard against its ears. It arched its back, screaming at all the pains it was enduring; she pushed both barrels against its chest, over its heart and fired. It flew back through the double hinged door and the kitchen flared. The door swung back open and another one entered the room only to leave this reality with a bullet through its heart and only half a head. She returned to the centre of the room, ejected the two near empty clips and put in two full ones.

Gillian was only half-concerned to notice that the sensual stroking had ceased; she drifted off to sleep with a smile on her face.

In the corner of the room, Zorga was curled into a tight ball of anguish; there was an almost constant stream of light pouring into his twisted body.

"Junior!" he called out and Junior burst into the room.

"Yes?"

"Stop this," Zorga indicated the river of light.

"Certainly," Junior replied and stood in the path of the onslaught. His body welcomed the light; Junior smiled in pleasure as he felt the power enter his body. *This could be considered to be initiating a take over*, he thought.

Zorga straightened himself up and saw Junior glorifying in his newly acquired strength.

"You may stop now," Zorga said but Junior seemed not to hear.

"I said stop!" Zorga bellowed and hurled Junior from his feet. The light returned to its original intent and Zorga stared out to its source, somewhere in the distance.

Junior picked himself up.

"I was unprepared for such a wave of liquidation," Zorga told him and Junior looked over at Gillian's naked body, asleep on the bed. He raised an eyebrow in appreciation of the sight.

"I did not get the chance to start the turn before this occurred," Zorga indicated the light. "What is happening?"

"Exactly as you ordered," Junior said, "you wanted her friends destroyed and so it is being seen to."

"But look at this!" Zorga shouted. "They must be destroying my entire army."

Junior shook his head. "Not at all, I just sent out the night battalions."

"Why just them?"

"They're old, they're lazy, they can't go out in the day and so are practically useless and there were lots of them. I assumed that in time they would be able to swarm them and win by force of numbers."

"These were some of my first acquisitions," Zorga said. "I'm not sure I approve of your callous attitude in disposing of them."

"But Master," Junior grovelled, "you know how much more exciting and invigorating the young ones are. Out with the old and all that."

"Yes, I suppose."

Junior waited to see if that was an indication of his dismissal. Not that he was eager to leave the vision of nubility that lay on the bed; it was just that if the conversation continued along these lines Zorga might begin uncovering information that Junior did not want him privy to at this present moment.

"We must offer our army some support," Zorga said.

"More troops?" Junior asked.

"No, no. Nothing like that," Zorga said. "Something along the lines of a distraction." He turned his attention from the city's rooftops to the naked body on the bed.

"Fetch me a drink, Junior."

"Yes, boss," Junior replied and left the room.

Cameron fired another round and searched his pockets for replacement cartridges; he found only two more. "I'm nearly out," he shouted.

"Me too," said Danny who had now only been firing in short controlled bursts.

"I think they've stopped," Cassandra called.

"They must be regrouping," Nutter said, "planning a different strategy."

"Right then," Cameron lowered himself to the floor and strapped a flame-thrower to his back and tucked a hand gun into the waistband of his trousers, "we move up. They'll have to come up through the bottle-neck of the stairs so only have a limited area through which to attack, leaving you guys defending in front with whatever ammo is left, and I can do behind with this." He patted the nozzle of the flame-thrower.

He marched out of the living room and into the splintered remains of the entrance hall. He turned towards the front door, pulled out the pistol and fired it twice through the front door. There followed a flash of light at which point he turned back to look at his three comrades and indicated to them that it was safe to follow.

Danny lifted the chain gun and another two machine guns that were still on the pile, Cassandra stuffed about a dozen clips down the front of her blouse and ran to the stairs, Nutter picked up another gun and about half a dozen magazines and followed after Cassandra.

Danny then noticed something that had been uncovered in the pile of arms.

"Cool," he said.

Cameron was systematically inspecting each upstairs room; kicking down the door, firing a burst from the flame-thrower followed by a couple of shots from the gun. Each room he treated reacted with a bright burst of its own. Cassandra got to the top of the stairs in time to see a frying vampire push past Cameron and run down the hallway towards her; she fired without a second thought. The vampire flew apart at the seams in a spray of light and Cameron caught one of Cassandra's stray bullets in the shoulder. He yelped at the sudden, sharp pain.

"Oops, sorry," she said.

"Be careful," he chastened and popped the bullet out, "I still feel pain you know."

Nutter came up the stairs. "I think they're attacking again."

"Where's Danny?" Cassandra demanded.

"He was right behind me," Nutter said and turned to see that there was no-one there.

Still in the living room, Danny was finishing off a neat little pyramid of grenades as the first vampire of the second wave entered the room from the window.

"You took your time," Danny said, stood and levelled the chain gun at evil intruder. This caused it to pause in its tracks; another half-a-dozen entered through the same portal. Danny smiled at their worried expressions, then he noticed the first one briefly glance over Danny's shoulder at the kitchen door. It smiled.

A broad smile spread across Danny's face as well. "'Cinemagraphic clichés' my arse. You guys must think I'm so fucking stupid."

At this, he edged over towards the living room door then turned quickly at the kitchen and sprayed the approaching vampire with a short burst from the chain gun.

As Danny backed to the staircase the vampires had filled the living room to capacity; he stood on the bottom step and smiled at them all.

"Danny? Are you okay?" Cassandra called from upstairs.

"I'm fine, darling. No worries."

The vampires that faced him seemed to be most amused at this brash statement until Danny pulled out another grenade and then they all remembered what they had seen him doing when they had first entered the room.

He pulled the pin and lightly tossed the metal bomb back into the centre of the room. The vampires were momentarily distracted by the gentle arc of their impending doom so Danny took the opportunity to sprint up the stairs as fast as he could. He reached the landing and shouted, "Fire in me hole!" and dived to the ground.

"Eh?" the other three questioned but soon had their answer as the explosion rocked the house's foundations. The blast raced up the stairs knocking Nutter and Cassandra off their feet, Cameron was standing outside the bedroom that was directly over the living room so found himself leaving the building via the bathroom window. He fell out into the back garden and looked back up to the house in time to witness the tidal wave of white light disappearing into the night sky.

He lifted himself to his feet and winced with pain as he fixed a broken bone in his leg. He then looked around him to discover he was surrounded by a couple of dozen vampires. He looked down at the ground and shook his head.

"You shake my nerves and you rattle my brain," he said and looked up, "too much love drives a man insane," the vampires were looking a mite perplexed but were still advancing towards him, "you broke my will, but what a thrill." Cameron shot straight up into the air and opened the flame-thrower on the circle of undead beneath him. "Goodness gracious, great balls of fire," he yelled.

The back garden lit up like a dancing bonfire as burning, screaming vampires ran around in circles, confusion and extreme pain.

Cameron soared up higher into the sky with the flames still pouring out beneath him. "I laughed at love 'cause I thought it was funny," he sang, and flipped a hundred and eighty degrees so the trail of fire whipped round and sprayed into an approaching air-borne creature of the night who promptly dropped out of the sky into the hellish chaos below. The circle of flames dropped onto Cameron as he twisted in the air and ignited the back pack of fuel. "You came along and mooooved me honey," he continued without concern of his predicament and dived into Dante's back garden, "I changed my mind, this love is fine," he rammed the flame-thrower's nozzle through the back of a walking, panicking pyre who instantly exploded into a shower of light. "Goodness gracious, great balls of fire."

"Kiss me baby," he unstrapped the burning fuel pack that fell into the outstretched arms of a vampire.

"Uh oh," it said as the metal ruck-sack of doom detonated in its grip and obliterated its body.

The light flared from behind Cameron's speeding form and he shuddered with pleasure. "Oooh, that feels good." Another leapt out from the darkness and fixed itself to him. "Hold me baby," Cameron sang at it and promptly twisted its neck round, snapping its spine. "I want to love you like a lover should," he told the free dangling head of the limp evil one as he returned his path to the skies once again. "You're fine, so kind," he sang as his velocity steadily increased to bloody-ridiculously-fast, "I'm gonna tell the world that you're mine, all mine." He suddenly stopped in his ascent but his passenger did not and continued straight up and disappeared into the midnight clouds.

"AAAAAAAAAAAAAAAAAAAAAAAHHHHHHHHHHH..." it said

Cameron landed swiftly in the back garden again, between the two remaining attackers. "I bite my nails and I twiddle my thumbs, I'm kinda nervous but it sure is fun."

The last two of the army seemed very unsure of what was going to happen as Cameron just stood there singing at them. They considered that to be torture enough.

"Come on baby, drive me crazy."

They advanced and Cameron plunged his hands deep into their chests, wrapping his hands around their hearts.

"Goodness gracious, great balls of fire," he whispered and squeezed.

Junior re-entered the room as the tsunami of fallen comrades burst through the window and struck Zorga with the force of, well, a tsunami really.

Zorga was propelled across the room, colliding with Junior

and knocking the chalice of crimson liquid from his hands. The pair of them smashed against the opposite wall with the golden cup of blood landing upturned on Junior's head.

"What the fuck is going on out there?" Zorga screamed from his upside-down position.

Junior licked the blood from around his face. "They are obviously better prepared than I expected them to be," he lied.

Zorga got to his feet. "Quickly, give me the..." he noticed the blood dripping down Junior's forehead. "Get another cup, now!" he ordered causing Junior to leap up and race out of the room once more.

Silence fell on the decimated student accommodation like a sudden coronary. Cameron was stamping out the last few patches of smouldering flesh in the back garden when the other three emerged in their various scathed and scraped conditions. Danny was brandishing one of his home-made stakes in each hand, eyes wildly searching the darkness for danger.

"'Fire in me hole'," Cameron tutted at him.

"Well it's something like that," he countered.

"Why didn't you just say, 'Get down, fucking huge explosion'," Cassandra suggested, and slumped onto the ground with a weary sigh.

"Oh well, don't anyone actually thank me or anything for wiping out fifty per cent of our problem in one fell swoop," he mumbled.

"If only I had one of these a hundred years ago," Nutter mused to himself whilst stroking delicate fingers over the muzzle of the gun he was still carrying. He looked up suddenly. "What's that noise?" he asked.

"What noise?" Danny enquired and turned his ear out to the darkness.

"Sshh!" Cassandra told him. "I can hear it. It's getting louder, it's coming from up there." She pointed skywards.

"AAAAAAAAAAAAAAHHHHHHHHHHHHHH!" the noise said.

Cameron snatched one of Danny's stakes from him, spun one-hundred-and-eighty degrees and threw it at a large oak tree at the bottom of the garden. The falling, broken-necked vampire's descent was cut short by the stake ripping into its chest and pinning it to the tree, it span like a Catherine wheel as light sparkled out of its body.

"Good shot," Danny commended.

Junior rushed back into the room at the very critical moment when he knew the battle must have been over. He handed the cup to Zorga and noted with interest the last vestiges of light seeping into his body. Zorga moved silently over to the bedside, lifted Gillian's body and sat behind her, cradling her head in his lap.

"You will see, Gillian," he told her recumbent form. "You will know what it is like to be a goddess at my side."

He placed the cup to her lips and they opened instinctively to the cold metal. He tipped it slightly so the warm red liquid just touched the top of her bottom lip. Her tongue emerged to the taste and took a sample back into her mouth. She smacked her mouth as the flavour raced around her taste buds, she opened her mouth further and Zorga tipped the glass more to pour the blood into her mouth. Gillian drank the fluid; it burned her mouth and seared the back of her throat. Her whole body started to tingle as more entered her digestive organs. She gagged, spat and woke herself up. The taste was automatically recognisable to her and she threw herself away from the cup at her mouth and off the bed. She tried to vomit the liquid up but it coursed through her body, she was disgusted at the situation. She stumbled across the room as the intoxicating liquor of life seeped into her brain and fucked up her vision. She could feel her fangs growing of their own free will. She screamed as the blood burrowed into her stomach and reminded her of what it was like to be alive. Her heart yearned to beat again, to have blood pumping around her body again; she needed to fill her body with that heavenly liquid again.

So this was what the blood lust was all about; not the feeding on blood – she knew that she did not need to eat to survive – but the lack of blood. Vampires abhorred the fact that mortals had life. Sure, the undead's senses had heightened exponentially, but because they had no grasp or need for the qualities or values of life, they no longer felt anything inside.

The feeding on blood changed that temporarily; it fired up their bodies into remembering what it was like to be alive; what is was like to feel again in one sudden shot. This was more powerful than any man-made drug; the rush was every emotion under the sun, experienced in a few seconds. Unfortunately the downside was equally as sudden, and the cold turkey seemed to last a lifetime. No rehab centre could wean you off this.

She threw her head back and stared at Zorga; she looked at the man who had turned her into this state of instant addiction. Her eyes glowed red with hatred and craving, he dangled the half-empty chalice of blood at her and smiled with satisfaction.

She needed that blood, she had to have it and at that point she knew that Gillian Kildress was dead.

They all fell into the seats in the living room, what was left of them and it, and admired their destruction.

"I think Gillian was right about our deposit on this place," Danny commented.

"I don't think that would have been a viable prospect anyway Danny," Cassandra told him, "I think I saw our landlord amongst the first wave."

"Still," Danny mused, "it was a bit lucky that you had to park round the corner, eh?"

Cassandra nodded in silence whilst staring out of the hole that used to be the window. "Gillian is going to be well pissed about you blowing her car up."

"It was an accident," Danny said in his defence. "I only meant to blow up the front room."

"Sorry I'm late," a voice called out from the front door and a middle aged, fat man trotted into the living room. "I hope you saved me some..." He stopped suddenly upon confronting the four exhausted executioners of evil. "Ah, don't mind me," he said.

"We won't," Cameron muttered, pulled the gun from his trousers and emptied the clip through the man's heart.

"Ah," he said and exploded. Not even Danny had the energy to admire the light show of another demising demon of darkness. He stifled a yawn in fact and idly flipped the stake in his hands.

Cameron cleared his throat loudly causing Cassandra to jump awake in her seat. The three mortals looked at him as if he was going to say something but he just hacked again, louder and rougher.

"That's attractive," Cassandra commented.

Cameron doubled up as his violent throat evacuation escalated further. He appeared to be in a great deal of pain.

Nutter walked over to him. "Cameron?" he enquired.

"GET THE FUCK AWAY FROM ME!" he growled and began retching. He pulled himself to his feet and Nutter backed away.

Cameron was experiencing the final stages of a severe vomiting attack, the bit where your stomach seems to be in an automatic mode of cramping and convulsing. Your body tightens up so much that your throat closes and you cannot breathe; your eyes water and saliva pours from your mouth but nothing comes up from your stomach.

"I saw this on 'Poltergeist 2'," Danny murmured.

Cameron fell to the floor in a tight ball and Cassandra dropped to his side. "What is it, Cam?" she asked desperately.

"Can't -" was all he managed before his throat clamped up again.

"We've got to do something," she implored to the other two.

"What?" they asked.

Cameron stretched his body and sucked in a hug lungful of air. "I need Gillian," he croaked between spasms of reverse peristalsis.

"We don't know where she is," Cassandra told him.

The cup rested in her limp hand. She looked despondently at the walls around her. Her chin was stained red from her over exuberant ingestion. This was not how it was supposed to be.

Zorga and Junior stood over her and smiled.

"Well, that wasn't so hard was it, Gillian?" Zorga asked but got no reply.

"I'm not sure that it's worked out the way you wanted it to," Junior commented.

"Nonsense Junior," he said, "the turning has been most

successful. Did you not see the way in which she literally begged for the cup?"

"Yes, but..." he, said dubiously.

"'But' nothing," Zorga cut him off with a touch of irritation in his voice, "she is mine now and that is what I wanted; it worked."

They returned their attention to the zombie-like state that Gillian was in. "So why is she like this?" Junior asked, waving a languid arm over her, "and not actually sucking you off as we speak?"

"It was never my intention to turn her into a slave," Zorga explained, "she was to retain her free will and sit at my side as an equal."

"Hmmm," Junior muttered.

Zorga sighed loudly. "What?"

"Firstly, it looks to me as though she could not control the blood lust," Junior said, "implying that she has just turned into one of your mindless drones.

"Secondly, even if she still has got her free will, what's to say that she still won't tell you to fuck off."

Zorga eyed Gillian suspiciously. "She wouldn't, would she?"

Junior shook his head in frustration. "I don't know," he said, "but it seems to be perfectly logical to me. She isn't of you and since she despised you in the first place she probably isn't going to turn to you now."

"But I have turned her though, haven't I?" Zorga said as if it were some sort of consolation.

"Yes you have, and if we're lucky it may create physical repercussions in her other half."

"That'll do for now," Zorga said with contentment and turned away to walk to the smashed windows that overlooked the city.

"It is very unfortunate that it has worked out this way, Gillian," he said to the night sky, "but it does seem as if you have reacted badly to the turning. It does seem as if you have become nothing but a minor pawn rather than the queen I had hoped for."

"What shall I do with her?" Junior asked in anticipation.

"Whatever you want to Junior," Zorga replied, "but first, let's see how well she reacts in close quarters with a mortal."

Junior laughed evilly at the plan, but also because he knew he was going to get a shag at last, even if it was nothing more than a twisted version of date rape. Hey, he was a vampire, he had absolutely no morals.

***

Penny sensed the presence from her position on the bed, the darkness seemed to wan slightly and she saw the outline of the door ajar, a figure standing there supporting the lifeless body of another which was dropped to the floor. The door closed and the darkness receded into the furthest corners of the room, Penny saw that it was Gillian's naked body that was lying there.

"My god," she muttered, "what did they do to you?" She leapt from the bed and ran to her friend's side. She tried to haul her limp body over to the bed but Gillian was just a dead weight.

Penny searched for a pulse, then remembered. She settled for lightly slapping Gillian around the face; eventually her dead eyes opened.

"Penny?" Gillian mumbled.

Penny was slightly startled to see that Gillian's eyes were a shade of deep red and that her canines seemed to be over prominent, but again she reminded herself of her friend's undead situation.

"Get away," Gillian said.

"What?" Penny asked incredulously.

"Get away from me."

Gillian's brain was a mush of conflicting opinions; she was happy to see her friend again; she was sad to remember that her friend was still captive; she was so weak from her recent experiences; she wanted to rip her friend's throat out to taste the sweet inner sensory overload running through her body again.

CRRRRRRUUUUUMMMPH.

Gillian shook her head slightly as the noise hit her. She frowned and listened for it again.

Nothing.

"Gill, are you -" CRRRRRRRUUUUUMMMPH.

Gillian started slightly and looked into her friend's eyes. Apparently Penny had not noticed it. It was a terrible sound, a noise that she recognised at some unconscious level but could not identify it upon demand. Like trying to remember the name of an actor that everyone knows, but for the life of you, you cannot think of his name at that precise moment; like, er, you know, in that film with the planes. Oh, this is going to annoy me for ages now.

CRRRRRRUUUUUMMMPH.

Gillian's face twitched with irritation.

"Gill? What's up? What is the matter?" Penny asked.

"That noise," Gillian replied, "it's driving me crazy, what is it?"

"What noise?" Penny enquired. "I can't hear any noise."

A penny dropped in Penny's head. "What did they do to you?"

Remembrance returned to Gillian's fevered mind and she bit into her bottom lip with shame, her eyes began filling up. "They made me drink blood Penny," she sobbed. "I think they turned me."

Gillian buried her head into her friend's chest for comfort and protection.

CRRRRRRUUUUUMMMPH! The noise was even louder and Gillian threw herself away from the tormenting sound that seemed to be coming from Penny's chest.

Oh, so that was what it was.

Penny looked scared.

Gillian tried to stop herself from salivating.

Cameron was convulsing more violently now, he did not seem to know if he wanted to arch his back in agony or tuck himself into a ball of pain. One thing he did know to do was to scream; his mouth was stuck open and an endless tortured cry was coming from his body.

"I think we had better leave," Nutter suggested.

"You are joking, right?" Danny asked.

"I don't like this at all," Nutter told them.

"I don't think Cameron's too keen on the situation either," Cassandra pointed out.

"Do you know what's wrong with him?" Danny asked Nutter.

"I could be wrong," he pondered, "but it looks like he is undergoing an internal struggle for the rights to control his body."

"And you can tell that just by looking at him?" Cassandra asked in a voice garnished liberally with sarcasm.

"I've seen this sort of behaviour before," Danny said and the other two looked at him in amazement.

"Oh yeah?" Cassandra asked. "'Return of the Living Dead' was it?"

"No," he replied with indignation, "'40 Minutes' actually. This guy was trying to come off crack or something, and this is how he reacted going through cold turkey."

"Oh no," Nutter said.

"What?" the two youths enquired.

Cameron could not get the noise out of his head, it was driving him insane. At first the taste of blood had washed through his body and he thought he was going to be sick, and by god, he had tried to be, just to remove the foul sensation. Then the drumming had started, three heart beats thumping away at his inner ear, he had become disorientated, pains straining at his stomach and head. He knew what it was and was desperately trying to fight it. He was losing badly.

"Blood lust," Nutter said.

Cameron was on his feet in an instant, sharp teeth bared menacingly, eyes shining evilly.

"HELP ME!" he roared.

Nutter drew his sword and stepped forward. "There's nothing we can do for him," he said but Danny stayed his hand.

"We can't; not him. There must be something we can do."

"YES YOU CAN HELP," Cameron growled. "YOU CAN OPEN YOUR HEARTS TO ME."

He was on them in a second; Nutter was tossed lightly across the room and he lost his grip on his sword, Cassandra watched helplessly as Cameron picked Danny up by his collar and bounced his head off a remaining piece of the ceiling.

"No!" she shouted and attacked. She jumped on Cameron's

back, gripped his head in a tight lock and twisted sharply snapping his spine. Danny was dropped to the floor and Cassandra fell off Cameron's back as he stumbled around the room trying to straighten his neck.

"Quickly," Nutter urged, "strike while he's distracted."

Danny got to his feet groggily and tried to clear the haze in his head. Cameron snapped his head back into place with a hellish grunt and returned his attention to the handsome young man with a great deal of blood in his body. He charged. Again Cassandra got to her feet to ward Cameron off but she was thrown aside and landed on top of Nutter who was about to attack.

Danny was lifted off his feet again and thrust against the wall.

"I'M SO HUNGRY!"

"Now Gillian," Penny said, "don't do anything that you might regret at a later date. Or in fact anything that I might regret now."

"I need you Penny," Gillian growled.

"And I need you to stop looking at me like that."

Gillian shook her head. "I'm so sorry but you have no idea what it's like, I can't stand the noise that's coming from your body, and you smell so tasty."

"Gillian, you really aren't attired in the best way to use talk like that; people might start getting ideas," Penny said.

"Very good Penny, but I'm afraid trying to stall me for time will not prevent the inevitable."

"That's why it's called the inevitable," Penny stammered, still trying to stall. "You can delay it though."

Penny had never known a vampire to move so quickly and with so much deadly precision; she was pinned up against the wall so suddenly that it blasted the wind from her body and left her desperate for breath.

"Why does your heart beat so slowly?" Gillian asked.

"Because of my longevity," Penny gasped.

"Eh?"

"Slow metabolism means longer life," she explained.

"That's why I'm immortal, because I have no metabolic

rate," Gillian hypothesised and Penny just nodded despondently.

"Cheer up Penny," Gillian said, "we can be best friends again in a moment."

Penny's arm swung up from her side and the pen she picked up from the chest of drawers next to her sank into Gillian's stomach. Gillian dropped Penny and stumbled away from the pain, Penny wasted no time in sprinting for the door. She had done this sort of thing for quite a few years so knew the next step as if she had rehearsed this moment before. She stopped suddenly when she was only a metre from her potential freedom; Gillian streaked past in a miscalculated attempt to intercept Penny. Instead of delivering the intended final, fatal blow, she just ran into the wall and bounced back across the room from whence she had come.

Penny continued with her escape and noticed that the room was becoming darker again; the midnight was creeping back through the walls to stop her. She pulled the door open and elbowed Junior on the bridge of his nose. *So predictable*, she thought and she kicked him in the stomach as he doubled up in agony. She ran as fast as she could down the corridor following signs for the emergency exit.

Gillian burst out of the room a second later and collided with the reeling Junior, he slammed into the wall and was dropping to the floor when Gillian caught him and pulled him up to her face.

"What have you done to me?" she growled.

"I..." was all he could manage.

"Where did she go?"

Junior pointed in the direction Penny had run and Gillian threw him roughly to the floor where he thought it the safest place to stay for the time being.

"I'll deal with you later," she yelled at him as she ran down the hall. He could not help himself but admire her naked behind as it disappeared around the corner.

Penny had considered it unwise to wait for a lift; what with not knowing how long it would take to arrive she also could not shake that scene from Omen Two from her fevered mind. Instead she had thrown herself into the fire escape and hurtled down the steps five at a time. She knew she could not keep up this pace for very long before she lost her footing or an ankle gave in, but then again she could not afford to slow down and admire the decor of this plush establishment.

She counted the floors as she continued her hazardous descent.

"Four," she puffed, "three," then she slipped. For the briefest of seconds her concentration lapsed to elsewhere other than where she was placing her feet and she miscalculated a leap, clipping the edge of the fourth step with her heel. She fell forward. Luckily she was close to a turn in the staircase and so landed in a pile on the flat floor. She sat in the corner panting heavily, looking back up the stair-well, awaiting either Gillian's or her initial abductor's advance. Neither was forthcoming.

"I fucking hate these moments of drawn out suspense," she puffed, picked herself up and continued her bid for freedom, this time paying more attention to where she put her feet.

"Two," she grunted, "one." She fixed her eyes on the approaching last turn, ready to strike out if, or rather when, the hiding creature of the night decided to lunge at her.

She passed the corner and dived to the floor, rolling halfway across the reception foyer and bumping straight into Zorga who was standing, waiting, by the entrance.

"Surely you didn't believe that I would actually allow you to leave us, did you?" he asked.

"It... crossed... my mind," she panted and suddenly reached out to strike him. He caught her hand easily and threw her into a chair where she stayed and tried to control her breathing.

"You will be most enjoyable," Zorga told her, "with all that extra oxygen you're feeding into your system. It will be most intoxicating."

She judged the distance from herself to the hotel entrance; she weighed up her chances of reaching it with her body still full of blood. Her estimations were 'too far' and 'as near enough to nil as damn-it-all', respectively.

Zorga was standing over her now, preparing to strike, and for a short moment she was actually looking forward to it, you know, fuck it all, why not? Life would not be so bad in the afterlife compared to the last day or so that she had had to put up with in this place, would it?

She looked into the eyes of pure evil and she realised that she was completely out of her depth here and that there really was nothing she could do to prevent her demise even if she tried very hard.

"I don't want to die," she whimpered.

"You will live forever," Zorga whispered to her.

"I've already been doing that for a while already and it hasn't been much fun so far," she replied.

Zorga's hands were on her shoulders, pressing her back into the chair, his mouth was descending on her neck. As it passed her ear she became extremely conscious of the complete lack of breath that she should feel brushing against her, it was like those first tentative moments between two nervous and excited lovers. She caught herself holding her breath in equal anticipation.

"Please no," she whispered.

There was a rush of wind and the darkness that was Zorga was replaced with the sight of the hotel reception again. Penny looked around in confusion and wondered whether that was it. Had it happened? Was that the indication of her passing over to the other side. She felt at her neck and discovered no signs of her being drained. She looked around her and decided not to question the reasons for her good fortune but make good her escape.

Upon standing she noticed a commotion in the dining area, Gillian was standing over Zorga's body, repeatedly smashing a bar stool over the back of his head. She turned to look at Penny with her crimson eyes.

"RUN," she ordered, and Penny did, not looking back once, not wanting to think of what had happened or what was happening to one of her dearest friends. Not wanting to know if she was being pursued or not. She just wanted to go home and be held for a long time.

The living room was still and silent. It seemed as if Cameron had been holding Danny for quite a long time, the pair of them just staring at each other. Danny noticed Cameron's eyes returning to their normal shade of dirty blue; the tension in his body suddenly washed off him and he lowered Danny slightly.

"Danny," he muttered, "if I ever do that again, don't even think about protecting me because I had no control over it. If it happens again you're going to have to try to defend yourself to the fullest. You're going to have to try to kill me."

Danny's eyes were wide with fear, he licked his lips and tried to compose himself. "I did," he croaked.

"Huh?" Cameron asked, and released his grip of the big man.

"I did try to kill you," Danny reiterated and motioned his head to Cameron's chest.

Cameron looked down and, for the first time, noticed the tight pain he had in his torso. There was one of Danny's home made, double-ended Ninja stakes sticking out of Cameron's chest. He staggered backwards and everyone watched him warily. He fell against the opposite back wall and the front point pushed out slightly.

"It's gone right through," Cameron said.

"Sorry?" Danny suggested.

"Right through my heart."

"I am so sorry."

"You really tried to kill me."

Danny shook his head. "No, no. I was just holding it in my hand and you ran onto it."

"Et tu, Danny?"

"You're not dying, are you, Cameron," Cassandra said rather than asked.

"It doesn't seem like it," he confirmed and Nutter fell back to the floor with a weary sigh.

"You can't even die like a proper vampire," he groaned.

"It does hurt," Cameron offered, "if that's any help at all."

"Do you need a hand to pull it out?" Danny asked.

"You stay the fuck away from me," Cameron warned and tugged slightly at the stake. "Ow," he whined.

"Oh come here," Cassandra said, walked to him and yanked the spike from his chest in one quick motion.

"Owwwwww!" Cameron yelled and hopped around the room.

"I bet you can't even pull your own plasters off, can you?" she asked rhetorically, and he just glared at her, rubbing his tit and pouting sulkily.

"So what was all that about?" Danny asked Nutter.

"I'm afraid that I'm not entirely sure about anything any more, Daniel," he replied and sat up. "Suffice to say, Cameron had an attack of blood lust."

"Why now and not before?" Danny asked.

"I don't know," Nutter answered.

"Why did it stop?" Danny asked.

"I don't know," Nutter answered.

"Why didn't I kill him?" Danny asked.

"I don't know," Nutter answered.

"What, not even some grandiose theory?" Cassandra chipped in.

"Right then," Nutter proclaimed and jumped to his feet. "Cameron's blood lust could have been brought on by two possible explanations; one, that his state of vampirism is slowly eating him away, instead of being an instant turn it could be like a cancerous growth slowly, gradually turning him. Two, and possibly the most likely explanation, is that he is empathically connected to Gillian due to them mutually creating each other, and it is her that has been turned and is suffering from the blood lust first hand; Cameron is simply suffering from sympathy pains. Blood lust by association."

"Why did it stop then?" Cameron asked with concern in his voice.

"You were conceived through love," Nutter hypothesised. "Love is controlled by the heart, when the stake pierced your heart the bond was broken."

"Either that or Gillian's been killed," Cameron said and Nutter nodded with resignation.

"Either way you still think Gillian's been turned?" Cameron asked.

"It is just a theory," Nutter explained.

"So why didn't he die when I stabbed him?" Danny asked again.

"Because he's a stubborn son-of-a-bitch," Nutter replied and made it absolutely clear that he wanted this non-stop questioning to cease.

"You should have let me go and get her," Cameron said to

no-one in particular.

"I didn't stop you Cameron," Nutter said, "I just told you that it wasn't the best option. Had you gone, we would all be dead."

The three mortals waited for a reaction from Cameron to show if he regarded the sacrifice of the one over the lives of the many.

He turned to them. "I know what you're saying, but it doesn't make it any easier to know that I may have to kill the woman I love."

Danny unconsciously reached out for Cassandra's hand and gripped it tightly. It did not pass unnoticed and did not make Cameron feel the slightest bit better; in fact, he felt positively sick with himself. What a situation to be in. What sort of a choice was this to have to deal with? Had he gone to get her when he told the others that he wanted to, he probably would have been back in time to save the day. Although he had only got back in the nick of time with the armaments he had found as it was, and if he had searched for Gillian first he might have returned empty handed and they all would have died.

But how could he turn his back on the woman he loved. After all these years of putting it off, pushing the realisation that he *did* love her to the back of his mind and never really telling her; he might never get the chance to tell her again.

He remembered his mother and became even more distressed at the repetition of his life; how much more regret for wasted time was he going to have to put up with? If he got out of this alive, he was going to see his dad and put things right between them. He was all he had left now.

"Cameron?" Nutter interrupted. "I think that it's about time we went looking for Gillian."

"No," Cameron said quietly, "it's too late for that."

The three looked at him in sympathy and fear that he was giving up.

"It's time that this ended," Cameron continued, "for good."

"Yeah," Danny agreed.

"Where do we start?" Cassandra asked. Cameron screwed his face into a visage of pure concentration.

"What's up with him?" Danny asked. "It's not happening

again, is it?"

Cameron reached out over the city once more, his mind traced over the contours of life and death, of light and darkness. He discovered a human, running scared through the streets but passed over it; he felt the flickering of a dying bulb of angelic brightness but would not let himself be distracted. His search slipped over a small area and Cameron retracted his senses to identify the reason for this, but again his mind swept quickly off this patch of the city. It was like he was trying to balance a pyramid on one of its points; just as he thought he had moved his mind to the slightest degree to settle on this elusive area he had toppled over to the other side. Instead, he scanned the immediate surrounding area and he surmised that he had discovered the heart of darkness.

"We're going to The Royal Lodge," he announced.

"You should have seen the expression on your face," Danny snickered, but nobody joined in. Not this time.

***

Penny had considered herself lucky to get this far without being accosted. She knew that the smell of her would bring every hungry night beast out into the streets, but the fact that it appeared that no-one was pursuing her made her more terrified than ever. The longer she remained alive the more she was convinced that she wanted to stay that way.

Of course it was at that point when she heard the movement behind her and she desperately tried to increase her pace. Her legs were hurting, her breathing was so erratic that it made her gag, she was tired, mentally exhausted and all she wanted to do was have a nice hot bath and pig-out on marshmallows.

The noise behind her was a scampering, snuffling sound; the sort of noise that a rampaging, asthmatic pig might make. She had a very bad feeling that she was going to die.

If she had conserved her energy she would have been able to put up a decent fight against a couple of lusting vampires. But then again, if she had conserved her energy then she would not have run as quickly and got as far as she had, therefore she probably would have attracted the attention of more blood thirsty devils than she would have physically been able to handle.

Her only option was to keep on running.

She hoped that it was not Gillian who was chasing her. If it was then she knew for definite that she would not be able to fight her. Well, she could not fight anyone at the moment so the hypothesis was a pretty redundant one to say the least.

Whatever it was that was chasing her had definitely got a lot closer, too fucking clo-

It was quite apparent that her mind was flying about in a state of delirium. Near-death situations will do that to a person. It is a very irrational state for somebody to experience and therefore it is very natural for them to go around thinking irrational thoughts like baths, marshmallows, and whether she could fight someone who was trying to kill her if she actually knew them or not. This is why she was not really concentrating on where she was going and why she nearly shat herself upon colliding with the dark figures that had just turned the corner.

Four bodies fell to the floor in a confused mass of flailing limbs, screams and swearing. Cameron stepped around the corner quietly and, without fuss, punched the pursuing vampire's head clean off its shoulders. It made a high-pitched whistling as it sailed back down the street without the rest of its body which just stood there, feeling a bit stupid.

Cameron thrust his hand through the decapitated demon's thorax and squeezed its heart until it squidged through his fingers as a mush of muscle. He turned his head away from the light as it illuminated the street brightly. Further down the road, a football sized beam of light zipped up into the heavens.

"AAH! AAH! AAH! AAH! AAH!" Penny said.

"Oh my god, what's happening?" Cassandra screamed.

"Screaming banshee of death," Danny replied frantically.

"Calm down, woman," Nutter grabbed at the hysterical girl's shoulders and shook her slightly. Her head looked up inquisitively at this voice of power and reason, and recognition set in.

"Father?" Penny asked.

"Penelope," Nutter confirmed with a sigh of relief.

"Penny," Danny and Cassandra cried, and leapt onto the girl with hugs of good fellowship.

Only Cameron did not display too many emotions of being overjoyed at the situation; now he was the only one from their group who had lost out in the relationship stakes. That was not to say that he actually wanted somebody else to die, not at all, but then again it is not easy to congratulate someone on their marriage when your partner has just told you that he or she has been having an affair.

The four reunited heroes scrambled to their feet and perhaps noticed Cameron for the first time.

"Oh Cam," Penny said and dashed to him, holding him tightly, "I'm so sorry, I don't know what they did. There was nothing I could do."

Cameron actually mellowed slightly upon the realisation that perhaps there were other people who loved his woman as much, if not slightly differently, as he did.

"Not your fault, Penny," he replied. "Are you completely okay?"

"I am now," she told him and added. "You're looking good."

He simply smiled at this but thought, *I'm not feeling too good.*

"We're going to The Royal Lodge, Penny," Danny told her.

"But that's where..." she started, and saw Cassandra nodding her head with full realisation of where it was, who was there and what events were likely to occur upon their arrival.

"You will be a lot safer if you come with us, Penelope," her father told her, and she assented with a silent nod.

As they continued their journey towards what they considered to be the final chapter, the young vampire slayers related all of their adventures thus far; Danny especially relished the part when he demolished half of the house in a well calculated, if not personally endangering, piece of battle strategy. Cassandra countered that it was simply some sort of sign of masculine insecurity displaying itself in the form of wanton destruction and big Arnie-esque explosions.

"So what did it symbolise when you was doing the 'Harvey Keitel' with two automatics blazing away?" Danny asked.

"Male symbolism of women as the weaker sex. Place a phallus in her hand to indicate her lack of one," Cassandra said.

"Yeah, well, that would be fine if this was a film," Danny said, "but somehow it doesn't really carry much weight in the face of reality. Firstly because nobody placed those guns in your hands and secondly because it isn't a bloke's fault that guns have become phallically associated. The gun came first, the symbolism after."

"Yeah, all right, Danny," Cassandra muttered, "we got the message."

"I'm sure it's a scientific thing rather than anything to do with male dominance," Danny continued, oblivious to the disinterest. "The shape of the gun makes it easier for a bullet to follow a directed path – pretty much like taking a pee. That's why guns aren't shaped like fannies, what with your sprinkler system and all."

On their way, both Nutter and Cameron kept quiet and removed from the conversations; Cameron was brooding over his failure to keep Gillian safe, and Nutter was trying to build up the courage to talk to Penny about the last fifty years or so.

"Aren't you going to say anything to him?" Cassandra asked Penny, and indicated with a backward twitch of her head at Nutter.

"Not yet," Penny replied, "I want to see how much he regrets everything that has happened. He can go first."

He did.

"Penelope?" Nutter stuttered. "Might we have a private word?"

Penny threw a quick glance at Cassandra who urged her to go with an elbow in the ribs. She fell back from the procession and Nutter walked up to her. They continued on their way side by side.

"Penelope," he started.

"Don't call me that," Penny interrupted. "It's Penny now."

"Very well," he conceded, and Penny was impressed; she had never known him to give in to something quite that easily. She knew that Penelope had been his first wife's name and that it meant a great deal to him. It genuinely looked like he was trying to make amends.

Penny was not going to make it easy for him though, fifty years cannot simply be forgiven by an acceptance of a name change.

"Penny," the word seemed to grate against his voice, "I'm not very good at this sort of thing as well you know."

"Or rather as 'I remember'," she told him.

"Quite. I believe that I have a lot of apologies to make to you."

Penny looked up at him, and instead of the stern, solitary figure of authority she had always remembered him to be, she saw a sad, lonely ageing man. She had to force herself not to just hug him there and then.

"At the time of our separation," he said and caught the harsh glare that she directed at him. "At the time when I sent you away," he corrected himself and she returned her eyes to the direction in which they were travelling, "I truly believed that I was doing the best thing for you."

"For me?" she cried out. "You didn't even consider to ask me what was best for me. You didn't even presume that I was a young adult trapped inside the body of an adolescent. It didn't even cross your mind that I might have been extremely confused and frustrated due to the mixed emotions and hormones that were flooding through my system. You're not stupid; and you never were. In any given situation you can always come up with a dozen justifiable reasons and explanations, so don't you dare try to tell me now that you honestly believed that you were acting in *my* best interests."

"What was best for us then," he attempted.

"No!" she shouted at him. "Not best for anyone but yourself. Throughout our miserable existences you slowly learnt how to dispose of your problems, swiftly and efficiently. When you came up against a vampire you killed it without question, whenever you thought that you were falling in love you allowed her to die, and at the first sign of me actually being curious about sex," Nutter grimaced, "yes, SEX! you automatically thought that I was an extension of the evil that you had condemned us to live amongst, and shipped me off to the first convent you came across, telling them all the gory details of my self, sinful, exploration."

Danny coughed self-consciously.

"Penel-" he caught himself. "Penny, have you ever thought

of the events from my point of view?"

"You had a burden and you removed it," she answered curtly.

"That's not true," he implored, "I loved you dearly. I still do. You were a young girl and a young woman at the same time and I was still having to look after you. Still having to protect you. After your mother died, I could have sent you away, but no, it occurred to me that you were someone I *could* love. My daughter.

"This thought was probably the worst and most selfish one that I have ever had in my entire life because, as you say, it 'condemned' you to live your life surrounded by evil. If I truly wanted you to be safe from harm then I should have given you to an orphanage or something at the very onset of your birth. Would you have been any less unforgiving if that had been the case?"

Penny could not reply. The consequences of such a possible past were causing her head to spin slightly.

"You were so young, Penelope," she let it pass, "you can't even remember the thousands of times I had to go out of my way to protect you and save you. You seem to have forgotten how much we were arguing during those final years.

"Yes, that time I caught you with that young man did scare me, but it also brought a great deal of clarity to our situation. I was not an adequate father for you, I was not bringing you up to the best of my abilities, and I could no longer guarantee your protection from harm – any kind of harm. So I sent you away for both our good."

Penny walked on in contemplative silence for a moment, slowly digesting this new point of view, this different way of perceiving her past.

"So what about the fifty-odd years?" she finally asked.

Nutter shook his head with remorse. "I don't know how to explain it, Penelope." It did not sound too bad to her the more she heard it. "I regretted my decision as soon as I had made it. I knew you would be angry with me,"

"Upset, perhaps," she interrupted, "even, deeply hurt, but not angry, not at first."

"I thought at first if I left you to your own devices, that

things would..." he searched for the right, diplomatic, words.

"Cool down?" Penny suggested.

"Yes."

"The longer you left me there, the more I thought you didn't want me, the more angry I got at you for dumping me," she told him.

"The longer I left you, the harder it was to come back for you. I got tangled up in a few, very long and arduous crusades that confirmed my beliefs that by sending you away I had acted in your best interests. Eventually I realised that decades had passed and it would be impossible for me to correct or resume our relationship again."

Nutter looked at Penny for a reaction of forgiveness, she looked up at him. "You're a useless bastard aren't you," she said and he nodded silently. She slipped her arm under his and leaned against his body. He squeezed her arm with his and they walked on in silence.

This just gets better and better, Cameron thought.

***

Gillian was walking the cold streets with an overpowering feeling of compounding shame, guilt, self-pity and maddening hunger. She was losing it, she knew, but she also knew that there was nothing she could do about it. The lust was slowly eating away at her, removing her sanity; all she had left was a solitary thought of Cameron and her love for him.

Saving Penny from Zorga had taken so much self control; instead of chasing after her immediately, Gillian had actually forced herself to call the lift and stood there, waiting for it. She hoped that it would take long enough for Penny to make her escape. However, as the lift descended she could still hear Penny's sluggish beat of life in her inner ear and could still smell her flesh. She really did want to open her up and drink deeply.

As the lift door opened in the lobby she saw Zorga leaning over the exhausted body of her friend. At first she charged to the scene for a piece of the action. At the last second she regained control of herself and altered her course to intercept Zorga. She lifted him off his feet and sent him hurtling through the glass double-doors into the bar. She had then grabbed the nearest heavy object – the bar stool – and repeatedly smashed him over the back of the head with it. It gave her a distraction away from Penny and it also gave Zorga something else to think about; and, of course, it gave Penny time to escape from the scene.

After she was sure that Penny was away, she decided to try and do some serious damage to Zorga – the head beating was just to keep him occupied for those few valuable seconds – now she set her mind on killing him outright. She flipped the bar stool one-eighty so that the feet of it faced down and then she plunged it into the head vampire's back, only to discover that his physical form had melted and that the room had filled with the same dense blackness that had consumed Penny's room earlier.

Junior then joined the conflict and sent her sprawling amongst the tables and chairs in the dining room. She got to her feet; she was angry, upset, hurting and desperate to do some terminal rupturing and rending. Upon seeing Junior and Zorga standing side-by-side, waiting for her next move, she decided to get out and assess her situation; her reality check if you like. So she went via the nearest window and was halfway down the road before she noticed that they had not even tried to stop her. She did not know that she had served the only purpose that she had been useful for.

Here she was, dressed in clothes that she had stolen from the first house she had come to, assessing her life, or death as it were, and she had come to the conclusion that she would probably be better off if she was dead.

Really dead.

Dead dead.

A couple of vampires erupted from a house and ran out into the street. They paused at the sight of her but then continued on their night-time revelry. She was shocked at first but when they went on their way she figured it to be the icing on the proverbial cake.

They think I'm one of them.

She wanted to find Cameron and tell him one last time that she loved him before she did what she had to do. She also knew that if he was still with the others, which she presumed he would be, then she would not be able to prevent herself from attacking and he would have to kill her to save them. That would be the better way to go; she had died in his arms once, a second time would not be so bad.

She searched for him and was mildly concerned that she had to turn back the way she had come in order to meet up with him.

***

"I want you to recall everyone," Zorga told Junior.

"Recall them?" Junior exclaimed. "Everyone is pushing out and gathering more acquisitions; there's nothing left for them here; they're practically at the edge of the city's border."

"Recall them now," Zorga instructed more firmly.

"But why?" Junior asked.

"Junior, I tire of your constant questioning and your annoying habit of taking matters into your own hands."

"I don't understand," Junior muttered with concern. "Lord," he added for security.

"Don't you forget it either. I am your lord," Zorga said. "I don't know what you've been planning, Junior, but I advise you to drop it. For your own safety."

Junior gave him a look of complete innocence and sincerity, implying that he really did not know what Zorga was talking about.

"They are coming for what they presume will be our final undoing, Junior, I want for you to recall everyone," Zorga said.

"Can't we beat them ourselves?" Junior asked, but already knew the answer.

"Of course not," Zorga bellowed. "The Professor could defeat you without raising a sweat, and as for that other one," Zorga seemed to shudder, "who knows how strong he is now."

"How do you know that none of them are dead?" Junior enquired.

"What, from your little plan?" Zorga's eyebrow rose with the disdain in his voice. "I am not so stupid to realise why you only sent out the night dwellers, Junior, and I agree with you, they were useless, fat, lazy, et cetera, and I commend you on your methods of rising up the ranks. But if you ever pull something like that again..." Further words were not required to be said or heard.

"They might have got a couple of them," Junior muttered.

"Trust me Junior, your plan failed with such honours that you really should not be standing before me now, you should instead be rotting in the ground."

'Failed'? Junior thought. *That's what you think.*

"What about Gillian?" he asked.

"I don't care any more," Zorga replied waving a hand dismissively, "she may provide a distraction every now and then but I can't see her being a threat to us any more."

"But she knows things," Junior reminded.

"And who is she going to tell exactly?" Zorga asked.

"Her boyfriend?" Junior suggested.

"Pah!" Zorga laughed. "He's watching over his mortal colleagues. As soon as Gillian comes within sniffing distance of blood again she'll try to rip their throats out. They'll have to kill her."

He chuckled.

"I believe this will be the final meeting," he said to himself. "It will amuse me greatly to have the Professor kneel at my feet in total subservience."

There came a silence between the two immortals as the elder mentally revelled in his presumed victory and the younger plucked up the courage to ask a nagging question.

"Doesn't it ever bore you?" Junior finally asked.

"What?" Zorga enquired.

"All this power relations stuff," Junior explained, "you only ever seem to be contented when your enemies have been personally humiliated before your eyes."

"And?"

"You're only happiest when you've got somebody able to fight against you. You could rule the world, you know?"

"It is the natural balance of light and dark, Junior," Zorga said. "One cannot exist without the other."

"Yes, it can," Junior said. "It can always be light or it can always be dark."

"But one is not truly appreciated without the other," Zorga pointed out.

"Are you 'appreciated' then?" Junior asked.

"I am here to allow people like the Professor the glory that they crave; to give parents a way to get their children to behave; to give people hope – if there is a devil, then there has to be a God. The Professor exists to provide beings like us amusing distractions."

Junior turned away and hoped that this 'amusing distraction' would be Zorga's last.

"Recall the troops," Zorga reminded him upon his dismissal.

"Yes, Master," Junior replied without hiding his sarcasm.

Zorga eyed Junior warily as he left the room. A wry smile crept over his lips as if an old memory of himself had been jogged by the youthful impertinence of his right-hand man.

"We used to respect our elders when I were a lad," he sighed, with nostalgic reverence.

"Now that is what I call black," Danny mumbled.

"Oh, do give it a rest," Cassandra spat, "I'm getting really fed up with you continually going on about how black everything is just when we're about to get trounced."

"I can't help it," he whined.

"Well, what bloody use are you going to be if all you can see is blackness?" she asked.

"Piss off," he replied.

"No, come on, I'm serious," she urged. "What is the point of you going in there if you can't see anything?"

"I can see stuff," he explained, "it's just that it's shrouded in black."

"Don't worry about it, Danny," Cameron said, "I can see it too."

"So what now?" Penny asked.

"Don't ask me, sweetheart," Danny said, "he's the brains of this operation," and indicated Cameron with his thumb.

"Cam?" Penny prompted.

"I think they're waiting for us to do something," he said.

"They know we are here," Nutter informed.

"Yes," Cameron said.

"So?" Penny asked again and everyone looked at Cameron

who was just staring up at the oppressive stance of The Royal Lodge Hotel.

"I don't know," he said.

They all joined him in watching the building, waiting for it to make its first move.

***

"What are they doing?" Zorga asked, staring down into the street from his room.

"Staring at us, I think," Junior replied from his side.

"Why are they not attacking?"

"I don't know."

Zorga frowned with consternation. "Are they waiting for reinforcements?"

Junior concentrated for a second. "No. There are no other mortals in the entire city."

"They should be attacking," Zorga said, aiming his comment more at them than at Junior. "The Professor never acted with such caution in the past. He would always be the one to strike first, to try to gain the element of surprise."

Zorga seemed to contemplate for a moment. He then turned away from the window and marched to the door. "Come, Junior."

"Where?" Junior asked, racing after him.

"Down there," Zorga said, from halfway down the corridor.

"We're going to confront them? On our own?"

"Yes."

"But you said..."

"I know what I said," Zorga said, "but it doesn't appear as if they are prepared to fight, does it?"

"I don't know," Junior said in a dubious voice. They called the lift which announced that it was already waiting for them, and they stepped inside, in silence.

The tinny muzak filled the cubicle and Zorga winced with distaste.

"Why is this noise still playing?" he asked.

"I haven't been able to find out how to stop it," Junior replied.

"There must be a player or something somewhere, surely."

"I'm telling you, I haven't found the source of it anywhere in the building."

With a violent yell, Zorga thrust his fist into the speaker from whence 'The Girl From Ipenema, Bazooki Dub Mix' was emitting. It sparked furiously and crackled noisily.

Zorga smiled triumphantly and silence resumed in the lift.

Muzak has an unfortunate effect on one's unconscious, the light, irritating, lilting tunes burn themselves into the listener's brain, and even after the airy sound is no longer present, one can still hear it as if it has possessed one's inner ear. Junior started absent-mindedly humming the tune to himself and received a surprising clip around the back of his head from his Lord and Master.

Only as the lift halted and pinged its arrival at their intended destination did they realise that the muzak could still be heard, faintly coming from the destroyed speaker.

Zorga growled.

Heaven help those individuals he planned to take that anger out on.

The five defenders of all that was pure and good were still staring at the ominous building which did nothing before them, when the two dark figures stepped through the main entrance and out onto the street.

Nutter nudged Cameron and nodded to the hotel's main door. "We have visitors," he said.

"What now?" Penny asked.

"Do give it a rest, Penny," Cassandra said.

"I just don't like standing around waiting for something to happen," Penny explained. "It was never like this in the past. We always leapt in and stormed the place. We're giving them too much time to get their armies together."

"Penelope," her Father said, "times have changed, things work differently now. We were never in this sort of position in the past."

"Cameron?" Danny asked.

Cameron's mind was a blank. Not the sort of blank when you cannot remember how to spell a simple word, remember a name, picture a face, and the like; a blank where he did not know any words, had no memory and no conception of what was occurring.

"I don't know," he managed.

Zorga and Junior stared across the road at their five adversaries.

"What are they doing?" Zorga asked again.

"They're a bunch of cocky bastards," Junior said, "I think they're taunting us."

"That is not the Professor's way," Zorga told him.

"I don't think the old man is in charge of this group," Junior said and pointed at the bright light in the centre of the group.

"Why isn't he dead, Junior?" Zorga asked.

"I haven't really had much opportunity to do anything about him, Lord," Junior complained, "you have kept me rather busy with other matters."

"Hmm," Zorga said, not content with his aide's excuse.

"Can't we at least shout some abuse at them?" Danny asked. "You know, rile them a bit?"

"I shouldn't if I were you," Nutter advised.

"So, what then? Do we offer them a rumble down at the rec' at play-time?" Danny suggested, and received a harsh look from the others.

Cameron was lost in awe. He was here at the heart of it all; this was all Zorga – the demon, the hotel, and the entire city. He remembered his dream and could picture himself drowning in the eyes of his god.

"We've lost him," Penny told the others as she stared deeply into Cameron's vacuous expression. "There's no-one at home."

Her words filtered through; "There's no-one at home." Was it as simple as that? He could feel himself slowly drifting away from reality and he did not know how to stop it; what was left to hold on to? No mother, no Gillian – everyone he loved was slipping away from him – and now himself. Was he just giving up? Returning to his old self; the mortal Mortice who always curled up into a self-protecting foetal ball and allowed himself to be carried with the flow.

His senses slammed into a black, solid wall of bad.

"He looks like a demented guppy," Danny commented.

"They're coming," Cameron said and made everyone jump. "Their army is coming."

"Here?" Cassandra asked.

"I knew it, I bloody knew it," Penny moaned. "If we stood around doing flap all then they would draw in all their troops and jump on us."

"Let's do it then," Cameron said. "Now."

"Okay," Nutter said.

"Yeah!" Danny enthused.

"Erm," Penny said.

"Oh, shit," Cassandra affirmed.

"They are going to strike," Zorga said, as the five going crazy in Leeds advanced towards their position. "How long before we receive reinforcements?"

"About five minutes," Junior told him.

"Bugger," Zorga said.

"Be prepared for anything," Nutter said. "Zorga is a highly trained…"

"Shit sucker," Danny interrupted.

"'Killer', is what I was going to say," Nutter finished. "He complies to no rules of fighting."

"Is that a rule of his?" Danny asked.

"Daniel, your levity of these highly stressful situations may, on occasion, ease the tension," Nutter told him, "but currently it is beginning to somewhat exasperate my patience."

"Sorry," he mumbled.

"Zorga," Nutter continued, "is a vicious combatant who will use any form of weapon available; physical, mental and emotional."

"Your point being," Penny decided to surmise, "is 'be prepared for anything'."

"Exactly, Penelope."

Her eyes rose skyward and she gently shook her head with disdain.

Zorga turned and ran back into the hotel, closely followed by Junior.

"What devilish tactic is this?" Danny asked and looked to Nutter for advice.

"Er," he said.

"Did he just run away?" Cassandra enquired.

"Maybe this is one of his unscrupulous attacks," Danny suggested. "Him legging it back into the hotel is actually mentally destroying our confidence and -"

"Shut up, Danny," Cameron said, and he did.

They walked into the foyer, cautiously eyeing the surrounding decor. Danny whistled his appreciation of the plush interior and received an elbow in the ribs.

"That way," Cameron said and headed towards the bar and dining room. The others followed in silence, Penny shuddered as they passed the chair in which she had almost met her end. She saw the shattered bar stool that had been discarded and the upturned tables and chairs in the dining room; she worried about Gillian's state of existence.

"They're in there," Cameron pointed at the double hinged doors that led into the kitchens.

Zorga and Junior were standing in front of the huge freezer, waiting. They were watching the double-doors that led back to the dining area. Suddenly they flew off their hinges and clattered to the floor; Cameron stood in the entrance with a very mean expression on his face, behind him stood his four compatriots of various shades of mortality.

"This ends now," Cameron said.

Junior sniggered and bit his lips together to suppress his laughter.

Cameron was thrown slightly by this reaction and contemplated that this could be some kind of trap, so he reached out with his mind in an attempt to identify any other vampires in the vicinity. There were none close enough to prove any great threat at this present moment.

"Indeed it does end now," Zorga said, "but I believe it will be our story that features in the epilogue of this little adventure."

Junior lifted the lever to the door of the freezer and swung the door open; once again the frozen air poured over the floor and swirled around the feet of everyone there.

"I have a very bad feeling about this," Danny said as the five heroes peered into the gloom in front of them. "It's too dark in there."

"Oh, there you go again, Danny," Cassandra chided, "if there were any vampires in there then Cameron would have..." she thought she saw movement from within.

There was a slight shuffling, then a hellish scream, and a silvery, glistening body hurled itself from the freezer at the group of enemies of evil.

It struck Cameron with the force of a speeding Volvo and he was knocked backward into his allies, sending them flying to the floor of the dining room.

"I believe that is what you would call a strike," Zorga said.

"Quite so, Lord," Junior agreed, "ten points."

Cameron looked up at the face of his attacker; the ice covered vampire had a look of extreme worry on its face. He was just about to hit back when one of the demon's arms fell off its body. It looked somewhat distressed about this and became even more upset when it tumbled to the ground as one of its legs sheared off at the knee. Upon hitting the floor, its head snapped off and its torso split in two across its chest. It howled pathetically and its jaw dropped off. It seemed to emit a fizzing noise and then a light burst from it and poured into Junior causing him to reel for a second.

"What happened?" Zorga demanded.

"I don't understand," Junior replied with absolute honesty.

From the vision of a Hell frozen over, more shambling vampire ice pops emerged. One attempted to raise its arms to reach out for the fallen freedom fighters; both limbs fell off at the shoulders.

"You have got to be joking," Cameron said to the confused demons of darkness. He stood and punched the harmless, armless aggressor in the chest; it shattered into a thousand fragments and a burst of light.

Two more vampires that came from the freezer rubbed shoulders during their struggle to be the first to enter the fray and stuck to one another. As they tried to pull themselves free of each other one split in half from its shoulder down to its navel and the other stumbled sideways, losing a leg to the corner of a work surface and its head to a saucepan that hung from a rack from the ceiling.

"I don't think we gave them enough time to thaw out," Junior told his Master as another soldier of his frozen army came out, slipped on its frozen feet and shattered on the floor.

The five disorientated defenders of decency watched with amazement and slight disappointment as, one after another, Captain Birdseye's army of frozen feeders of blood emerged, made a menacing motion, then toppled to the ground in a tangle of frigid limbs. They shook their head and grimaced in embarrassment. They had not noticed that Zorga had legged it again.

***

Gillian had joined the ranks of a few other vampires that were mindlessly making their way back to their base. They paid her no attention and Gillian unconsciously returned the compliment; they meant nothing to her now. All that she was concerned with, and focusing on, was the heightening aroma of living flesh and the impending battle that she was being drawn to.

***

Danny was getting frustrated every time he attempted to stick one of his stakes in the chest of one of the fractured vampires that had not self-destructed, it just split apart even more.

"It's like trying to nail plates to the table," he complained.

"But you're getting the right result," Cassandra told him as another shaft of light erupted from his ministrations.

"But I want a stake to stick in their body," he said. "It seems a waste of time to have made all of these if none of them are actually going to skewer their hearts."

Cameron rubbed at his chest absent mindedly.

"I'm worrying about you again, Danny," Cassandra told

him.

Another burst of light and another expletive from Danny later. "That's all of them," he declared.

"Right then, let's get on with it," Cameron announced and they all marched back into the dining room to witness the first of the recalled vampires enter the hotel lobby.

"Shit," Cassandra said.

"Quite," Nutter agreed.

"What's the plan then?" Penny asked. "One for all and all of that?"

"Everyone for themselves, I think," Danny said.

"Hit hard, hit fast," Cameron said. "Hit first."

"Let's do it," Danny said and passed a few stakes out to Cassandra and Penny. Nutter unsheathed his sword and breathed heavily in anticipation.

The foyer had filled with undead.

"Deja vu anyone?" Danny asked.

"I'll try and take out as many as I can," Cameron said. "I think you lot should stay together and watch each other."

"I completely concur," Nutter said.

With the battle strategy decided Cameron lifted one of the circular dining tables nearby, turned its legs forward and propelled himself with it in front into the distending crowd of vampires, who then found themselves being liberally tossed aside without a second thought from their antagonist. A couple of them were dispensed with by a protruding table leg through the tit, a few more were stripped of various limbs, and a lot more were given severe fractures and busted innards.

The missile of man and mahogany slammed into the side wall of the foyer with a sickening crunch of wood and bone. Cameron turned to face his brothers of physicality but not flesh. The pathway he had created was closing in as the vampires regained their composure. The dead sea filled again and Cameron was cut off from his mortal mates but he did not worry for their safety, each of them, he knew, could look after themselves most admirably. If not themselves then at least each other. The first came to him within arm's length so Cameron lengthened his arm and smashed its face in.

The others worriedly briefly for Cameron's safety as they

watched the path closed around him but then, noticing the front line staring at them and grinning maliciously, they quickly concentrated on their own safety.

"I don't suppose you have any more grenades, Danny?" Cassandra asked.

"No," he admitted.

"Thank god for that," she sighed, and he shot her a hurt look.

"Yes," Nutter said, "at least we now have some semblance of a chance of getting through this with our lives."

Danny stared at him in amazement. "Was that a joke?" he asked.

"Quite possibly," Nutter replied.

The vampires advanced and Penny slipped her shoes off her feet, Nutter rolled his head around on his shoulders as if warming up for an aerobics class, Cassandra was muttering something under her breath and Danny looked as if he was about to fall asleep.

One approached within five metres. Nutter lunged forward and returned to his place so quickly that the vampire barely realised the metal blade had pierced a hole through its chest and out through its back. It erupted violently, causing its fellow aggressors to cower for a second before resuming their steady approach.

"It's the blood lust," Nutter commented. "All notions of personal safety become negligible when there is the possibility of feeding."

"Thanks for that," Danny said, and Cassandra's muttering started to become slightly louder and more coherent.

"Shitshitshitshitshitshitshitshit," she was saying.

"Stay loose, Cass," Penny said, and bounced lightly on her toes, preparing herself.

"Here we go," Danny announced.

"Oh, fucking shit," Cassandra said.

Penny went in first and delivered three lightning fast kicks to the left side of her nearest assailant's head; its neck cracked with each blow, finally dropping forward limply on the third. She leapt forward with a Ninja "Hah!" and plunged one of her stakes deep into its chest and removed it again with equal speed.

Another approached her from the side and she executed a round house kick to its face sending it flying across the tables. She flipped over the stake that she had used in her first victim so the point was directed down her arm, towards her body. She thrust the blunt end backward with both hands so that the tip travelled under her shoulder and into the stomach of the vampire that came at her from behind. *So predictable.* It doubled over and she grabbed it in a head-lock. Another came forward so she lifted herself into the air and kicked that one in the face with both feet, sending it back from whence it had come. She then allowed her body to drop to the floor with the vampire still tightly locked under her arm. They both hit the deck, she snapped its neck up ninety degrees and the stake in its stomach thrust up through its spine. She rolled over onto its back, pulled the stake out, flipped it around and returned it to its body just below its left shoulder blade.

She leapt to her feet brandishing a double pointed stake, stepped back out of the path of two vampires approaching from either side of her and stabbed both of them, alternately, with the one stake.

Nutter had charged at the group of vampires that came for him. He sank his blade through the chest of the first and continued advancing and so skewering another vampire that followed closely behind the first and a third behind that one. He withdrew his sword as each one exploded with its own individual display of pyrotechnics. He swung the foil out to his right, slicing it through the rib cage and heart of a vampire that was attempting to attack his flanks. He brought the blade back, facing front, and defaced the front of another eager feaster.

Danny and Cassandra watched the opening moves of the Father and Daughter tag team in awe and amazement.

"Check out Cynthia Rothrock and Zorro," Danny muttered, and felt slightly impotent upon noticing the squadron of vampires that had advanced on his position with him holding only a couple of sharpened sticks as his defence.

He laughed sheepishly.

Cassandra screamed and barged Danny out of her way as she ran forward and smashed a dining chair over the front vampire's head. It crumpled to the floor and she kicked it in the face with a great deal of force and pleasure. She knelt on its neck and brought one of the shattered spikes of chair down into its chest; it screamed and blew up.

Another loomed directly over her head. Danny tossed her a stake he was holding; she caught it neatly and rammed it upwards, straight into the vampire's body, just below the rib cage. It rose into the air, over Cassandra's crouched form then fell to the floor in front of Danny. He dropped to his knees, clutched the stake still protruding from its gut, and twisted it up under its rib cage and into its heart.

Cassandra swiped her right foot out in a tight circle knocking several attackers off their feet. She leapt into the air and brought a heel from one foot and then the other down into the bodies of two floor prone blood suckers whilst Danny jumped forward and delivered a fatal blow to another before it could come to its senses and get to its feet.

Danny's throat was clasped in a vice-like grip, he was lifted off the floor and brought face to face with imminent demise.

"Not again," Danny wheezed.

The vampire that had him in its clutches changed its expression from a victorious grin to pained confusion, and Danny noticed a silver tip gently ease its way through his captor's breast. He turned his head away as it disintegrated brightly and opened his eyes to see Nutter standing in front of him, blade thrust forward. Nutter turned and sent another demon on its way to the afterlife without fuss.

"I didn't even get a chance to thank him," Danny said. "Who was that masked man?"

"That was the 'Lone Ranger', Danny," Cassandra told him, "not Zorro."

"Oh yeah," he remembered, but this little nostalgic quote of popular fiction seemed to instil him with a burst of strength and courage.

"Come on then," he shouted. "You hell spawn of Janet Street Porter."

This seemed to confuse both the offensive and defensive teams.

"What?" Cassandra asked.

"You know? The teeth," Danny explained.

"But that's her front teeth, vampires have big canines," Cassandra told him.

"What about 'Nosferatu' then?" Danny begged to differ.

"That was a film, Danny," Cassandra replied, "you know, fiction?"

And with that, the battle resumed with neither side showing any sign of gaining an advantage. Nutter and Penny swiftly and effortlessly despatched their opponents and lent a helping hand to Cassandra and Danny every now and then. Cameron was not diminishing his enemies' numbers as such, just diminishing his enemies, limb by limb. But what the night breed lacked in strategy, teamwork and basic fighting ability, they made up for in there being a fuck off multitude of them.

STOP THIS! came a cry from the reception desk and both warring factions turned to see what Zorga's problem was. Danny took this moment of distraction as an opportunity to dispel another vampire. He thought he was being very sneaky and careful until the dispatched-one exploded with the most ferocity thus far.

Everyone turned to the scene of interruption and Danny grinned nervously.

"Nice one, Daniel," Nutter commended.

"This is absolute chaos," Zorga screamed. "It was never like this in the old days. You youngsters are undisciplined and untrained, you think you can win by sheer weight of numbers and have no sense of protection for your own existences."

Junior winced slightly at this statement.

"Enough," Zorga continued. "This will end now, as it began. You and I Professor, as it should be."

Nutter nodded to the challenge.

"No!" Penny yelled and ran to her father's side. "You can't beat him."

"But I have to try, Penelope," Nutter said to his daughter, holding her chin gently in the palm of his hand. He then turned to Zorga. "You. Outside. Now."

Nutter marched towards the front entrance. Perhaps Zorga had psychically eased the blood lust in his minions, or maybe they had enough sense of self preservation not to go against their creator's desires; whatever the reason, the vampires simply parted without a sound and allowed Nutter a path across the hotel foyer to the main entrance. Zorga lifted himself from the desk and drifted over their heads. They both stepped out of the hotel and down to the middle of the street. Vampires and mortals alike, followed suit, filing out into the street to claim a prime position to witness the ultimate battle.

Cameron rejoined his friends.

"He can't beat Zorga," Penny told him.

"It's all right," Cameron said, "I don't think he intends to."

"He is Ben Kenobi," Danny said and then remembered something. "Sorry Penny, I didn't mean that he's going to, you know, sacrifice himself so that -"

"Shut up, Danny," Cassandra told him.

The two timeless ones faced each other in the middle of the road.

"This is how it should end," Zorga said, "the two major pieces in a final, fatal confrontation."

"Yes," Nutter replied, but did not say it with conviction.

"Scared?" Zorga asked. "Recognising your own mortality at last?"

"Perhaps," he answered, and looked over to where Penny was standing, "but I think it has more to do with understanding a better reason for living."

"Hah!" Zorga laughed. "I do believe that you are getting old."

"Shut up and get on with it," Nutter told him and added, "shit sucker."

There came a triumphant cry of "YES!" from the surrounding crowd, which brought a smile to Nutter's face and a look of absolute fury to the face of Zorga.

Zorga charged at Nutter, screaming with anger as he rushed through the air, Nutter side-stepped lightly and flicked his sword deftly.

Zorga stopped as he flew past Nutter's position, turned and looked down at his chest; three neat slashes had been delivered to his shirt in the shape of a letter. Zorga looked up in bemusement.

"For 'Nutter'," Nutter told him and laughed.

"You have changed Professor," Zorga told him, "you do not

seem to adhere to the rules of honourable engagement any more."

"But you haven't even asked for my Father's blessing," Nutter said and laughter rippled through the audience.

"Do you truly believe that by making me angry you will defeat me?" Zorga asked.

"This time I will succeed," Nutter announced. "I have defeated a Prince before."

"'Defeated a Prince'?" Zorga roared with laughter. "I make Vlad look like a fucking mosquito. I made him. You don't want to fuck with me old man."

Zorga charged again, lifting Nutter effortlessly and tossing him through the window of a DIY shop opposite.

Cameron remembered something about surnames and turned to Penny. "He beat 'Vlad'? Wait a minute. He's not... I mean Nutter, your father, he isn't... is he?"

Penny shrugged. "He seems to think so, sometimes."

"Excuse me?" Danny interrupted. "Hadn't we better help out."

"When he's ready," Cameron told him.

"What is that supposed to mean?"

"Look to the wind, listen to the stars; there will you find the truth, Daniel," Cameron said.

"You already look like Nutter, now you're beginning to sound more like him every second," Danny said.

"Just call me 'Grasshopper'," Cameron countered.

She approached the crowd, flanked by a couple of dozen recalled vampires. They all wedged in tightly at the perimeter of the audience and tried to see what was happening; none of them appeared to be interested with the aroma of mortals except for Gillian, but now she could not move. She was getting more distressed at the noise of heart beats at their various tempos, and her hunger was beginning to really hurt.

She was getting angry.

Nutter dusted the glass from his body and shook his hair at the ground, loosening a fine shower of crystal rain from his silver mane; he tutted at the thought of having to find little shards in his pockets for months to come. He shook out his shoulders, sighed quickly and stepped back through the window (or rather the empty frame) on to the street.

"Shall we try that again?" he asked Zorga.

"My pleasure," Zorga replied, and charged again.

Nutter dropped his sword, picked up a five litre can of 'Dragon's Blood' gloss paint and swung it up in a high arc, letting go of the handle at the peak of the curve. The can continued up until it reached Zorga's head, at which point it stopped. Zorga continued his attack until his head came in contact with the paint can, at which point he sort of stopped – part of him stopped. His head stopped.

His body swung out in front, his arms still outstretched for his intended target. His legs began to circle upwards as if his head was now a stationary sun that the rest of his body must orbit, which it was doing until gravity remembered where it was and what its specific part in the proceedings was.

Zorga fell to the road with the can of paint still attached to his nose. The can split open and the bright red liquid contents exploded over his head and chest...

***

She saw the crimson flow forth and grimaced with the frustration of not being able to sate the pains in her head, stomach and heart. With a great deal of effort she managed to pull one arm above her head.

It was not hers.

The vampire next to her screamed in pain as it became detached from its limb. She rammed her elbow down onto the shoulder of the vampire in front of her, its collar bone cracked upon contact, but there was nothing it could do to retaliate because it was also packed in as tightly. She pushed down and lifted herself up enough to pull her other arm free; this was worse than that 'Carter' gig she had been to when she had needed to go to the toilet halfway through 'Sheriff Fatman'.

***

...He spluttered as the paint poured into his mouth and up his nose, vampires do not need to breathe but sometimes they forget this, and sometimes when they have the wind knocked out of them it is a natural reaction to try to suck some back in.

Nutter picked his sword up again, leapt forward and pinned himself onto Zorga's chest, the silver blade glinted in the moonlight as it was poised over Nutter's head, pointing downwards.

Zorga knew it was over.

No one had noticed the commotion taking place in the crowd to the side until now, a loud scream echoed along the street and sounded as if it was getting louder to Nutter's aural senses. It was actually getting closer.

Gillian slammed herself into Nutter lifting him off Zorga's body and sending him tumbling down the street and causing him to lose his sword in the process.

"Why Gillian," Zorga spluttered, "I knew you would see sense."

Gillian momentarily took this opportunity to kick Zorga in the face, the back of his skull cracked against the concrete. She did not really know why she had done it; something about the man upset her.

Now, where was she? Ah yes.

Nutter was reaching for his sword as she pounced on him. Pinning his shoulders to the floor with her hands, she hissed evilly at him.

"Gillian?" he stuttered and a moment of recognition passed over her twisted features. "It's me, Nutter, remember?"

If she did remember then she did not like the memory because she bared her teeth menacingly at him. His head seemed to shrink into his shoulders as he tried to hide as much of his neck as possible, as if he actually thought it would make any difference.

"Gillian?" Cameron said and she turned to identify this interruption. She looked up at him and seemed to regain some composure.

"Cam?" she whimpered.

"Get off him," he said softly.

"I can't," she replied.

"Please?" he asked and held out a hand to her.

She looked from Cameron's proffered hand to Nutter's scrunched neck – "Please?" Nutter whimpered – then back again.

"I can't," she repeated and lunged forward.

She did get off, perhaps not voluntarily, but she did get off him. Just as she bent for Nutter's throat, Cameron grabbed her by the back of her neck and lifted her into the air. She wriggled in his grip like an adult cat that had been grabbed by its scruff and was in for a damn good defleaing.

When they were about fifty feet in the air he stopped ascending and pulled her towards him. She clawed her nails across his face in anger but he did nothing to retaliate, he just looked into her eyes. She calmed slightly and the redness of her irises waned accordingly, but not completely. The three deep gouges in his cheek refilled with flesh.

"Help me," she muttered. "I can't control it."

"I don't know what to do," he replied.

"Do you love me?" she asked.

"You know..." he started.

"I mean *truly* love me?"

This threw him for a second. *I say I love her and she asks if I truly love her. What's that mean? I love her means I love her. How can I love her more than loving her?*

"You've got to kill me, Cam."

Ah.

"If you truly love me then you'll do it. There isn't any turning back from this, Cam. You don't know what I'm going through just trying to talk to you, something inside is telling me to rip your face off because I know that you're the enemy now."

Ah.

"Cam?"

"I..." he tried to think of the right words, "can't."

She bit her lip and closed her eyes from the disappointment, she buried her head into his chest.

"You don't understand what you're asking," he said, "I can't kill you because I do love you so much. If it was Danny asking then, like a shot, he'd be dead, but not you. There must be something we can do."

She re-opened her eyes, her bright red eyes.

Cameron felt his stomach open and swore later that something large, red and wobbly fell out of the hole.

He threw himself away from the pain and clutched at his gut, suddenly realising that his hands were unable to hold his insides in and the woman who had just excavated them both at once.

Gillian was a falling angel. She smiled gently at the thought of her demise, the release from her inner torment, then she hit the ground and the smile was removed rather swiftly from her face. She felt the back of her head cave in. The impact thrust her brain forward hard against her the inside of her forehead. Her teeth shattered and she bit through the end of her tongue. Her jaw snapped and crushed down into her throat. Both of her shoulder blades fractured into a thousand splinters and every vertebra shot out of place as her body twisted ninety degrees at the trunk. Her ribs folded in and punctured both lungs and all of her limbs fractured in a multitude of places and splayed awkwardly from her body.

"Arrw," she groaned.

Cameron scanned the floor around him as he landed, searching desperately for something that he was sure had fallen from his stomach. Unsuccessful, he healed himself and dashed to Gillian's side.

"Shit, shit, shit."

The others came over and stared in horror at their broken friend.

"You lot should get back," Cameron told them.

"Yeah right," Danny said. "What is she supposed to do no-."

There was the sound of multiple bones straightening and fixing themselves, the muffled noise of burst organs returning to their intended shape, kind of like, 'C-C-C-C-LACKSHLP'.

Then Gillian was gone. Danny's sentence had not been finished but it looked like he was about to be.

"Why's this always happen to me?" Danny protested.

She pulled his head sideways and lunged her mouth into his neck. She closed her eyes in rapture as her teeth punctured skin, bit deep into flesh and she heard the moan of pain. That struck her as a bit odd – a moan of pain and not a scream of agony? She sucked furiously at the flesh but no warm metallic liquid came forth, so she bit harder. It was then that she opened her eyes and saw Cameron standing in front of her with his arm firmly locked in her mouth. His jaw was clenched shut as he endured the pain that she was inflicting upon him.

"Finished?" he asked, and she withdrew. "I told you I wasn't going to be able to kill you, Gillian, but that didn't mean I was going to allow you to kill someone else."

"YOU'RE FUCKING PATHETIC," she howled at him. "ARE YOU GOING TO KEEP ME LOCKED IN A CAGE FOR THE REST OF OUR EXISTENCES?"

"No," he replied and pulled her into his body. "I know now, I truly love you." he whispered in her ear.

The redness emptied from her eyes, her canines retreated into the top of her mouth. She inhaled sharply and blinked rapidly as shock and realisation sank in. Then she smiled.

"I knew that you would," she sighed and closed her eyes.

He lowered her body gently to the floor and looked guiltily at his comrades who all looked in abject horror at the stake that protruded from her chest.

"Oh, my god," Cassandra gasped and threw herself at Danny's body; he wrapped his arms tightly around her.

Penny's mouth was hanging open. *Any second now,* Cameron thought.

Nutter gave him a solitary nod of approval.

The tears welled in Cameron's eyes and he looked down at his lover's body; someone was going to pay for this, with interest.

"Why didn't she burst?" Junior asked of his paint splattered Master.

"She was the light," Zorga replied, "it has nowhere to go. It was where it was and where it would remain."

They noticed Cameron staring at them. "I want to kill you two so badly," he shouted.

"I do not suppose that he means he is going to make a bad job of killing us, does he?" Zorga asked.

"No," Junior replied.

"This is a final battle between the two major pieces of this game," Zorga told Cameron, and looked to Nutter for confirmation.

"I think this pawn," Nutter indicated Cameron, "has just been queened."

Cameron shot a hurt look at Nutter. "I may be a bit camp, but that's going too far."

"Are you telling me...?" Zorga shouted at Nutter.

"I've been substituted," Nutter said.

"The next batter's been called to the plate," Cameron reiterated.

"You can't do that," Zorga complained. "This is *our* fight."

"I can't be arsed any more," Nutter said. "This has gone on for too long, I'm old and very tired. I resign."

"You can't," Zorga ordered.

"Can too," Nutter said.

Zorga turned his attention back to Cameron who was looking decidedly pissed off.

"You dancing?" Cameron asked.

"What?" Zorga demanded with a whole bundle of mixed up emotions; anger, confusion, frustration, and a bit of 'I don't want to go to bed yet, mum'.

"Oh shit," Junior said.

Cameron did not rush, did not charge headlong into the pair of them, he simply stepped over the dead undead body of his girlfriend and walked over to them. Zorga diffused himself into a cloud of blackness that swirled away leaving Junior to face the ominous approach of Cameron. The red paint that had been on Zorga 'slapped' to the floor.

"Ever dance with the devil in the pale moonlight?" Cameron asked.

"I did have to massage his feet once," Junior replied and Cameron hit him.

The surrounding crowd erupted into two parts. Firstly there were those standing directly behind Junior who erupted as he piled straight through them due to the physics of Cameron's assault. The second eruption was perhaps because of this or perhaps because Zorga was no longer present and maybe he was no longer holding his army at bay. It could have been that they just got fed up with waiting. Whatever the reason, the gates of hell seemed to give way and the battle for the mortals' circulatory system resumed.

"Shit," they said and started running down the road, away from the swarm.

The hungry hordes of hell dashed past Cameron as he salmoned his way against the current to the stunned body of Junior.

Junior watched him approach again, this time through bleary eyes. "Wait," he puffed, "let me explain something."

Cameron did not stop to listen, instead he kicked Junior in the crotch which hurtled him another two-hundred yards up the road. Cameron continued in his calm, determined progression.

"It doesn't have to be like this," Junior shouted at Cameron and strained his testicles out of his body, back into their appointed place. "We can help each other."

Cameron picked him up by his leg and threw him against a lamp post, the top half of the street light buckled forward from the impact, smashing its head on the road.

"You owe me," Junior shouted.

"And I'm paying you back," Cameron told him and raised his fist above his head in preparation for a fuck-off hard punch.

"For the guns I mean," Junior yelled and brought his hands up to his face in defence.

Cameron paused. "What?"

Junior lowered his arms. "You'd all be dead if it wasn't for me, I put that lorry of guns there for you to find."

"How did you know that I would find it?" Cameron asked.

"I put someone there to call to you," Junior told him.

"Why? Why did you save us?"

"Because I want Zorga out of the way," Junior said, standing up. "I want to take over."

Cameron looked confused.

"He's old, useless. He doesn't know how to run this organisation, I do. You wiped out his entire army when they attacked; his personal army. He has no acquisitions left except through me, and they're all personal, expendable quick profit accumulators."

"What about Gillian?" Cameron demanded.

"Very unfortunate," he replied slightly too bluntly

considering his predicament, but Cameron let it pass for now. "I couldn't show him that I was up to anything, I had to keep him distracted."

Cameron seemed to think about this for a moment.

"We can get rid of him together," Junior said. "It would be a lot easier than one on one."

"And what about you, afterwards?" Cameron asked.

"You understand our situation, don't you?" Junior asked. "We are natural, we're like lions, or sharks, we exist."

"Lions and sharks aren't evil," Cameron told him.

"I'm not evil either, but he is. That's why when I become top dog, things will be run differently. We'll become like another species of life or something. Everyone will know about us; David Attenborough will do a 'Life on Earth' special. Something can be sorted out."

"This is getting ridiculous," Danny commented as he punched another vampire in the face when it came a bit too close to the fleeing mortals.

Nutter deftly evaded the clutches of another as it leapt forward for a rugby tackle.

"I don't think I can run much more," Cassandra gasped; she had already discarded her shoes and was holding on to her breasts as she legged it along the street.

"We can hardly stop and make a stand now," Penny stated as she looked over her shoulder at the street full of undead that were sprinting after them.

If the vampires had been slightly more intelligent then the four heroes would have been ripped to pieces by now, but they were reacting purely on some selfish instinct. Each one wanted a taste and so they were fighting and tripping over each other in their desperate attempt to fill their yearning bodies with the liquid of life.

Nutter squinted at the road ahead and a smile spread across his face. "I think it's time to stop and make a stand." He pointed ahead at the dark green lorry that lay abandoned at the side of the road.

"I don't understand," Penny puffed.

"It's an army lorry," Cassandra said and then groaned. "Oh

no, not again."

"Cool," Danny enthused, and pumped his legs faster, breaking away from his friends to get the first dibs on whatever was stored inside.

He dived into the back of the lorry to discover nothing; it was empty. He charged forward into the cab as the others climbed into the back and saw that the keys were still in the ignition.

"This'll have to do for now," he muttered and ignored the cries of panic and frustration from the passengers in the back.

He turned the key and the engine roared to life; he floored the clutch, forced the gear stick into place, ...

"Why is he taking so long?" Nutter asked.

"He's still taking lessons," Cassandra told him.

...he listened for the balance point in the engine's noise and eased his foot off the clutch whilst pressing down on the accelerator.

The vampires were at the back of the lorry.

His foot slipped and the lorry lurched backwards, ploughing into the unfortunate group who thought they were going to get the best pieces; they merely ate spinning rubber.

"Shit," Danny spat and Cassandra moved forward to sit next to him and turned the headlights on.

"Put your foot on the clutch," she said softly and he did, "put the gear stick into neutral," he did, "now into first," she said slightly more forcefully and he did.

"Push down onto the accelerator and ease off the clutch."

Penny screamed from the back as a vampire clambered into the lorry, which gently moved forward.

"Ease off the clutch," Cassandra urged, and the lorry moved a bit faster. A vampire slammed itself against her door. "Take your foot off the fucking clutch!" she screamed and the lorry jerked forward twice, the engine spluttered.

"Footbackontheclutch," she yelled and the engine resumed a more even rumble.

The vampires that had mounted the lorry had been thrown clear when the lorry had kangarooed, but now others were replacing those who had been shaken off. Nutter and Penny were fending them off from the back as best as they could considering they did not have any weapons.

The lorry picked up speed. "Now foot on the clutch," the engine whined desperately, "off the accelerator, move up to second gear, foot off the clutch and ease on to the accelerator."

The lorry was approaching twenty-five miles per hour and was breaking away from the mass of vampires, but some were still crawling over the outside of it.

"In a couple of minutes we'll be taking that turning on the right, just beyond the traffic lights, see it?"

"Uh huh," Danny confirmed.

"Don't slow down, don't look in the mirror, don't indicate."

"Gotcha."

The lorry travelled around the corner, gently clipping the kerb and shaking all the passengers.

"Foot on the clutch, off the accelerator and move up into third."

"I'm not sure if I'm ready for this," Danny said.

"You've got to do it at some time Danny," Cassandra told him. "The examiners won't let you drive around the town and *not* expect you to go into third."

The engine whined, slowed, the gear box crunched in protestation, then it picked up again and accelerated.

"Good," Cassandra praised and Danny smiled. She looked in the side mirror at the mass of chasing darkness that was getting more distant by the second; she noticed something else.

"You see that lamp post on the left?" she asked him.

"Uh huh."

"I want you to drive as close to it as possible."

"Okay," he replied and steered the vehicle closer to the kerb.

The vampire that was hanging on to the side of the lorry edged its way on to Cassandra's door at which point she pushed it open. Both vampire and door were torn from the lorry as they collided with the lamp post that the truck raced past with mere inches to spare, she poked her head out of the cab to inspect her handiwork, as a movement in her peripheral vision caught her eye.

"Emergency stop," she yelled and Danny instinctively slammed his feet on to the brake and clutch. The backs of their seats thudded as Penny and Nutter experienced, first hand, the full force of Newton's laws on the conservation of momentum. The lorry screeched to a halt and half-a-dozen vampires that had been travelling on the roof flew further down the street. The pursuing mob began to catch up again.

"First-gear-foot-off-brake-onto-accelerator-ease-off-clutch," she ordered and the lorry started off again.

"Foot-on-clutch-second-gear."

The lorry jolted as they drove over the scattered bodies in front of them.

"Third-gear."

The gear box crunched slightly but otherwise they accelerated steadily.

"Fourth-gear."

The lorry went faster.

Nutter stuck his head forward. "I think we're clear."

"Hadn't we better get back for Cameron?" Danny asked.

"That means turning 'round though," Cassandra said.

"Right," Danny said.

"I think we're still a few lessons short of a three point turn," Cassandra informed him without attempting to hide her sarcasm.

He lifted his foot from the accelerator, pushed both onto the clutch and brake whilst lifting the handbrake and turning the steering wheel.

"Oh bloody hell," Cassandra said as the world span.

Cameron shook his head to clear the fog, he saw Junior standing over him still holding the smashed light from the lamp post.

"You stupid, stupid son-of-a-bitch," Junior said.

"At least I'm not an ugly, stupid son-of-a-bitch," Cameron replied and received another wallop across his face from the light head.

"I mean, you really actually considered it didn't you?" Junior laughed. "You really thought that we would team up and kill Zorga didn't you? What made you think that I'd want you around when I'm in charge, I'm not going to want anyone alive who might get in my way."

"I found the prospect of a 'Wildlife on One' study of your

sex life an interesting idea," Cameron said. "And this week," he did in his best David Attenborough impression.

"You're outrageous," Junior laughed.

"We discover a new species of human,"

"You just can't stop yourself, can you?" Junior laughed louder.

"That is so spineless it can actually fuck itself."

Junior stopped laughing and lifted the light again. "Even when you're on the brink of painful and inevitable death, you just can't stop mouthing off."

"I've always found it to be the perfect distraction," Cameron said and threw himself into Junior, lifted him from the ground and carried him flying backwards.

The lamp post came as quite a surprise to Junior as it ripped through his back and out of his chest. He was almost as surprised to realise that Cameron had not let go and was still pushing him along the pole even though the metal had penetrated Cameron's chest and was plunging out of his back.

Eventually they stopped moving and the pair of them dangled on the pole. Junior looked down at the metal that protruded through his body. He started laughing.

"You missed," he gasped, "it went through my right side. You missed my heart. My right and," he laughed even louder, "your left, your heart." He then looked up into Cameron's undying face.

"How?" Junior asked.

"Apparently I'm a very crap vampire," Cameron replied through gritted teeth then leaned forward to rip Junior's arms from their sockets. He then gripped the lamp post in front of him and pushed himself backwards, easing himself gently from the pole. He collapsed on the floor and waited until his spine had fixed itself, at which point he stood, walked over to the left side of the dangling Junior and ripped the stumps that were already growing from his shoulders. Junior screamed.

The darkness around them coalesced at the end of the broken lamp post; it gathered to form Zorga. Junior smiled, Cameron just admired the special effect and wondered how he did it.

"Hello," Zorga said to the two young men.

"Hi," Cameron replied.

"Lord?" Junior said and indicated his predicament on the pole avec no arms.

"Yes, I see," Zorga said. "I also heard. Everything."

Cameron smiled.

"I only said those things to throw him off guard, Lord," Junior explained.

"I see," Zorga said, "so even when you had him at your mercy, you were still throwing him off guard were you?"

"Er," Junior said.

"You've been sussed, mate," Cameron commented and leant on his shoulder, pushing Junior across the pole.

Junior gasped as the edge of the metal neared his heart, he looked to Zorga for help.

"Dear boy," Zorga said, "you assisted me in destroying the love of his life; the rules of engagement state that I must allow him to have his retribution."

Cameron leaned against Junior slightly harder and bones cracked. "Does that include my retribution with you?" He did not really know the word but hoped that it worked in the way he used it.

"You can try, of course," Zorga said.

"Right oh, then," Cameron said, stood upright and rubbed his hands together. He took a step forward then paused. "I nearly forgot." He stepped back to Junior's side. "Bye," he said and pushed so Junior's body crunched all the way across the pole, mashing his heart.

Junior screamed in ultimate agony, betrayal and frustration; he had been given everything and it was all being taken from him. He really wished he could -

He did not finish that thought.

Zorga prepared himself for the light that exploded from Junior's dying body but Cameron stepped forward into the path of the light and accepted the lot.

"Oh I'm sorry," Cameron said, looking into the irate face of death, "was that yours?"

"You dare...?" Zorga roared.

"You'd better come and get it then," Cameron said and then shot into the air singing 'The girl from Ipenema' for a reason that completely eluded him at that moment.

The lorry slew around the corner and rose up on to two wheels as the vehicle tried to attain take off-velocity whilst gravity and driver tried to keep it on the floor (the driver being the only part of that partnership that really wanted it to stay on its wheels, gravity did not give a monkey's which way up it stayed on the floor, just as long as it stayed there).

Seconds after clearing the corner and tearing down the road, a motley group of vampires ran after the lorry, except for those that limped, hopped and crawled.

If you looked closely at the lorry as it passed you might have noticed a few bits of body stuck in the radiator.

"BRAKE!" Cassandra screamed and Danny slammed both feet onto the appropriate pedals.

The wheels locked and screeched down the road. Eventually it stopped.

"Why the urgency?" Danny demanded.

"You nearly went over Gillian's body," Cassandra panted.

Danny leapt out of the cab and ran to the front of the vehicle; Gillian's body was still lying there, her head was resting against the front wheel. He reached over her and gingerly pulled the stake from her chest, he figured that they would need something to try to fight off the ensuing attackers.

"What's that?" he heard Cassandra ask from the back of the lorry.

"Shhh," came the reply.

Danny ran to the back to see Nutter passing a large box from the lorry down to Penny.

"What's that?" he asked and made everybody else jump.

"It fell from one of the overhead racks," Nutter said and Danny's eyes lit up.

"You mean it's a gun?" he asked, dropped the now-pathetic-in-comparison-stake and stepped forward to take the wooden crate but was intercepted by Penny.

"No," she said, "it's not a gun and you can't have it."

"What is it?" he asked again with hands twitching in anticipation.

"I believe that it is called a 'bazooka'," Nutter told him and

Cassandra groaned.

"Oh, wow," Danny gasped. "Please let me use it."

"No," Cassandra said. "You're too dangerous."

"Yeah, well, I bet none of you lot know how to use it," he said, and they looked at each other hoping that someone would say, "Well, actually..." No one did.

"That settles it," he said and grabbed the box.

"Do you then?" Penny asked.

"I've seen films," he said.

"And I'm sure that these films told you exactly how to use one did they?" she enquired.

"It depends on what type it is," he mumbled. "They showed you how to use one on 'Beverly Hills Cop 2' and 'Falling Down' as well. It's easy."

The other three looked at each other then noticed the alarming closeness of their pursuers. They handed the crate over and he 'whooped' with joy as he ripped the top of the box off. He lifted out the half-metre long grey metal tube with the care of removing a baby from its first bath. He flipped it over and inspected the buttons and switches. One caused the tube to extend sharply, a sighting flipped out from the casing then a handle flipped down. Danny lifted it to his shoulder and aimed it at the closing mob; the three humans dashed around behind him.

"Are you sure that you're aiming the right end?" Cassandra asked.

"Er," Danny said, and the three humans dashed to the side of him, at the opposite shoulder.

"Well, it should be this button here," Danny said, and pressed it.

There was a sudden whoosh as the rocket burst from the aimed end. "All right!" Danny exclaimed as the missile sailed into the approaching crowd.

The ground shook, shop windows imploded, the noise was deafening, especially if you were at the receiving end of it.

The mini-mushroom swept up into the air and bits of flaming bodies rained down.

"Dan, Dan; the man who can," Danny shouted.

"And the man who invariably does," Nutter mumbled under his breath.

They all looked up as the smoke drifted into the sky, it was then that they noticed the area of dense blackness that hung in the air.

"Danny?" Cassandra asked.

"It's just black."

And Cameron was surrounded by it. It probably would have suffocated him if he thought it necessary to breathe. It was doing something very painful to him, it was pressing in all over, trying to squeeze the dead life from his body.

AT THE END OF EVERYTHING IS DARKNESS, CAMERON, Zorga said from everywhere. THERE IS NO PLACE THAT IT DOESN'T TOUCH, EVEN ON THE SUN ITSELF ARE PATCHES OF DARKNESS.

Cameron strained against the pressure. "Yeah well, light is... better," he pathetically strained against Zorga's argument and Zorga laughed loudly.

EVEN YOU KNOW THAT IT IS TRUE. DARKNESS ALWAYS PREVAILS.

"Yeah... well," he groaned, "you're a wanker." In the face of defeat, a childish insult always prevails.

Cameron felt the darkness close in even harder. "Shit sucker," he added for a laugh.

The pressure increased further and Cameron pushed out with everything he had.

The blackness became awash with light and a body fell from the sky into the pack of regrouping, rehealing hunters. They clambered around the fallen form.

"Who was it?" Penny asked. "I couldn't see properly."

"It was black," Danny said.

"They were both wearing black, Danny," Cassandra said and then remembered. "You mean...?"

"Yeah, that's Cameron coming down here."

As the descending body came closer they saw that it was Cameron, slightly flustered, slightly thinner, but Cameron none-the-less.

"You okay?" Penny asked.

Cameron strained and his body inflated to its normal dimensions. "I am now," he replied.

"Is it over?" Cassandra asked.

"You're joking right?" Cameron enquired and she shook her head. "No, not yet," he said.

There came a low roar of anger from the diminished army of darkness and Zorga rose from their midst.

THAT'S IT, he screamed, NOW I'M REALLY PISSED. And they all charged.

"Oh great," Penny groaned, "that's really done it."

"I think she may be right," Nutter professed.

"More than she really knows," Cameron agreed and picked up the discarded stake. He threw it at the rapidly approaching Zorga who caught it easily at the point before it entered his body. He laughed his defiance loudly and accelerated his army forward.

They were on them.

Cameron snatched the bazooka from Danny's grasp, deftly side-stepped from Zorga's path and swung the weapon at the stake that the speeding demon still held at his breast, point inwards.

The end of the bazooka struck the blunt end of the stake and it ripped through Zorga's breast plate, heart, then back.

Zorga continued forward, his troops stopped in their tracks as they all felt his pain, the stake continued on its trajectory from Zorga's body and penetrated one of the attackers that now stood motionless behind.

Zorga stopped and turned to look at the mortals and undead alike. He then looked down at the gaping hole in his chest.

"What happens now?" one of the vampires nearest Cameron asked.

Cameron turned to it and raised an eyebrow. "Well, you know what happens when 'Bagpuss' goes to sleep."

"All his friends go to sleep," it answered and Cameron nodded.

"I think we had better leave," Nutter announced and the others agreed by lifting their legs and sprinting away from the scene.

"I'll wait here," Cameron said to their backs, "just to make sure." But they never heard.

Zorga screamed loudly, a scream for every death he had ever caused. He clutched at the hole in his chest and wondered if he could repair his heart but knew that this was the end, the liquidation of all assets.

As the vampires that surrounded Cameron began to convulse and groan in pain, he became unsure as to whether staying put had been a good idea. He decided that it definitely was not a good idea when the undead next to him exploded dramatically and its light rushed past him.

"Yep, I think that that's fairly conclusive. Wait for me," Cameron yelled to anyone that might care to listen and began running.

One after another, the vampires of the city of Leeds exploded with extreme ferocity. Cameron held his hands up to his face, warding off the onslaught of flesh and bone, he noticed bodies of light entering the street from far over the horizon.

The last four mortals looked back when they had decided that they were a safe distance away; the end of the street was blindingly bright; only Danny, with sunglasses, was able to stare at the super nova without straining his eyes too much.

"Here comes Cameron," he announced and they slowly made out his silhouetted form sprinting out of the wash of whiteness.

He ran up to their position and stopped next to Danny. "I wish I'd brought my camera," Cameron said.

"Cool," Danny commended and patted his friend on his shoulder.

"I have a very bad feeling about this," Nutter said.

"It's too big to be a -" Danny started but then got the same feeling.

"Why are all the lights focusing on that one spot?" Penny asked. "Surely they should be flying off in every direction."

The glare was dying, shrinking, withdrawing to a single point that at first looked like a six foot column, then became humanoid in shape; very Zorga-esque in fact.

"Fuckinghellshitfire," Cassandra surmised.

"I really thought that that was it," Cameron said. "What happened?"

"I would presume," Nutter started.

"Save it for after," Cameron told him and marched back to the spot he had just evacuated.

"I'd like to know," Cassandra told Nutter as Cameron strode away.

"I think that Zorga has just recalled the power that was stored in every vampire he had created in an attempt to heal the wound that Cameron had caused."

"And he succeeded," Penny said.

"It appears so, doesn't it," Nutter mused.

Zorga stood there smiling at the approaching form of Cameron.

"You just won't let it rest, will you?" Cameron asked.

"I should thank you," Zorga said, ignoring Cameron's protestations.

This threw Cameron for a second. "Eh?"

"I've never recalled all of my investments before because it always seemed like wasting all of the time that was spent investing in all of them. Life, or should I say death, has been getting very boring and I desperately needed something to brighten it up. At first I thought a bit of death and destruction would do the trick, then yourself and your lovely woman came along and livened the place up for a bit, but not so much that I had never seen before."

Cameron's eyebrows shot up in surprise.

"What? Did you believe that you were the first to be born through love and not lust? How very short-sighted of you.

"Do you know what you have done for me?" Zorga asked and Cameron shook his head. "You've given me a clean slate to work from. I don't have to adhere to any more rules, I don't have thousands of mindless undead following me around day and night, I don't have any," he thought for the right words and looked at Cameron, identifying it straight away, "responsibilities. You know what that's like don't you? Doing whatever you like, not giving a shit about anyone but yourself. You remind me very much of myself, when I first came to the world."

"I'm nothing like you," Cameron spat in defiance.

"Oh but you are," Zorga retorted. "I recall glorying in the

excitement of being a superman for a couple of decades before it started to be as exciting as putting my socks on in the morning.

"How long do you believe that you can act all high and mighty, defender of the Earth, before it all becomes rather dull and uninteresting for you too? What do you do when all of your enemies are defeated and all who are left are you and the mortals? How many times do you think you will get upset when you see another friend die and know that you could have kept them alive for eternity as well? How many times will you allow yourself to fall in love before it all becomes too painful and you have to make yourself immune to it all? How long before you start using people? Start getting into relationships that you know will never last, that no excess of emotion will be spent on that person. Start getting into relationships that are no longer driven by love but purely driven by lust.

"That's when you enter my world; it only takes one taste. It only takes one thought of 'if she was just like me, we could live together forever'. Can you deter that temptation for all eternity?"

In the face of arrogance...

Cameron hit him.

"I nearly felt that," Zorga said.

"Shit," Cameron deduced.

"There's nothing personal about all of this any more," Zorga told him and rose into the air, "but it really does have to be a completely clean slate."

The sudden gale caught Cameron off guard and he stumbled backwards slightly, but then he gritted his teeth and pushed himself against the rising tornado. It felt like his flesh was being ripped from his bones, bits of tarmac had been drawn into the wind and were gradually sand-blasting his skin away. He shielded his eyes from the onslaught with one arm, he reached out with the other, trying to find Zorga to pull out some of his major organs, but all he could feel was the twister that increased its intensity around him. That struck him as a bit odd; he could actually feel the wind around him as if it were a tangible, pliable object; he grabbed it.

With every action there is an equal and opposite reaction. Zorga had produced this raging twister by constantly accelerating the wind in a tight circle around Cameron. Now that

Cameron had discovered this ability to move and control the very air around him, he did so. The tornado stopped and what Zorga had been pushing around suddenly pushed him back, he flew dramatically off as if he were a hockey puck shortly after 'hockey three' had been called. He slammed into a wall and stuck there, groaning lightly.

Cameron pulled a shard of glass out of his cheek and shook the gravel from his hair. "Let's give the special effects people a rest, huh?" he suggested to the firmly embedded Zorga.

Zorga pulled himself free of the brickwork that had moulded around him and floated down to the ground. "Do you want the first hit?" he asked Cameron.

"After you, I insist," Cameron replied and Zorga hit him.

What glass that had escaped destruction from the earlier explosion shattered now as Zorga's fist created a sonic boom of Concorde proportions against Cameron's face.

Cameron nodded politely to Danny as he jogged back up the road, returning to where Zorga had just sent him hurtling.

"Always take the first hit," Danny advised him.

"Yeah, cheers, pal," Cameron replied and popped his nose out of his face.

Zorga was waiting patiently for Cameron's return with his arms folded across his chest. "Your tur-"

When reality seeped back into Zorga's consciousness, he assumed that he had been kicked into orbit. He was suspended in mid-air without any wilful effort on his, part, then he realised Cameron was holding him up by the throat.

"Glack," Zorga said, and Cameron dive-bombed the ground below, with Zorga's head outstretched in front.

The four mortals struggled to stay on their feet as the ground shook beneath them from the two vampires' impact. A gentle hail of hot concrete rained down around them as they peered into the gloomy crater in the middle of the road. They heard movement, then saw a body fly out of the hole towards them.

Cameron fell to the ground a few feet away from their position and groaned. "I don't think I can beat him," he mumbled.

Zorga arose from the depths and stepped onto the road.

"We need some heavy artillery again," Danny said and Penny and Nutter looked at each other.

"Well, actually," Nutter said, "there was this but we didn't want Danny to know."

Nutter pulled his hand from his pocket and showed that he was holding a dark metallic egg the size of his palm.

"Holding out on me, huh?" Danny questioned and reached to take the grenade, Cameron held him back.

"When I say," he said.

He fired his body at Zorga again wrapping his left arm around Zorga's head and grabbing his jaw with his right hand; they lifted once more into the air.

Zorga growled with annoyance and struggled with wild confusion as they soared higher. Cameron pulled his left arm up and right hand down; Zorga's mouth snapped open wider than should be physically possible unless you were one of those lizard aliens from 'V'. Zorga howled in pain as his mandible snapped loudly in his ears.

"Now," Cameron yelled at the ground and came to an unpleasant conclusion that he was very high in the air.

"I couldn't possibly throw it that high," Nutter told the youths around him so Danny snatched the bomb from his hand, pulled the pin out and stretched his body as low to the ground as he could.

Cameron felt Zorga's mouth tighten as muscles and bones tried to fix themselves, he strained to keep the two sets of teeth firmly separated.

Danny threw his body up as hard as he could and the grenade flew up towards the distant figures. "It's going to make it," he said.

"Why don't you give it up?" Cameron asked the struggling Zorga. "It must have been like this when you took over. Why can't you just accept that it's over? Out with the old and all that."

"Gare has owngly egger geen ge," was Zorga's reply and Cameron almost felt sorry for him until he saw the grenade cease in its ascent towards him and hang in the air, inches from his grasp.

"Shit," Cameron said.

"Shit," Cassandra said.

"It's coming back down," Penny said.

"Run?" Danny suggested.

Once again, Cameron angled himself into a dive and made him and his captive tear headfirst towards the ground in an attempt to catch the metal globe of mass destruction. They caught up with it and Cameron moved his left hand to hold Zorga's jaw open and reached out to the grenade with his now, free right hand. He grabbed it and rammed it towards Zorga's tightening mouth but it fumbled in his hand and he just managed to thrust it up Zorga's nose and split one of his nostrils with it.

They both hit the floor a millisecond later, Cameron felt his right collar bone shatter, his neck snapped painfully and his hips jarred out of their sockets; he lay there, broken on the ground without the energy or inclination to fix himself. It seemed to him that he had failed. He heard the muffled pop from Zorga's head as tendons and muscles pulled his jaw bones back together. Oh yeah, the grenade would go off of course, and it might even rip a nasty wound in Zorga but he doubted that it would kill him.

Zorga started chuckling at what Cameron presumed was the victory that he was about to enjoy; he had failed Gillian, Nutter and the others, his parents, himself and now, possibly, the entire human race; that was not too much of a burden to carry, was it?

Zorga stood up and turned to Cameron. His hands were pulling at his mouth and Cameron saw that the grenade was firmly jammed in it. Obviously as Zorga had hit the ground face first, the grenade had been pushed through his top set of teeth, which were currently returning to their proper shape and entrapping the bomb firmly in place.

"Ooo ung," Zorga said.

Cameron decided that a good strategy now would be to fix all his broken bits – pop, pop, pop – and get safely outside of the imminent blast radius.

His legs pumped furiously as the grenade exploded over his shoulder and on the shoulders of his enemy. He rejoined his friends, and only when he saw the looks of abject disgust and horror on their faces did he turn to witness the scene behind him; Zorga's torso and legs were staggering awkwardly in the road, light poured from the hole in the top of his body. His arms that had been blown away were already regrowing from their shoulder sockets, somewhat slowly, but definitely growing. The light that leaked from the middle of his shoulders was only coming out in spurts as skin and bone enclosed the wound but got torn away again from the sheer pressure of Zorga's death.

"Is he trying to make his head?" Cameron asked.

"It seems so," Nutter confirmed.

"Can he do it?" Cassandra enquired.

"I've never seen it done before," Nutter confessed, "but then again most of everything that has happened today has been firmly outside of my field of experience."

The arms had ceased to grow and seemed to be faltering as stumps at the elbow, the light was erupting in shorter bursts as a head-shaped bubble of skin kept inflating from his shoulders, bursting and deflating, then growing again.

"Shouldn't we do something?" Danny asked.

"We don't have anything to do 'something' with," Penny reminded him.

"That's what I thought last time," Danny said and threw a look of betrayal at Nutter who just shrugged his shoulders and kept his attention fixed on the scene ahead.

Zorga, with whatever was left of his senses, his consciousness or instincts of survival, was transferring the growth of his arms to the more immediately desperate areas. His limbs were shrinking and his head was becoming more solid and head-like. His eyes burned red hatred at the five champions of evil every time that his face inflated to a state at which they could stare out at; his mouth was set in a grimace of ultimate concentration. Then it all burst again with another spurt of light, collapsed in on itself and started the cycle once more but becoming more solid with each attempt.

"It's just like watching a continuously exploding zit, isn't it," Danny observed.

Zorga's head was completed, the top of his skull would just split for a fraction of a second before sealing itself again, then, at last, it was solid and Zorga laughed with triumph and with genuine joy. Only at that last desperate moment – so close to absolute death – did he realise how much he really wanted to live. The struggle was over and he had defeated oblivion again;

it was like a rebirth; a chance to begin enjoying the beauties of existence again. But first he had to rip his enemies' arms from their shoulders and drink their blood through their open eye sockets.

Zorga stopped laughing and looked up at Cameron's knees and the other three pairs of legs that approached him. He looked down at the concrete that his neck was resting on.

"I suppose you must be the 'head' vampire?" Cameron asked.

"No!" Zorga screamed in defiance and shook with anger. He rolled over onto his ear and attempted to bite the nearest foot to him.

"How the mighty have fallen," Cassandra said.

"I will reheal and return to rip the hearts from your chests," Zorga announced.

"'Tis but a mere flesh wound," Danny said, "I've had worse."

"I will feed on the blood of your unborn children!" Zorga roared.

"Only if we give it to you in our unborn children's baby bottles," Penny told him.

"I will sup on the amniotic fluids of your children's children. I will flay the sagging skin from your grandparents' bodies and piss on their twitching flesh. I will find every living member of your families, rip their necks out and fuck their open throats. Your mothers, fathers, sisters and brothers will all drown on my hell-driven spunk"

Nutter rejoined them after retrieving his sword.

"I will use all of eternity to kill every single last one of you," Zorga declared.

"You will shut up and go to hell," Nutter told him and drove his sword through Zorga's ear.

ARSE! Zorga screamed and snuffed out of existence as a cigarette butt does when it is tossed into the toilet bowl.

***

During the week that followed, the four mortals discussed at great length as to the whereabouts of Cameron. After Zorga had been shished to death by Nutter's reclaimed blade Cameron strolled silently to Gillian's body and lifted it from under the front of the lorry. He held her in his arms and took off into the moonlit night sky. Nobody had considered to call him back because they all thought that it was reasonable enough that he desired some time to himself to gather his thoughts. When they returned home, but decided to break into the house next door to stay, they were mildly surprised that he did not come back that night at all, and did not make any contact with them as to his well-being whatsoever.

More armed troops came to town and the heroes were asked lots of questions concerning the whereabouts of the entire population of the city centre. They thought it the best policy to answer that they knew absolutely nothing about any disturbances over the past couple of days and that they must have slept through it all.

What? Even the mass destruction of the house next door?

Really? Explosions you say? I thought they just had their telly turned up a bit too loud; well, you know what students are like.

Then the army were called away and a very smartly dressed man and woman turned up, asked Nutter a few things and then left again. Nutter did not mention what they had asked and Danny only wanted to know if their names had been Scully and Mulder but Nutter said, "No".

They waited for Cameron for a while longer and then decided that they should really get on with their own lives, and it was on that seventh day that all four of them had their relative shock number of ten out of ten.

"You're going where?" Cassandra asked Penny.

"We're going to take a trip to Paris for a while," she replied, "that's where I was brought up. Mostly. And we're going to catch up on the past fifty years."

"I suppose you've been forced into retirement," Danny said to Nutter.

"It appears so, Daniel," Nutter answered, "and I don't even have a pension scheme to collect."

"What about you two?" Penny asked.

"We're going to go to Cass's folks for a while, until we

work out what she has to do to finish her degree," Danny said.

The door swung open and Cameron marched into the room. "I don't know," he puffed, "if you don't leave a forwarding address how is a person supposed to stay in touch?"

"Where have you been?" Penny demanded.

"We've been worried sick about you," Cassandra finished.

"I've been believing very hard," Cameron said, and they all looked confused.

"What did you do with Gill's body?" Penny asked.

"We've been worrying sick things about you," Danny finished.

"I will reveal everything to you," Cameron declared, "as soon as I get a cup of tea inside me."

"Cameron," Nutter said. "We would like to know what you've been up to now."

"Pah!" Cameron spat and made everyone jump. "None of you have a sense of dramatic tension."

There was laughter from the doorway that sounded like angel song to one person in the room.

"Hello, everyone," said a voice that, a week ago, everyone presumed would never be heard again.

The four mortals looked up to identify the voice; there then followed the sound of their jaws dropping. Cameron ran to the girl at the door, picked her up in his arms and swung her round in a circle.

"How are you feeling?" he asked.

"Great," she answered.

"But how?" four voices asked.

"Who said 'Frankenstein' was bloody stupid?" Cameron asked.

"Actually that was me," said Gillian from Cameron's arms.

"But that's only because John Cleese was in it," Danny muttered.

SHE'S ALIVE, ALIVE! BWAH HA HA HAR!!!

<u>An End</u>

(but for a brief dream)

The armadillo with the hairy knees!" she exclaimed.

Its dewy eyes watched them warily, then the corners of its mouth widened and it laughed evilly,

"You fools," it yelled. "You superstitious, incompetent fools. All the time, you never considered that it was me, the armadillo with the hairy knees. Only now does the full weight of the matter come to your attention, and knowing now is just too late. Because you can't defeat me, I've survived more nuclear holocausts than you've had hot ants."

It was obvious to all present that something was wrong.

"Ants? Ants? You don't know what it's like to snuffle around on the floor, day in, day out, eating nothing but ants. It's horrible.

"But now, aha! Who's laughing now? That's right, me, I'm laughing because I can laugh. I have sentience beyond your pathetic comprehensions and I am unstoppable. I am invincible, I am..."

The juggernaut trundled over the procrastinating animal without a second thought for its invincibility.

They all looked down at the bloody smear down the road.

"I guess that that's it then."

"I suppose so."

"Funny thing, life, isn't it?"

"Yeah, hilarious."